PENGUIN BOOKS

DOWN IN THE VALLEY

David M. Pierce was born in Montreal, Canada. He lived for some years in London, where, among other things, he wrote songs for the pop group *Meal Ticket* and acted in a Shakespearian theatre group. He co-authored a musical with fellow Canadian Rick Jones and has written songs with Jeremy Clyde. His other publications include three volumes of verse and a cookery book, written with singer Annie Ross. He has written two other books featuring private investigator Vic Daniel, *Roses Love Sunshine* and *Hear the Wind Blow, Dear*, both published by Penguin.

DAVID M. PIERCE

DOWN IN THE VALLEY

PENGUIN BOOKS

PENGUIN BOOKS

Published by the Penguin Group
27 Wrights Lane, London W8 5TZ, England
Viking Penguin Inc., 40 West 23rd Street, New York, New York 10010, USA
Penguin Books Australia Ltd, Ringwood, Victoria, Australia
Penguin Books Canada Ltd, 2801 John Street, Markham, Ontario, Canada L3R 1B4
Penguin Books (NZ) Ltd, 182–190 Wairau Road, Auckland 10, New Zealand

Penguin Books Ltd, Registered Offices: Harmondsworth, Middlesex, England

First published 1989
10 9 8 7 6 5 4 3 2 1

Made and printed in Great Britain by
Richard Clay Ltd, Bungay, Suffolk
Filmset in Monophoto Sabon

For my folks

I invented many things herein – including all of the people – but not Los Angeles or the San Fernando Valley. God knows who invented those.

CHAPTER ONE

Bits and pieces.

Why is nothing ever simple?

Why don't things have a beginning, a middle, then an end like a date with a Catholic girl? Why aren't they neat and uncomplicated like a double shot in a clean glass?

If I was the type to wax lyrical, I'd compare my average week with doing a jigsaw puzzle missing a substantial but unknown number of the border pieces. For instance when I walked in the back door of the Mo Kee Café he didn't even look up but went on slicing Chinese health food with his foot-long chopper.

'Money or else Small Claims Court,' I said, being humorous as he was maybe four foot six standing on a case of soy sauce.

'No money,' he said. Instead he offered me a piece of white radish on the end of his machete. I lifted him up with one hand under his chin and sat him on the work table in a pile of bean sprouts.

'Money,' I said.

'Later,' he said. He carefully dropped the machete so it stuck in the floor an inch from my almost-new white loafer, then shouted something. Two of his co-workers came trotting in from the dining room. What was I going to do, declare war on the whole Yellow Peril again?

I left, shaking my fist at the wily Oriental. He was an ex-Viet-boatperson and still owed me $750 for a job I'd done him. All right, if charm didn't work I'd have to try something else – I could get clever or I could get mean. As I'd already tried getting clever once or twice before in my life without a lot of luck, that left mean.

I drove back to where I worked thinking over the possibilities and was at my desk writing him a nasty letter on Department of Immigration stationery when Timmy went by the front window and peeked in inquiringly. I shook my head, as in get lost. He wobbled his in understanding and went up the line to pester my neighbors.

At that time I had the end unit in a small, L-shaped shopping area at the corner of Victory and Orange, right next to a vacant lot where from time to time in the gentle California evenings I could hear the sounds of bottles breaking and ethnic voices raised in loud dispute about everything and nothing at all. And, recently, during the muggy California afternoons, I had started to hear the nasal voices of schoolkids discussing the important events of the day in dialogue like 'Pass the joint' and 'Don't Jew the end'.

On the other side of my office was the Nus' Vietnamese take-out, next to that a video rental outfit and one more along a Taco-Burger franchise run by the handsome Señora Morales. Finally, next to her around the bend of the L was the Armenian shoe repair establishment of Mr Amoyan. I hoped Timmy wouldn't pester him as I liked the old gent; we used to loll on the wooden bench outside his shop in the late afternoons sometimes watching the high-school girls and the young moms go in and out of Taco-Burger, shaking our grizzled heads sadly at the follies of youth and our own lack of it.

As for Timmy, well, like the San Francisco Giants, he was one of God's less successful ideas.

I met him the first time six weeks earlier when the first real smogs of April were settling on the San Fernando Valley like cheap hairspray on a home permanent. Someone whapped me on the shoulder with a broom handle as I was opening up my office; I turned around ready to kill and found myself looking at someone more than a boy but less than a man, with an innocent, round moon face and vacant blue eyes. He was obviously mentally retarded but from what medical cause I neither knew nor particularly wanted to know.

But Timmy was harmless; he could talk, sort of, and all he wanted was to sweep the front of my office for me. He had a shopping cart borrowed from the local Ralph's supermarket full of assorted cleaning junk, newspapers, bottles, old rags, some toys, the usual precious collection of those who have nothing.

So he swept my stoop, with great care, and I gave him a buck. A few days later I got him a real job. I had a visit one afternoon from a Mr Christo Papanikolas who was getting fed up with being ripped off. He and various other members of his clan ran the busy Arrow Liquor Mart two blocks up Lankershim Boulevard and he'd been hit three weekends in a row. After he left I was mulling over the standard ways of dealing with a problem like Mr Papanikolas' – dogs, alarm systems, selling out and buying a mink ranch – when along ambled Timmy.

Light bulb flashed, and now Timmy spends his evenings sitting on a chair atop the freezer at the back of the Arrow Liquor Mart with what looks like a one-handed cannon on his lap but is really a nautical flare pistol, $40 from any merchant chandler, no license required. Mr Papanikolas, now a friend for life, informs me there's been no hint of trouble since Timmy started riding shotgun except for the time he pointed the thing at an ancient bag-lady picking up her weekend bottle of port and shouted at her, 'Move an' you die, bitch.'

Aunt Fat'ma baked me some of her special halvah, which was terrible. Nephew Yuri asked me to help him with his English homework. I asked Mr Papanikolas to please pay his bill promptly – two cases of Christian Brothers brandy, twelve quart bottles of Canada Dry ginger ale, and a large jar of imitation pepperoni Hot-Stix. He did. To each his own.

So now we're up to date, everything's right with the world except what isn't, and I'm at a second-hand desk in a third-hand office trying to outwit a half-pint Oriental cabbage-chopper. Do not get me wrong, I'm not prejudiced, only against people who owe me money. And Germans. And male Japanese. And girls who smoke cigars.

The phone rang.

I looked at it with mild surprise, then picked it up. It was a lady, or at least a female, with a voice like corn syrup on a short stack of buttermilk pancakes.

'Mister V. Daniel?'

'That's right,' I said. 'V. (for Victor) Daniel.'

'Victor Daniel, will you be in your office at one o'clock today?'

'If you can give me a good reason why.'

'Mr Lowenstein, vice-principal of St Stephen's High School, would like a word with you.'

'That'll do nicely,' I said, and hung up. I wondered what Mr Lowenstein, vice-principal of St Stephen's, which was an academy of lower learning about five minutes' drive west of me, wanted. Maybe just to check out my Hawaiian shirt collection, which was not without a certain small fame in those parts. Luckily there are a lot of huge Hawaiians in the world.

I had an hour to wait til I found out so I switched on Betsy, an Apple II computer with most of the important trimmings except a matrix printer, and my letter to Santa about that had long been in the mail. You might care to know that Davy Crockett's rifle was also named Betsy. I loved Betsy. I had loved many times before in my life – two cars, a tree house, a lefty genuine cowhide first-baseman's mitt, a lady, somehow, but I loved Betsy madly. The only problem was it had taken me years to learn how to work the fool thing and I was still making mistakes of an embarrassingly elementary nature like forgetting to take the lens cap off, but who's perfect?

I was involved in a bizarre game some freak had programmed; it had to do with a mythical Asian town of which the game-player was the satrap or khan or whatever you call it and you had to decide how much grain to plant. I was getting on to it, though. I punched in 'Plant 200 kilos'.

'Thank you, oh Wise One,' the computer said.

I was just about to enter 'Kill 200 peasants' when someone came in the front door in such a hurry he not only forgot to knock, he forgot to leave his baseball bat outside. I didn't know whether he was after me or Betsy but I'd fight to the death for either one. Luckily, although he was the same color, Hank Aaron he wasn't, and he missed us both by a mile. I pulled the bat away from him with one hand and gave him a crisp backhand across the chops with the other, then delivered a short but sweet tap on one of his knees with the old hickory and that took care of that.

'Haven't seen you for a while, Mick,' I said. 'How're things by you?'

'Terrible, fuck-face, thanks to you,' Mick said. 'Now I got a broken leg, too.'

'Also, you're not swinging properly,' I said. 'I think you got your weight too far forward.'

He limped to the door, went out, was about to slam it, thought better of it, and contented himself with expectorating sloppily on the sidewalk. Good, that took care of him for another month or two. A while back I'd helped a pal do a repo on Mick, only in this case it wasn't merely his car or his furniture, it was his whole house plus contents. He was nine months behind on the payments on a $75,000 mobile home and was also trying to sell it with full title so I took him pool playing one night and let him hustle me for a few bucks while my pal moved a rig into the park, hoisted up the mobile home and took her away. Being of a suspicious nature, Mick suspected me and used to drop around once in a while when he was on uppers and make some half-hearted attempt to decapitate me.

Where was I? Oh yes. I entered 'Liquidate 200 peasants'.

'Done, Merciful One,' the computer said.

CHAPTER TWO

Just after one fifteen a man who I presumed was Mr Lowenstein peered in the front window briefly. I peered back at him. Then he knocked and came in. I switched off Betsy and stood to meet him. He was about six foot two but I could still eat a bowl of soup off his head without reaching up, being a tidy six foot seven and a quarter last time I looked.

'Mr Lowenstein?'

'Correct. Mr Daniel?'

'Correct.'

We shook hands without making a big thing of it. He sat heavily in the chair on the far side of the desk and reached for a crumpled pack of Winston Lites.

'It destroys me not being able to puff away in school,' he said. 'I fully realize it is good for me but it is also murdering me. Funny. It used to be the teachers who smoked but now we're not supposed to so all the wretched children are sneaking fags and we're sucking peppermint-flavored sugar.' He lit his smoke with an old-fashioned Zippo.

'Never had the habit,' I said, watching him inhale so deeply it almost made his toes curl. Mr Lowenstein was a handsome man in his early fifties with harassed gray hair parted in the middle, solidly built but not overweight, wearing slacks and a contrasting gabardine jacket with a yellow hanky in the pocket. I was wearing tan slacks and a gorgeous short-sleeved shirt from Oahu featuring tropical drinks and palm trees.

'Please don't think me impolite but may I put a question or two to you first?' he asked.

'Shoot,' I said.

'You are indeed a properly licensed investigator for this city?'

'For this whole wonderful state,' I said. 'Renewable by the licensing board every year if I've been a good boy.'

'How long have you held your license?'

'Six years here and before that, four years back East. In Illinois.'

'I see,' said Mr Lowenstein, nodding. 'And do you have anyone in authority who might vouch for you?'

'I have a bank manager,' I said. 'He could vouch I pay my bills. And I have a brother who is a Louie in the L A P D. He could vouch something although I'm not sure what, brothers being what they are.'

Mr Lowenstein looked at me. I looked at him. Then he looked at the computer.

'Must be very helpful in your line of work,' he said.

'Yours, too,' I said. 'I know my brother finds them of great assistance. All in all, they are quite the coming thing.'

'Um,' said Mr Lowenstein. He sighed and stubbed his cigarette out in an ashtray I had that was shaped like a piano, in fact it came from Del's Piano Bar down on Independence where I was wont to pass the occasional idle hour.

'Very well,' he said, making up his mind. 'Here it is, sir. I'm sorry to say we have a good deal of trouble at present at my school and we seem to be completely unequipped to handle it. The use of drugs has become so widespread the pupils are almost taking them openly. I know some of the older boys are selling them on school property. And a young boy in one of my classes was stabbed last week, in the parking lot.'

'Dear me,' I said, as some sort of reaction seemed to be called for.

'Dear me is right,' he said. 'Mr Daniel, I do not care what those degenerate pea-brains do when they are off the school grounds, although I suppose I really do, they can inject battery acid straight into their soft adolescent brain cells if they so desire and some of them likely are already doing so, but I am affronted when they do it almost before my very eyes, understand me? When they return from lunch coked to the gills, or whatever the expression these days is, or when they come back from the gym looking like the living dead or giggling insanely at my mild witticisms. And I would very much like it stopped before it goes any further, understand me?'

I said I understood him.

'Excuse me for getting worked up about it,' he said, lighting up again. 'But I suppose I am worked up about it and getting more worked up every day.'

I said I understood that too. He gave me a small smile, then looked at his watch.

'Chemistry at two o'clock,' he said. 'I actually enjoy teaching those morons. Strange.'

'Unbelievable.'

'So what do you think about it all, Mr Daniel? Any ideas?'

'I think we better talk again when we've got more time,' I said. 'Then I could have a look around, then we could talk some more.'

'After school today?'

I said I couldn't make it.

'Ten tomorrow at the school?'

I said I'd be there.

'Fine.' He got up to go. I got up too.

'Eh, please don't misunderstand me but it might be best if you came looking sort of, how shall I put it, nondescript?'

'I'll try,' I said. I saw him to the door; he smiled again briefly and left. I smiled briefly at his back and went to sit down again. Nice guy, for a teacher.

I dumped his stubs out of the ashtray into the wastepaper basket, turned the computer on, put in a clean disk, coded it and entered 'St Stephen's, 14 May 1984.' Then I punched in Mr Lowenstein's name, looked up the school telephone number and entered that, and then, as I couldn't think of anything else, I switched disks again and slaughtered some more peasants, an occupation I can highly recommend.

A few minutes later, Mrs Morales' cute daughter went by

and gave me a wave. I gave her one right back, another occupation I can highly recommend.

At five minutes past four I ran a check on my appointments for the rest of the day – Valley Bowl and Mrs Lucy Seburn – then started packing up for the night, everything of value going into a monster of a safe that took up most of the floor space in the bathroom at the back.

My car was parked right in front where I could keep an eye on it during the day although it was only a clown car, a beat-up pink and blue Nash Metropolitan. Definitely not one of my automobile heart-throbs: a 38 Chevy coupé, duff gray with a rumble seat, and a 53 dark green Hudson Hornet with a necker's knob on the steering wheel. Was I hot stuff in those days. Wonder what happened? But I must admit the Nash was starting to grow on me.

Down Victoria to Apple, past Dave's Corner Bar, right at the Longhorn Grill – Happy Hour 4.30 to 7.30 – up Flamingo Drive past the Irish Bar, then out and lock up at the Valley Bowl, J. D. Curtain, ex-pro bowler, your genial host. The place was still fairly quiet, only four lanes being in action, but in another hour all twenty-four would be jumping with league competitions.

John D. was in his office, Big Sally at the snack counter told me. She only had one customer, a kid drinking a milk-shake, so I took pity on her and let her make me a tuna fish on white toast.

'So how's your love life?' she asked me.

'Unbelievable,' I said truthfully.

'Mine too,' she said. 'Unbelievably vacuous.'

'Is that good or bad?' the kid drinking the milkshake wanted to know.

'Go look it up,' I said.

'What a good idea!' the kid said. 'Thank you, sir. I'll rush immediately to the nearest library.'

I gave the callow whelp a withering look, then settled up with Sal, leaving her a quarter tip. She gazed after me somewhat wistfully, I thought, as I made my way down past the row of Space Invaders and pinball machines toward John D.'s office. Perhaps she was sweet on me. Perhaps she just liked all her big tippers.

I found my friend sitting at his cluttered desk perusing a smudgy-looking bowling news letter.

'How's it going?'

'It's going,' he said. 'How about you?'

'Likewise I'm sure,' I said.

He smiled. John D. was a well-set-up man, in his early forties, I suppose, dressed in faded warm-up clothes. He hadn't put on a pound since his days on the pro tour, unlike some I could mention. Without my asking, he tossed me a set of master keys he took from a board on the wall behind his head. I caught them deftly, got out my checklist, and betook myself off to earn my daily bread.

First I warned the staff to expect strange events in the next half hour, as I always did, like bells ringing unexpectedly and the patter of large feet overhead, then I gave John's entire security system its monthly physical, including going out on to the roof to check the skylight and wandering out back to check the sliding doors in the loading area where his deliveries came.

All systems were go as far as I could see, but a large floodlamp in the parking lot was out which meant I had to go down to the storeroom, get the ladder, climb up and replace it, which I did without managing to fall off, for once – some years ago I started suffering inexplicably from vertigo, and it wasn't getting any better. Lucky for me my mountain climbing career had already ended by then. Likewise my part-time job as a tree surgeon.

When I was done, I washed up and made my way back to John D.'s office.

'Safe for another month,' I said.

He waved me into a worn director's chair and began doing some warm-up stretches.

'Something's going on,' he said, breathing in deeply through his nose.

'It's called Life,' I said helpfully.

'Must be one of the girls in the cash booth.'

'I still think it's Life,' I said. He started on some painful-looking knee-bends.

'I'm all-league now six nights a week, I can figure within a card or two what I should take. I'm comin' up forty to fifty bucks short.'

'How many girls work there?'

'At night, three,' he said. 'They're supposed to rotate so there's always two on together, but you know girls.'

'I wish I did,' I said. 'Do they work there during the day?'

He shook his head. 'Too quiet.'

'How do they get paid?'

'Cash,' he said innocently. 'Simplifies the book-keeping.' Yeah, it simplified the book-keeping all right, for the IRS.

'Every Friday,' he added, and began forcing himself away from the wall in a series of upright push-ups. It hurt just to watch him.

'How much?'

'Too much,' he said. 'Four dollars twenty-five an hour, one fifty-three a week, casual labor, no withholding.'

'Slave driver,' I said. 'Well, an extra fifty bucks a week isn't exactly going to change their lifestyle, I mean one of them isn't going to suddenly show up for work in sables driving a Maserati coupé.'

'So?'

'So it'll probably take a little outside work and a little luck and a great deal of professional expertise, and as none of those are covered in our contract, it'll take a little pocket money from you.'

'What else is new?' He picked a battered bowling ball off its donut-shaped stand from a shelf crowded with trophies, and hefted it. 'Won a little money with this mother-roonie in my day,' he boasted. 'How much is little?'

I told him it could take half a day, maybe a whole one. He said do it. I said send me the girls' employment sheets or copies thereof. Also, if he had them, copies of the nightly receipts for the past month.

'Consider it done, amigo,' he said, swinging the ball over his head. 'Ever tell you about the time I won in Dearborn with a two hundred ninety-nine in the last game?'

'Yes,' I said, and left. Another nice guy. Two in one day, might be a Valley record.

Back in the car, I checked the time – five fifteen – turned on the radio and headed out into the rush hour for my last chore of the day, Lucy Seburn, Mrs, but not by much.

'Down in west Texas, the town of El Paso . . .' sang the radio.

'Once took a ride on a Mexican crab,' I sang.

CHAPTER THREE

Mrs Lucy Seburn lived some twenty minutes' drive east in one of Burbank's ritzier streets, in one of the street's ritzier homes, graveled driveway and all. It even had a name – Mariposa, or butterfly. Feeling more like a moth I parked around the corner on Rivera out of sight of the house, facing back the way I came as I figured I knew Mrs Seburn's routine by this time because it has been the same for the last six Thursday afternoons.

At five forty-five promptly she emerged from her cocoon, got into her new black Toyota and drove it down towards Rivera where she turned left away from me, made a right on Laurel, right on Acacia, hit the Ventura Freeway, got off at La Cienega and made her way, driving carefully, to a health club out Ventura Boulevard, into which she went with a springy gait.

I jotted down her route and the times in question, as usual, parked at Moe's hotdog stand across the street as usual, had three hotdogs, mustard and relish only, double fries and a root beer, as usual, and listened to country music for an hour on the radio, as usual.

When Mrs Seburn came out, looking refreshed, I noted the time and then followed her home. Would you believe for that sort of child's play I actually got paid money? Every Friday I sent by messenger service a typed-up report of the lady's keep-fit routine to her husband at his business address in Century City. Every Monday he sent me back by the same messenger service $82.50 cash. I had concluded after the first time that the attractive Mrs Seburn was having it off and I don't mean her cellulite, although maybe that too. All the other customers of the health club entered carrying holdalls of one kind or another, usually with a combination lock dangling from the strap somewhere. I found out from a guy I knew who used the West Hollywood branch of the same club what the procedure was – clients always brought their sweats and tights and woolly socks with them, placed their street clothes in lockers and secured the lockers with their own combination locks, which the management preferred as keys were too easy to lose on Nautilus machines or during aerobic dance freak-outs.

Needless to say Mrs Seburn was always holdall-less; presumably she told her hubby, if she told him anything at all, or her maid, if she spoke Mex, that she left her gear at the club. Only me and de Shadow knew better. And hubby, by now, of course. I'd also taken a peek at the Mr Universe at the front desk and figured we could get a deposition out of him without cleaning out the piggy bank. Furthermore, to support my deductive evidence of Mrs Seburn's extramarital activities I also had some nifty shots taken with a long lens of her kissing a young hunk who usually walked her out to the car. She was young and pretty. He was young and pretty.

I was old and jealous.

And what was a nice, clean-cut kid like me doing in that line of work in the first place? Eating. Most gents in my trade with a certain – how shall I say it? – class loudly proclaimed they didn't do divorce work. They did; so did I. I didn't like it all that much but I didn't mind it either, like Canadian whisky, like a lot of things.

The traffic had thinned out by then, or at least gotten as thin as LA traffic ever gets, which is clotted. I drove home, which is where the heart is, everyone says. It's also where a first-floor, 2br, all mod cons, new C & D, security garage, on Windsor Castle Terrace, talley-ho, just after the freeway overpass, is. It was OK if you liked shit-brown carpeting and cottage-cheese ceilings. The owner, who lived downstairs in the other unit, was Mrs Phoebe ('Call me Feeb') Miner, a tough old gal with blue hair who didn't care what I did as long as I did it quietly or somewhere else.

I got some grapefruit juice from the fridge, switched on the TV to the news channel and began typing up Mr Seburn's report on the portable Olympia I kept under the bed, finishing up at about seven thirty. I phoned Mae to see if she was back.

'She'll be back tomorrow,' her roommate reluctantly told me. 'I don't know when.'

I said, 'Thanks a million.' Mae was a legal secretary almost, meaning she did the work without the pay, for a snazzy ambulance-chaser who had an office in Studio City and a $200 wig. She had taken a month's leave of absence to go home to Peoria and bury her mom.

All right.

There were other fish to fry for a Nash Metropolitan owner who still had a few moves.

I called Linda with the skinny legs. No answer. I called a number written on a cocktail napkin from the Two-Two-Two. No answer.

Good. I didn't want to go out anyway. I watched some garbage on the TV for a while. I liked police and detective shows best, they were so accurate, so true to life, so wonderfully real. Just kidding, Mother. Then I washed my glass and went to bed with a good book. Not as good as *The Amboy Dukes* or *God's Little Acre*, but good. It was set in Hawaii. Then I went to sleep.

At least the Sandman was home.

The following morning I didn't bother opening up the office. I had some underdone pancakes and three cups of forgettable coffee at a counter joint, then presented myself right on the dot of ten o'clock to Mr Lowenstein's secretary over at the high school. A sign on her desk said: 'Miss Shirley, Apple of the Teacher's Eye'. Miss Shirley was wearing an off-the-shoulder scoop neckline salvaged from an MGM 50s musical, showing plenty of adorable tanned skin still warm from some giggly beach party. White pop beads. Bright orange fingernails. She was, at first sight, that Hollywood classic, the gorgeous dumb blond, as out of place in a school as I would be singing 'Hi-ho, hi-ho' with the Seven Dwarfs. Strangely, her lipstick had been put on carelessly, almost amateurishly.

She smiled at me when I entered her office, smiled when I told her my name, even smiled kindly at my tan suit, dark brown shirt, rust tie, brown loafers and impressive-looking Oxford-red, gen-u-ine leatherette briefcase with the fourteen-carat gold clasp. I kept my hand over the fourteen-carat gold initials as they weren't mine.

'Well, hi there,' she said.

'Hi yourself,' I said. I wondered if the school held night classes for aging buffoons who were still vulnerable little boys at heart. I was leaning towards her deep blue eyes to ask her when she said I should go right in.

I sighed inwardly and in I went. Mr Lowenstein smiled at me too.

'I know,' he said. He was replacing a couple of tomes in a bookcase. 'Unfair, isn't it?' I didn't bother pretending I didn't know what he was talking about, or rather, who. 'I have to look at it all day.' He shook his head sadly.

'No job is perfect,' I said. 'I don't suppose she can type too.'

'Like a demon,' he said.

We sat at opposite sides of his metal desk; it had a new IBM Selectric typewriter attached to it on a swiveling shelf. While I was taking a clipboard out of the gen-u-ine briefcase I thought of something.

'Where's the principal's office?'

'Down the hall.'

'Ah,' I said. 'He doesn't want to be involved.'

'You are a male chauvinist pig,' said the Vice. 'The principal is a she, not a he. Also, you're wrong, she cares, deeply, but she's helpless.' He looked out one of his windows, the one that overlooked the parking lot; there were more wheels lined up out there than in North and South Korea put together.

'She's a good woman,' he said. 'Very bright, excellent administrator, more than well qualified, first-class teacher, but she is perhaps just a touch old-fashioned, if you take my meaning.'

I indicated that I did.

'Now that she is out of the way, care to do some work?'

I indicated that I cared by taking out a black felt-tip, courtesy A & A Aaron Bros, Opticians. He talked, I made notes. I asked some questions and made more notes. After a while it became clear that if I was going to get anywhere at all it wouldn't be by being Mr Nice Guy.

'So what?' he said.

I asked him if he wanted all the details as I went along.

'You better believe it, old buddy,' he said. 'Include me in. I'm a big boy too now and also that's what they pay me for. You want something in writing, no doubt.'

I said it's always better that way.

He buzzed the intercom and in swayed Miss Shirley.

'Miss Shirley, Mr Daniel.'

She smiled at me.

'With an "e",' I said. I don't know why, I'd never said it before in my life.

'We need a piece of paper, dear,' Mr Lowenstein said sternly. 'One copy for Mr Daniel with an "e", the original in the safe. It will cover these points: St Stephen's, via its agent, me, hires Mr first-name Daniel . . .'

'Victor,' I said.

'. . . Victor Daniel, of address here . . .'

I obliged with my office address.

'. . . to investigate the use of illegal substances on school premises, to collect evidence of same if possible and to terminate same if possible.'

I looked at Miss Shirley to look at Miss Shirley, and to see her reaction; she was gazing vacantly out of the window, the one that didn't overlook the parking lot.

Mr Lowenstein continued: 'He will report at least weekly in writing to me or my agent, you.'

I managed somehow to hide my glee.

'I will take full responsibility for all his actions. His fee will be enter fee here . . .'

'Two bills a day plus reasonable expenses,' I said.

'Put it in,' he said. 'Paid weekly. This agreement will continue until the stipulations of the contract have been met or by decision of either one of the contracting parties. Anything else?'

'Mr Daniel will have full access to all files, card indexes, computer print-outs, etc., that he deems necessary to fulfill said contract,' I said.

'Put it in,' he said. 'Anything else?'

I shook my thinning pate; Miss Shirley shook her platinum curls.

'OK. Date, witness and we'll sign them as soon as you have them ready.'

'See you,' she said, and sashayed out. We both watched her go.

'She certainly upsets one's attention span,' said Mr Lowenstein.

I agreed.

'I called your brother down at Central,' he then offered.

I figured he had or otherwise we wouldn't have gotten this far. 'So how is he?'

'Fine, fine. Says he's working too hard.'

'Oh, well,' I said. 'He was always the over-achiever in the family.' I told him I'd better try and leave before the classes broke as I didn't want too many kids to get to look at me and my natty wardrobe as I'd soon be returning in some other clever guise, one that would give me a good excuse to hang around the premises as it was unlikely that I could pass myself off as a high-school student even if I did put on a beanie and a T-shirt that said something catchy like 'Everyone over 21 sucks'.

He agreed. We chatted about football and the weather for about the amount of time it takes to spend ten bucks in an

LA cab, i.e., very little, then Miss Shirley flounced back in with the contracts, gave them to her boss, then flounced back out again. The Vice and I both read copies without finding any mistakes, then signed on the dotted lines. I said I'd call him later when I'd figured out some sort of approach, and left. I told Miss Shirley the same thing. I wished she'd stop smiling at me like that, it would give a Civil War statue ideas.

CHAPTER FOUR

Back at the office I opened up, put the contract in the safe, retrieved the telephone, called the messenger service, who said they were already out the door, retrieved Mr Seburn's report from the gen-u-ine briefcase, put it in an envelope, sealed and addressed the envelope. The mailman hadn't come yet so I got out the clipboard and began thinking about St Stephen's and making the occasional note.

Obviously the problem was infiltration; if I couldn't infiltrate, who could, and would? I tried to remember what it was like being at high school and while I recalled some vivid details of my pitifully few years there, at least half deeply embarrassing, came up with nothing helpful. Timmy ambled by and peered in hopefully; I waved him away. The messenger boy puttered up on his Yamaha 175. I paid him $7.50, got a receipt and handed over the report. The kid was wearing a sort of uniform, and that gave me the beginnings of an idea. I shut up shop, got into the car and headed out into the world, the brave new world, not as easy as it may sound when your brave new California world is an unholy mix of the tedious and the garish, stretching from the Hollywood Hills north to the San Gabriel mountains, the tops of which were already disappearing into thick air. Good thing I'm not the sensitive type.

At a Sergeant's Supply Store on Sepulveda I bought a pair of painter's white overalls, size X-L, a painter's cap and a twenty-foot metal pocket ruler with automatic rewind. What the hell; I threw in a new pair of white Adidas-imitation sneakers and a two-pack of white tube socks, putting the bill away carefully. I had to go to three car rentals before finding what I wanted, a small, well-used (beat-up) unmarked panel truck; it even had a ladder on the roof rack. I took it for three days, did the necessary paperwork and for an extra $10 had a peon follow me home in it.

He waited while I changed into my whites, then I drove the truck back to the car rental and dropped him off. He said, 'Have a good day.'

I said, 'Adiós, amigo.'

I drove back along Victory to the school, having a little trouble with the shift into second, and did a slow circle around the school property until I spotted what I'd been looking for and what no school in the US of A would be without – a nearby junk-food emporium. This one was on Greenview right across the street from the back of St Stephen's; it was called B & B's, a solidly built wooden shack with the usual signs advertising Coke and Seven-Up, plus a few plastic benches next to its own small parking lot into which I wheeled smartly in case anyone was watching – it was twelve thirty by then and B & B's was jumpin'.

One of the two phones in the back was free; I dialed Miss Shirley. She sounded funny.

'I'm eating my lunch,' she said.

I told her that was a mighty fine idea and I would do the same and then stop by the school and start to work.

'I'll hold my breath,' she said.

I put away some fries and three hotdogs, mustard and relish only, not bad but not as good as Moe's, then sucked at a root beer and watched the assembled juveniles at their play, which seemed to consist mostly of insulting each other both physically and verbally. Some things never change. A cute girl at the end of the bench I was on nodded at me and said, 'How ya doin'?'

I said, 'OK, thanks for askin'.'

Unfortunately I couldn't spot anyone rolling reefers, rolling drunks, shooting up or popping caps. I did see the cutie nick her extra catsup packets and also spied two adventurous lads in the front seat of a new Ford 4 × 4 sneaking hits of beer from a paper bag, but that was all. 'I laughed with them, I quaffed with them, I let them rob me, but that was all!' my pop used to recite from some unknown source to make us kids giggle.

'Death, where is thy sting?' my mom used to answer him back, from some other unknown source.

A couple of kids in soccer gear came trotting across the street to assorted wolf whistles from the wits in the crowd; I noticed a large sign over the back entrance to the school that said: 'Sat. 10.00 a.m. – SOCCER – Blitz Vrs Runners'.

When I'd gotten all the mileage I could out of two root beers I dumped my trash and the cute co-ed's in a nearby bin and went up to the service window again; the owner's city permit to operate was thumbtacked up just inside the opening. The red-faced man in a paper chef's hat and dirty paper apron who had served me before came over and slid the protective screen open. He had the smile of a man who wants to be liked but is rightly afraid he isn't. Maybe he had a canary. He for sure had a set of expensive false teeth.

'What can I do you for?' He had a couple of fingers missing on his left hand.

'Just a toothpick,' I said. 'Sorry to trouble you.'

'No trouble,' he said, passing over a small box.

'Nice place,' I said, helping myself.

He shrugged. 'Yeah.'

'Would you be one of the Bs in the sign?'

'Nah,' he said. 'Everyone asts that. It was there when me and the wife bought in so we just left it. I'm Art.'

'Jim,' I said. 'Bidding on a painting contract at that establishment of higher learning across the street there.'

'Oh yeah?' He leaned his elbows on the counter and gave me his idea of a smile again. Everyone was smiling at me today; maybe it was my deodorant. The two kids in the Ford left, burning rubber, and went all of fifty yards to the school lot.

'Fuckin' kids,' said Art, the red-faced philosopher.

'Yeah, well,' I said. 'See you later, pal.'

'OK, pal,' said Art, retrieving the toothpicks and sliding the screen across again. So much for any ideas I had of skillfully pumping Art.

I shifted the van across the street without burning any rubber and, trusty clipboard in hand and new tape measure in pocket, walked down the empty hall of the Admin wing to Miss Shirley's office.

Miss Shirley was in, fresh makeup lavishly applied, curls combed or tousled or teased or whatever it was she did with them. She raised one imperfectly drawn eyebrow at my get-up but otherwise was all business, at least as far as a dish like her could ever be business.

'I would like,' I told her, 'a short tour, then to meet the head of your school security and then access to your computer outlet, in that order, please.'

'Follow me, Picasso,' she said.

And the tour was short, all I really wanted at that time was a look at the storerooms and the kids' locker rooms. So I looked at the storerooms – they were rooms in which things were stored – then saw the locker rooms, of which, it turned out, there were two, one for each sex, unsurprisingly. They were located in the sports wing that ran off at an angle from the other buildings right next to the gym, which was also unsurprising. The lockers were the usual metal type in rows two lockers high, each numbered and with a built-in combination lock. Then the vision called Miss Shirley escorted me down endless halls to the office of the head of security, a Mr Dev Devlin, to whom she introduced me and to whom she spelled out my bona fides. Then she left; I couldn't stop myself from watching her go but did prevent myself from whistling. Maybe I was growing up after all.

On the way to Devlin's office I was trying to figure out why the place felt so different from schools in my day. It looked different, of course, with color-coordinated icky pastels on the walls instead of good, honest poop brown and puke green, and the desks seen through the occasional open classroom door were different, of course, being contemporary work areas instead of good, honest, too-small, carved up wooden horrors. And in some of the rooms the kids were bent over computers instead of books, and the color of the blackboards was for some reason green now, like tennis balls are green and hair is green but the main difference, it came to me, was the halls were quiet. In my – admittedly short – day, schools were designed to be as noisy as possible, why, God only knows, probably money – reason anything out and sooner or later you get to that – but these halls were quiet, foam-backed lino on the floors, acoustic tiles on the walls and ceilings, movable screens set up as baffles . . . what the hell. Maybe the kids were noisier now so it all evened up.

Oh. Something else happened on the way to Devlin's office. I broke up a drug orgy.

We were going by the boys' washrooms just opposite the lockers when I heard with my little ear something that began with 'scuf', as in scuffle. As classes were in progress at that very moment it didn't take but a trice to deduce that what was probably going on was boys doing something they weren't supposed to be doing.

I excused myself nicely to Miss Shirley and went in and sure enough, a small group of St Stephen's finest ne'er-do-wells were sharing a joint. My entry caused a brief flurry of muffled laughter and stall doors abruptly swinging shut, then all was quiet. The place was thick with the sweet smell of good pot. I relieved myself noisily at one of the urinals, tucked away Old Faithful, got out my new pocket rule and, whistling, began measuring things.

'Well, she's about ten by ten,' I said ostensibly to myself, then stooped down and had a quick peek under the stall doors. Under one of them I counted four feet, under the one next to it, six. I made some noise over by the window and one of the kids slipped out and went to wash his hands. He gave me a quick glance in the mirror to see who the hell I was and what the hell I was doing.

'What do you think about canary yellow?' I asked him.

'What?' He was a big kid with a sort of modified Apache cut.

'Canary yellow!' I said. 'It'll look darling with forest-green trim.'

'You like a painter?' the kid said, drying his hands.

'A decorator,' I said. 'A color coordinator, if you prefer. Painter!' I shuddered delicately. A second kid snuck out when my back was turned and exited rapidly. 'Mind holding the end of this a teeny minute?' I offered him the end of the rule.

'Yeah,' the kid said. 'All right, you guys,' he said to his friends. 'It's just some jerk-off.'

'Well!' I said. 'Jerk, maybe.' The rest of his pals emerged, gave me looks varying from contemptuous to downright hostile, then they all trooped out with appropriate horseplay at the door. After a minute I followed them. One of them was talking to Miss Shirley.

'For Mr Bonds,' he was saying with that innocent look kids put on when they're lying through their teeth and which grown-ups put on when they're lying through their false teeth. 'For the game.'

'Well, you better get on with it then,' Miss Shirley said. The kid took off. 'They're marking something called the pitch for Mr Bonds for the game Saturday,' she told me.

'They're also getting smashed in the boys' washroom,' I told her. 'And a "pitch" is what the Limeys call a soccer field. I do a lot of reading,' I added.

'I do a lot of standing around waiting for you,' she said. 'Let's move it, Pablo. I've got work to do.'

We moved it. Well, I walked it, she moved it.

CHAPTER FIVE

Mr Dev Devlin was tough, if you took his word for it, and I was more than willing to.

He looked pathologically normal, with the stereotyped mien of the ex-Marine, and I soon found out that's exactly what he was. His office was small and appropriately spartan although there was a vase of fresh daffodils on the battleship-gray metal desk and several pictures of the Irish countryside up on the walls. Confirming his Marine connection, just inside the door was a large framed photograph of him as a lieutenant in Vietnam; he came over to look at it with me. There was something about his walk, a hesitancy, he lifted one foot a little higher than the other, I wondered if he had a partial prosthesis of some kind.

'Just before Tet,' he said at my shoulder. He smelled of Old Spice, the GI's favorite, and he-man cigarettes. He was in a dark blue para-military outfit with red 'Security' flashes on each sleeve and a metal name-tag that said 'M. Devlin, Chief Sec.' above his breast pocket. His holster was snapped shut but by the size of it he was packing something more than a BB pistol. Shorter than me but with a weightlifter's build, his muscles showing plainly through his shirt. Square face, light brown hair a little longer than regulation but not much. Also, he was not pleased and he told me so, standing there in front of the photo of one of his life's Golden Moments.

'I don't like it, Vic,' he said.

'Gee, I'm sorry,' I said.

He gave me an unpleasant glare and pointed at a nasty-looking aluminum chair. I sat down; big deal.

'I don't like outside security coming into my school,' he said. 'Not one little bit.'

I was going to say I was sorry again but I hate being redundant. He paced up and down behind my chair showing me how much energy he had; I didn't bother watching. I figured he'd calm down in a while and he finally did.

'What's going down, Vic?' He took a swivel chair across from me and straightened an already straight pen and pencil holder made from a brass mortar casing.

What's going down? A good question, Dev ol' boy. Miss Shirley had told him my name, status and that I'd been hired by the vice-principal, but that was all. I was debating with myself how much more to tell him; on one hand I needed inside help, and who better than he to provide it? On the other, sinister, hand was the disquieting thought that if he was such a hot-shot he should already know what was going on so why hadn't he done something about it? If you have a highly trained, logical mind like mine, this would seem to lead to two possibilities – (1) he wasn't such a hot-shot or (2) he had his own reasons for sitting on it. I thought I'd start by working on (1), but it seemed a little direct to open up with 'Are you or have you ever been a hot-shot, Dev?' so I asked him instead, 'What do you know about computer thefts, Dev?'

He shook out a Camel from a pack he kept in his top drawer, lit up with a kitchen match, then put the pack away again.

'You mean of the things themselves?'

'No, I mean using the things to steal other things with.' He looked a little lost. I really felt sorry for him.

'Well, I read about it,' he said. He kept his cigarette cupped between thumb and first two fingers as he smoked. 'That what you're doing here?'

I nodded solemnly. 'It's my specialty, Dev. It can be mighty tricky, too, I can assure you.'

'Oh, yeah?' He looked relieved; I thought I'd relieve him some more.

'Yes, indeed. Oh, by the way, Mr Lowenstein asked me to

specifically tell you his bringing me in in no way reflects criticism on your department.' Kissing ass is good for the soul, said St Francis. 'Speaking of your department,' I said, doing my soul some more much-needed good, 'how do you manage to stay on top of a job like yours? It must take some organizing, having responsibility for a place this large, to say nothing of its contents, both animate and inanimate.'

Dev brightened; he told me, one pro to another, how he had the job organized, and it was impressive evough. More often than not a security system is only as good as the specific demands the insuring company has listed, but that wasn't good enough for Dev. All requirements for locks, dead-bolts, window-jams, alarm systems silent and otherwise, firedoors and escape routes, fire drills, internal security and all the rest had not only been met but more than met. He had two properly licensed assistants who worked school hours on alternate days and the routes and times of their meanderings were changed by him arbitrarily and irregularly. He organized street-crossing patrols of goody-goody students and when necessary for special events, goody-goody parking monitors.

He also divulged that he slept in a small, self-contained apartment at the far end of the science wing near the front of the school and his nightly patrols were altered as well in irregular patterns. He informed me he was licensed to carry a weapon on the premises while on duty and had fired it twice in the course of said duties, both times into the air and both times to prevent car thefts. H'um – it looked like the Loot was a hot-shot after all, which left the above-mentioned possibility number (2) – a whole different can of worms.

'Wow,' I said, after he had run down a bit. 'Sure wish my job was as exciting as yours.' He then expressed polite interest in mine so I told him a little about my boring occupation, how it was a lonely one-man job, hinted that computer thefts were often linked to purchasing departments (a red herring) and then took my leave with a considerable amount to think about. A lot of fancy footwork from Dev is one thing I thought about.

Ten minutes later Miss Shirley had me installed in an empty office two doors down from hers. She told me what language the computer on the otherwise bare table spoke and asked me if I spoke it too.

'Un poco,' I said modestly. 'Just enough to order a drink and get something to eat.'

'Ha ha,' said Miss Shirley.

I limbered up while she went to get me some programs I'd requested and when she came back holding them to her chest like a small girl holding schoolbooks I asked her, 'I know it's a long shot but are you by any chance Marie Wilson's daughter?'

She said, no, she was the only daughter of Mr and Mrs Shirley and who was Marie Wilson anyway, then she left me to my toils.

I switched on, signed in and asked the computer if St Stephen's had a cadet corps.

It did.

I asked the computer to run a list of members.

It did.

I asked for a print-out of same; it rattled me off one. I asked the computer if St Stephen's had a gun and rifle club or facsimile of. It did, and obliged me with a list of members, acting president M. Devlin. There were seven names of students that appeared on both lists. I asked for and immediately got a print-out of the names, addresses and phone numbers of those seven, obtained by cross-connecting with the student directory. Ain't progress terrific?

I looked up Dev's file while I was there; it told me little that I didn't already know but I saw and noted down that he had used as a reference when he'd first applied to St Stephen's a former employer, one Sheriff W. B. Gutes of Modesto, California. I also memorized Miss Shirley's home number in case of emergencies. Listen, be prepared; and if Macbeth ever said a truer word than that in his life I never heard it.

There wasn't much more I could do til school broke so I

switched off, tidied up, took back to Miss Shirley what I had borrowed from her, then asked if I could borrow her typewriter for a sec. She sighed deeply and batted her blue eyes at me; maybe I was getting somewhere.

'Listen, Dopey,' she said. Maybe I wasn't. 'Use the printer, that's what it's there for. It prints things.'

'Thank you,' I said meekly. I went back to the empty office, switched on, and typed in a résumé of my work so far and my plans for the rest of the day. I asked for two copies and got them without any sarcastic 'Done, merciful one' comments. One copy I kept, the other I handed over to Miss Shirley for her boss. Then I said farewell and split the scene, as the kids say.

Or used to, anyway.

A hard, maybe even a bitter woman, that Miss Shirley. A hard, bitter, frustrated ball-breaker, I knew the type well. What man these days doesn't?

After only a couple of wrong turns I found the science wing and noted where the door to Dev's apartment was. Then I took myself over to Art's for a much-needed snack. I hadn't had anything at all in my stomach for a good hour and a half. I managed to finish two of Art's mediocre chili dogs, then got some change from him and put in a call to the Modesto, CA police department.

The desk sergeant was in.

Was Sheriff Gutes still in charge there?

He wasn't but he dropped in most afternoons to complain about something. The desk sergeant sounded like one of the things the sheriff complained about was him.

Could I reach the sheriff at his home?

I could if I knew the number. And if the sheriff was home.

Could I have the number please?

The small-town wit finally gave it to me and a moment later I was actually speaking to the sheriff, or ex-sheriff, to be precise. Were sheriffs still called sheriffs after they retired or took off for Florida with a blond and a suitcase full of small, unmarked bills? Anyway, I was going to tell whatever he called himself that I worked for California Casualty or some other fictitious insurance company and as Mr Devlin's contract with St Stephen's was about to be renewed we had to run an obligatory check on him. Then I thought to hell with all that, the sarge had given me the impression Gutes was straight to the point of being a nuisance about it so I decided to be straight right back and see what happened. It wasn't really important anyway, it was just curiosity.

After introducing myself, I said, 'Sorry to disturb you, sir, but it's about an ex-employee of yours, Dev Devlin.'

'You aren't disturbing me, son,' said a mild, old man's voice. 'I wish you were. What about him?'

'He's head of security at a high school down here,' I said.

'Where's down here?'

I told him.

'What's the weather doing?'

I told him.

'What's Dev doing?'

'Well, that's just it,' I said. 'He doesn't seem to be doing much. When he worked for you, would you say he was a smart cop?'

'I would say that.'

'Did he know about things like drugs?'

'Be hard not to these days, even in Modesto,' said the old gent.

'How long was he with you?'

'A good three years.'

'Know what he did before that?'

'Straight army.'

'If you don't mind me asking, was he honest?'

'As honest as most,' the ex-sheriff said. 'Course you don't get the opportunities up here in the sticks a fellow might down there in the big time. Also he was working under me.'

'How would you sum him up in a few words, if you had to?'

The old man thought for a moment.

'Hard-working. Moody. In pain a lot.'

I told him I got the picture, thanked him and hung up. In pain a lot? Who wasn't?

CHAPTER SIX

I was ordering a root beer to go when I remembered something so I wedged myself back into the phone booth and called Mr Lowenstein. I was cool with Miss Shirley, who put me through.

'You have been busy,' he said.

'I try,' I said modestly. 'I presume you've read my full and detailed report, pardon the paper it's written on.'

'I have it in my overworked hand this very moment,' he said. 'Mr Daniel. I'm not trying to tell you your job but for goodness' sake remember pupils have both rights and parents these days.'

'They would have, wouldn't they,' I said, 'at least parents. But I also have to remember just what I'm up against. Anyway, one or two quick things — do I assume you want to keep the cops out to try and minimize any publicity?'

'You certainly do,' he said. 'Next.'

'Why didn't you use your own security men?'

'I decided not to,' he said shortly. 'I decided an outside investigator might be more . . . objective.'

'I see,' I said. 'And how did you come up with me?'

'My wife and two children bowl,' he said. 'Very occasionally they talk me into going along with them. As I refuse to make an ass of myself by even trying to knock those foolish wooden objects over, I normally spend most of the time talking with Mr Curtain, a man I've come to admire somewhat over the years.'

'I see,' I said again.

'Next,' said Mr Lowenstein.

'That's it,' I said. 'Thanks.'

'Thank you,' he said politely, then hung up.

'Objective, eh,' I said to the dead phone. 'That's me all over.'

As I fought my way out of the telephone booth that was designed for midgets I noticed there was only one car left in Art's parking lot, the one sporting a car-phone antenna. I went into the washroom at the back; it was surprisingly clean, with a heavy smell of disinfectant. I looked through the wastepaper basket; there was one empty packet of strawberry-flavored cigarette papers, either from a sissy or from someone trying hopefully to mask the highly individual aroma of burning pot.

Then, braced with the soft drink, I got myself as comfortable as possible in the front seat of the van back in the school parking lot and waited for the last classes to let out for the day. The first trickle of liberated youth started just after three thirty, then the volume increased steadily until the lot was in full action, doors slamming, brakes squealing, engines revving unnecessarily, kids calling back and forth. The soccer field, or 'pitch' as I liked to call it, and tennis courts filled up, so did Art's. Dev put in an appearance and strolled about keeping the lid on things; twenty minutes later it had all pretty much calmed down. I wasn't looking for anything in particular, just getting the feel of it all. Nor is it true to say that I was waiting for Miss Shirley, whose car, who knew, might just happen to be at the garage that day and who would love a drive home in a dirty van with a dirty old man. Anyway, I did not see her; maybe teacher was keeping her in late.

So I drove home by myself, changed clothes and vehicles and made it back to the office just before rush hour. I waved to Mrs Morales, opened up, picked the mail off the floor and leafed through it – no employment records yet from John Curtain so I could put off thinking about his problem for the weekend. I didn't want the chore of getting Betsy out and setting up, but habits are habits and good ones even more so, according to Miss Manners, so I did and transfered all my notes, names and addresses, receipts, the contract, the report to Mr Seburn and the one to Mr Lowenstein in abbreviated forms on to their appropriate disks, then cut up all the now superfluous paperwork with a shredder of my own invention – a large pair of pinking shears and a deft left hand.

What the hell. 'Occupy yourself ceaselessly,' said Solomon, 'it sure beats thinking.' Then I attacked the rest of the mail.

There was some bank interest from a ninety-day deposit to enter, also a certified check for $200 from Mr Raymond Millington of St Charles, New Mexico. I'd been looking on and off for over three months for the Millingtons' runaway daughter Ethel Catherine Anne, age fifteen, last seen at the Taos Trailways bus station 2 February. She wasn't really last seen then, hundreds of people had hopefully seen her since, it's like Columbus discovering America when it wasn't even him, it probably wasn't even America then, and there were assorted millions of people here already, but that's the way it was always put, last seen.

I'd so far tried all the usual things as well as several unusual ones but I wasn't getting anywhere and didn't want any more of the old man's money – I didn't know for sure but I saw him as an old man – bearded, mournful, maybe a farmer. So I got out the typewriter and on my officially headed stationery (from Mrs Martel, next to the post office) wrote him a note withdrawing my services and telling him that if I went on I felt I'd only be wasting his money. I kept his last check because I'd earned it. Most of it, anyway. My leg started hurting about then so I got up to stretch it.

There were two more missing-person letters in the mail, one from Utah, the other from Santa Barbara. God knows how the writers found me. Not that I wasn't capable but as a one (occasionally two)-man operation I'd be far down on a list of potentially helpful agencies where manpower is what's needed, not brains. I don't suppose there are many things sadder than a missing-person letter with its list of physical characteristics and you know it's one of 500 copies. And in the photograph that comes with it the subject is always smiling; of course who keeps a picture of someone crying or frowning, or takes one for that matter, but still.

I answered both letters, saying I couldn't take on any more clients right now but I would keep the pictures with me and keep my eyes open as I went about my daily business. Sure.

By then it was getting on to six thirty, hell, time I was getting out of there. I dug the phone out and called Mae. She was back. Sure she'd see me later, just for a drink or two though cause she was beat.

'I can imagine,' I said. I tidied up, put everything away, locked up, mailed the letters in the corner box, waved to Mrs Morales but she didn't see me, and burnt just a touch of rubber on my way out into the traffic.

Home. Showered the body beautiful, shaved the visage divine and patted on some aftershave Mae had given me in my stocking last Christmas. As five months had gone by and there was still plenty of it left and it had been a small bottle to begin with you might think I didn't care that much for it and you might be right. Then I donned some out-dated Valley leisure wear, drank a weak brandy and ginger and idly ruminated about Art, Dev, Mr Lowenstein and with one, cute, untidy exception – faceless high-school students. I didn't think about Miss Shirley. Then I put the top up on the car and went to pick up Mae.

A lady on the radio told me to stand by my man. I said I would.

Mae and I had a drink or two at the Two-Two-Two, one at Dave's Corner Bar and a quick one over at Sandy's where the local post office workers were just starting to get into it. Great invention, bars, I'll take them over the steamboat or cotton gin any time. Hell, over the wheel, too. And all I ask in a bar is three little things – that within it is for ever twilight, that it serves booze and that it serves me. There's not a lot wrong with bar girls either, they're something like actresses, seldom ugly, seldom teetotal and seldom celibate, but usually heavier.

After Sandy's we had a bite of overdone pasta at Mario's and a couple of glasses of house burgundy which she liked but I could have lived without. Mae said she was OK, she was relieved it was over, her sister had been no help at all and her father, long divorced from her mom but still living reasonably nearby, hadn't even bothered to show up. Couldn't let a little thing like a funeral interrupt his afternoon canasta session, she said without malice. Nice girl, Mae. Nice big, blond girl, big appetite, worse clothes sense than mine even, no games. She was wearing a mother-of-pearl locket that had been her mother's and before that her grandmother's, and kept touching it to see if it was still there. I thought she had something on her mind other than what she had just been through, but I didn't press her about it.

We wound up back at her place; she and her hyper-active girlfriend Charlene shared a small house off Sepulveda that smelled strongly of cats, which made sense as there was always at least a dozen living there at any one time. Charlene was out for once on a date; God only knows what he was like and where they were, maybe go-carting in Encino. Mae made us a nightcap and we went to bed.

'Just for a cuddle,' I warned her. 'Been a tough week.'

'Very amusing,' she said.

We were sipping and cuddling and watching a barely watchable Burns & Allen re-run when she said, 'Jay-sus, what's that?'

'What's what?'

'That.' She turned on the bedside lamp and pulled down the sheet. 'That.'

'Shark bite,' I said.

'Not very amusing,' she said. 'You didn't have it when I left.'

She touched the foot-long scar gently. It was on the top of my left leg, on the inside. I leaned over her and turned the light off again, giving her a kiss on the way there and on the way back.

'Well?' she said.

'Well,' I said, 'I was in the Oasis, way out Ventura. You know it?'

She shook her head.

'Just after you left. I was drowning my sorrow.'

She made a noise indicating disbelief. 'Drowning your thirst, maybe.'

'Anyway, it was getting late. For lack of anything better to do I was shooting the breeze with this garden furniture salesman who'd just lost his job so he was sleeping in his car. Well, I bought him a couple of drinks and he felt bad because he couldn't return the favor so to cheer him up I bought him a couple more and bought the old girl behind the bar, Martha, a couple too, she'd just had all her tubes out so she wasn't too cheerful either.'

'Sounds like a fun soirée,' said Mae. 'Sorry I missed it.'

'Two guys had been playing pool, waiting for the joint to empty out. Young kids, drinking beer. Harmless. One Mexican. One hippy. The hippy jumps the bar, whips out a bread knife and holds it against the old girl's throat while she empties the till.'

'Oh, God,' said Mae.

'While he's doing this his pal is holding his hand in his pocket like he's got a gun, covering us two, i.e. me and the ex-garden furniture salesman who's sleeping in his car. I figured he was full of shit, if he had a gun he would have shown it, so when his amigo let go of Martha I decided to get clever.'

'Uh-huh,' said Mae. 'What else is new?'

'I caught him a good shot on the side of his cabeza with a pool cue. He dropped the money and the knife. As I figured, his small-time compadre didn't have a gun but he pulled out a knife from a sheath on the back of his belt where it was hidden by his shirt and he caught me one.'

'You're lucky he didn't cut your testimonials off,' she said.

'He was trying,' I said.

'Brilliant,' she said. 'Totally brilliant.'

'I know, I know. But what are you going to do? You put up or shut up, especially when you're my size.'

'Well, you could shut up once in a while,' she said. 'Specially when you're smashed.'

'You know what? My personal physician says it's OK for me to resume my love life again if I stay on the bottom and don't move anything but my eyelashes. Next week I can curl my toes.'

'You'll be lucky,' Mae said. And so I was.

CHAPTER SEVEN

The following morning Timmy was burned to death in my office.

I was there at the time looking up the names and phone numbers of some students I planned to have a word with later that day. If I'd been a little less paranoid I'd have made out a list Friday afternoon and kept it with me but there you go. That time in Chicago the Corsican button-man tried to tattoo my head and shoulders with the firing pattern of a sawn-down shotgun had come about because I had a piece of paper in my wallet I should have left at home or burned or eaten.

So, Saturday morning, feeling pretty good all things considered, I parked in front of the office at about ten thirty, waved to Mrs Morales, opened up, took the garbage out the back and was unlocking the safe to get Betsy when I heard the front picture window shatter. I poked my head out of the bathroom to see what the hell was happening, figuring it was probably that loser Mick again, when the whole office went up in a whoosh of flame like it had been hit with a load of napalm. Maybe it had. I smelled my hair burning. I did have a fire extinguisher but it was by the front door so I couldn't get to it even if I'd wanted to. Fat lot of use it would have been anyway.

It seemed impossible a fire could spread so quickly; I soaked a towel under the tap, put it on my head and crawled to the back door and out, crawled like the bad old days on the obstacle course at Fort Meyers when sadistic, gung-ho creeps fired live 30-30s up your rectum. Thank God it was garbage day and I'd already unlocked the back door.

I lay on the asphalt out back for a minute. I saw my pant

40

legs were smoking and rolled over and over in the dirt. I probably shouted a bit too because I frightened the worms out of the alley cat who lived next door and nothing frightened that molting feline. Then I heard someone else shouting, then a siren. I hobbled around the side of the unit through the broken glass at the edge of the vacant lot. When I got around to the front, flames were shooting out through where the plate-glass window used to be. Mr Amoyan was trying to get close with his toy fire extinguisher but someone was holding him back.

'Your friend went in,' he said when he saw me but I didn't know what he meant. Then he went on about something else but I didn't know what that meant either. It must have sunk in though because I remembered it later.

I sat down suddenly in the parking lot; some kind citizen pulled me further away from the blaze; Mrs Morales gave me a paper cup of something I didn't drink. I saw the Nus helping their cousin carry cartons of merchandise out of his store, as if the stuff wasn't hot enough already. Mr Amoyan said something in Armenian I didn't understand. I said something he didn't understand right back.

The first of the fire engines came around the corner, some of the crew jumping off and going into action before it stopped. I noticed it said 'Class One' on the door of the fire engine; nothing but the best, as usual.

It was all over in a surprisingly short time, maybe six or seven minutes. By then the fire was out completely, there wasn't even much smoke left. My unit was the only one touched. A fire marshal who had arrived in a bright red Pontiac made his way cautiously into the ruin.

'There's a fatality in here,' he called back. 'Male.' I noticed Timmy's shopping cart lying on its side in front of the Nus'; some of his belongings had been carried by water from the hoses down past Mrs Morales'. A plastic ray gun floated like a boat in the water. I seemed to recall Mr Amoyan saying something about my friend going in and guessed that my friend Timmy had gone in all right, to try and help his friend, me, out. Goddamn it anyway.

The paramedics arrived. The one who wasn't the driver smeared some cooling jelly on my face, cut away what was left of my almost-new chinos and began on my legs. Ouch. The fire marshal came out looking angry. I asked the driver to get him for me; he brought him over.

'My office,' I said as best I could. 'I was in there. What happened?'

'Looks like a brick first, then a bottle of gas,' the marshal said, turning away for a good spit. 'Burns like hell for a few minutes, then goes out.'

'You take him to the hospital now, please,' said Mrs Morales. The paras already had the stretcher out; they lifted me effortlessly on to it.

'When are you coming to visit me?' I whispered to Mrs Morales.

'You shouldn't be talking, pal,' said the driver.

'Why should I visit a crazy man like you?' asked Mrs Morales.

'I can tell you what you're doing wrong with your tacos,' I said.

The paras snapped down the legs of the stretcher and wheeled me to the ambulance and then slid me in, one jumping up behind me, the other closing the door behind me. Then the one in the back began giving me oxygen.

'Just in case,' he said.

'In case of what?' I asked, but he didn't answer.

The driver took off. I could feel awful things happening to my legs, I imagined I could feel skin oozing off, like baby Blobs. The para who'd cut off most of my trousers had thoughtfully left me my pockets for future use like a true member of the medical profession; I pointed to the one with my wallet in it. The para got it out. I stopped sucking oxygen long enough to tell him, 'Insurance.'

He nodded, found my Kaiser card and redirected the driver.

I was damned if they were going to take me to County, I'd wound up there once before when I'd been shot, mugged, stomped, rolled and a few other things downtown near the flower market and it was six hours before they got around to me. Not because they didn't like me or because of something I said, but because bleeding slowly to death from a stomach wound was way down on their list of emergencies, they had dozens of more serious cases to look at first and more arriving regularly at the door. I found out later they got about 400 emergency patients a day and about half of them were critical, having been stabbed, shot, slashed, smashed, run down by cars or life.

Anyway, finally some Samaritan saw me passed out on the floor and screamed loudly enough to get me some attention. I woke up in the intensive-care ward not feeling well at all. The men on both sides of me were handcuffed to their cots; both had been shot in the stomach during separate robbery attempts. And, although I know this part of it wasn't County Hospital's fault, maybe, the second day there we had an earthquake and bottles and IVs were crashing all over the place. Luckily I was high as a kite on painkillers.

One funny thing happened while I was at County, or it seemed funny at the time. Most of the patients in the ward were on restricted intakes for one reason or another which meant they (and I) got only a thimbleful of water to drink every four hours for the first couple of days. We all took it pretty well except one nerd across from me who'd had a perforated ulcer and he bitched and moaned and complained non-stop that he was dying of thirst. However, he couldn't move to do anything about it, he had a tube coming out of his ass, another one out of his dick, one up his nose, the IV going into his arm and a fifth tube sticking out of a hole in his chest.

Well. We woke up one night to find the silly bugger sitting on his bed sipping hot chicken soup. 'Ahhh, is that good,' he was going. He'd somehow shut off a couple of his tubes and taken the other two and the IV stand with him and shuffled his way to the coffee, soup and cocoa dispenser on the floor above. What that horrible, salty, instant muck did to his stomach must have been murder because he had a relapse the following day and a very angry nurse wheeled him out back down to the operating room. Served the stupid fucker right, was the general consensus. So much for County. But it did the job, and free, and there's not many places you can say that about today.

Well. They got me over the hills to Kaiser on Hollywood Boulevard without hitting anything and an hour later I was tucked into bed, mildly but not unpleasantly doped up. I'd had some more jelly and new bandages put on in emergency and been told that I'd live. The other good news was I had only first-degree burns that would heal in time without even leaving a blemish on my smooth, baby-like skin. The bad news was that it would be a day or two before I could get out of there and start blowing up places myself.

The night passed, as nights eventually do.

Sunday morning.

Sunday morning in Kaiser.

Six thirty of a Sunday morning in Kaiser. An old hag masquerading as a nurse's aide said I had to get ready for breakfast. I said I didn't want any breakfast, I wanted to go back to sleep. She said it was Sunday. I said I knew that. She wanted to know if I wanted a visit from a minister, priest or rabbi of my chosen faith. I said I might consider a lama but I really wanted to go back to sleep. I also wanted a 'Do Not Disturb' sign on the door because it didn't take the Queen of the Gypsies to foretell a lot of nosy visitors in my near future.

The first one came at 10.01, one minute after official visiting hours began. It was my brother. His name is Anthony, called Tony. He came in and gazed sadly down at me. I gazed sadly up at him. A lot of people think we look alike, maybe

44

we do. His wife Gaye never thought so. We get along pretty good, considering what he owed me. He was wearing shorts, sneakers and a sweat-top and was carrying a paper bag.

'Brought your lunch?'

'No, brought our breakfasts.' He took out two large containers of coffee and gave one to me. I could smell the booze in it even before I wrestled the top off.

'You allowed to drink this?'

'Sure,' I said. 'They told me my lungs were like a newborn babe's, no damage whatsoever due to my cleverness in not breathing at the wrong time.'

'With that thing on your head, you look like Turhan Bey, was that his name?' my brother said. 'How's the rest of you?'

'No problem,' I said. We both blew on our drinks. 'How'd you find me so fast?'

He took a sip and shuddered. 'Routine detective work,' he said airily. 'Friend of mine, you know Lew Marks? He saw your name on the case sheet and called me. I called the paras. So what happened, stand too close to the barbecue again?' He was referring to a time when we were kids when my new birthday shirt caught on fire because he pushed me accidentally on purpose into the barbecue where Pop was cooking supper.

I told him what happened. He whistled.

'Are you lucky, Vic. Any idea who did it?' He sat on the other bed in the room, an empty one by the window. Folded up against the wall next to it was a portable screen, next to that was an IV stand.

'You better believe it,' I said. 'I don't have so many enemies I don't know who they all are. I'll tell you about it sometime.'

'Well, ex-cuuuse me!' He pretended to be deeply offended; I knew and he knew I knew he could get all the details that were going from the investigating officer who was no doubt out in the hall waiting his turn to badger the poor invalid.

'How's Mom?' I asked him after a while.

'Same. I haven't told her anything yet.'

'Well, don't,' I said, sipping away, feeling the warm brandy slide down a grateful throat, take the turn and head for home. 'You mind keeping her for another week?'

He waved it away. 'Sure, easy.' Mom wasn't well. I would look after her for three weeks, which is why the extra bedroom where I was living and also why I was living in the Valley of Death at all, then Tony and Gaye took her for their turn. It worked out OK for her, not so well sometimes for me or Gaye, whom she didn't like, and I was with her there, but all of us involved had come to realize the hard way that the other choices were even worse. The change-over was supposed to have happened that afternoon, now I had a week to get myself together. The week would be added on to my next stint, Gaye would see to that.

'I gotta go,' my brother said, getting off the bed with a groan. 'I'm playing soccer with the kids.'

'Do you good,' I said. 'Tell them Uncle Cinders says hello.'

'Anything else I can do, anytime, you let me know, kid.' I liked the 'kid'. I was two years older than him.

'Funny that you should mention that,' I said. He groaned again. 'There is a little something. I need a guy checked out, it won't take you a minute, one call.'

'Can't it wait? I gotta go.'

'No.' I passed him the phone. He sighed heavily and began dialing.

'It would help if I had the name.' I gave it to him, and a license-plate number, which he relayed to whoever he was talking to down at Central.

'How's Betsy?' he asked while we waited.

'Fine,' I said. 'How's yours?' His didn't have a name like mine.

'Fine,' he said. We waited. Then he passed me the phone. I listened, thanked the man and hung up. In the old days it would have taken a week.

'Who was that?' I asked my brother.

'Morrie,' he said. 'You don't know him. He's weird. He smokes a corncob like Popeye's.'

'That's weird, all right.'

'Well, see you.' My brother chucked his empty container in the wastebin and made for the door. 'Don't do anything too stupid, OK?'

'You know me, Tony.'

'Yeah. Call you tomorrow.' He left. I finished my breakfast and chucked my container after his, missing by a mile. Maybe I should have seen that minister, priest or rabbi of my chosen faith after all.

CHAPTER EIGHT

'Messy, messy!' said my next visitor from the open door. 'If it isn't the Shriek of Araby!'

'Go away,' I said.

He didn't. He came all the way in, closed the door carefully, tiptoed over, retrieved the container, deposited it where it belonged, then beamed cheerily down at me. 'And how are we feeling this morning, h'um?'

'Fine until recently,' I said. He giggled and bounced up and down on his little piggies. I don't know what the height minimum is for cops these days but from the size of him it couldn't be much, suddenly my life was being overrun by trolls. This one was attired in the Johnny Carson look – powder-blue jacket too tight at the waist and too large in the shoulders, tan slacks, narrow tie, tiepin.

Wow.

'Lieutenant Maynard Conyers, West Valley,' he said. 'ID on request.'

'Forget it,' I said. 'One look at your picture and I'd have a relapse. Besides, you must be a cop because if you weren't and you said you were, who would believe you?'

'Woke up cross, did we?' he said. He looked around the room for a minute, then walked out and came right back in with a straight chair. He put it beside my bed, sat on it, then took out from his jacket pocket a large, new-looking notebook bound in yellow leatherette. 'Thinking caps on,' he said. 'Work time.' He didn't fool me at all although he probably met lots he did. Protective coloration I do believe it's called, he was as trustworthy as a Siamese fighting fish before supper, and about the same size.

'Mr Daniel. I've read your medical report. I read the case

48

sheet and talked to the two patrolmen who answered the first call. I talked on the phone to the fire marshal. I saw what was left of your office and it's a mess. I talked to a Mrs Morales, a Mr and Mrs Nu and a Robbie Brunner, some in person, some only by phone so far.'

'Who's Robbie Brunner?' I asked him, just so he'd think I was listening. I did want to ask him how my Bowman & Larens safe was but I didn't want him to get the idea there was anything interesting in it.

'A passer-by,' said the lieutenant. 'A helpful passer-by who pulled you away from the fire. My conversations have led me to the suspicion that there exists in this cruel world some party or parties unknown or maybe known who don't like you very much.'

'Good work, Lieutenant,' I said. 'Smart thinking.'

'Thank you,' he said. 'Any idea who?'

It so happened that I'd been doing some thinking that morning mainly because from six thirty to ten o'clock on a Sunday morning lying in a hospital bed there's not a lot else to do frankly except to feel sorry for yourself. I didn't even have any grapes to peel. What I thought was first of all I couldn't be sure the fire had been intended to hurt my person as against my office as I'd been out of sight at the time in the bathroom so it might have been meant only as a warning. It was also possible of course that the maniac who did it was parked across the street waiting for me to open up, but I seldom did on weekends. I also didn't know if a brick and bottle would go through a window and a closed venetian blind; if not, the perpetrator, as the fuzz love to put it, would be obliged to wait until the blind was up which it only was when I was in the office.

Why you may ask did not said perpetrator chuck his brick in through the back window? Because there was a grill over the back window is why. Even from the front there wasn't a lot of risk though, there was only a narrow sidewalk between the car park and my frontage, you could throw anything you wanted without getting out of the car, and the exit from the parking area was only some ten feet from my door and running down back of the building was a handy alley.

So I'd cogitated about all that. I also cogitated about Mr Lowenstein and his beloved human zoo and what might happen to it if all the shit hit all the fans. I also cogitated about a seven-letter word spelt REVENGE and tried not to cogitate too much about Timmy.

Thus it was that I said to Lieutenant Conyers, 'Yes, I do have an idea who doesn't like me.'

'I'd love to hear about it,' the lieutenant said, 'if you can spare the time.'

I told him about the attempted robbery at the Oasis way out Ventura Boulevard some weeks ago, about Martha, the hippy and his amigo. Hell, I even told him about the ex-garden furniture salesman with his big thirst. I told him I thought I'd caught a glimpse of the Anglo in front of my office in a green Chevy just before it happened. I told him before he asked that the kid could have found me easily enough as my name had been in the local paper after the foiled holdup. They'd actually used the word 'hero', I informed him diffidently.

'Really?' he said. 'Well! Wait till I tell the wife.'

I'd given a full description, I went on to inform him, of the dynamic duo to the cops at the time and it would be on file somewhere. I told him a considerable amount of believable crap, in fact I might have believed it myself if I hadn't known I was making it all up. Then the strain of it all must have gotten to me because I came over all funny, fluttered my eyes and rang for the nurse.

'Heart-breaking,' the midget muttered. Whether he was referring to my Camille imitation or the Oasis yarn I will never know.

The nurse came in surprisingly quickly, I didn't even have time to think up the reason I'd rung for her. Luckily I didn't need it for as soon as she saw the suffering etched on my wan face she started right in.

'Have you been bothering Mr Daniel, Officer? We cannot have that.'

'Bothering him? I've been giving him the third degree, I just put the rubber hose away before you came in,' the halfpint said. 'Got any electrodes I can borrow?'

I moaned weakly and closed my weary eyes. The lieutenant got up, put his notebook away and picked up the chair.

'What year Chevy?' he asked me.

'It was a 63,' I said. 'Large dent in the door on the driver's side. Bumper sticker that said "Police Are Human Too – Bribe One Today".'

'I'll maybe come by tomorrow when the miracles of modern medicine have had a chance to work,' he said to me. 'Ta ta, Florence,' he said to the nurse. He left with the chair. Cops. Maybe they are human – that's the trouble with them.

The nurse asked me why I had rung. I said I wanted a roast beef on onion roll easy on the mustard and four Mogadons. She said she could let me have two aspirins and padded out to get them. She came back with them in a few minutes. I told her I was hurting and didn't want to be a big baby but I would appreciate something stronger, she said no more drugs until the doctor had seen me again which would be on his two o'clock rounds.

She left; I phoned Benny. It was time to get off the pot.

Benny was my buddy. We played chess over at his place about once a week; I'd learnt that highly irritating game in a Louisiana guest home for bad men. I had plenty of time – three years is a lot of days and about twice as many nights. My roommate Herbie, a thoroughly nice chap who used to rent his sister for short periods of time to his friends, taught me, it only took me about a year to learn the moves, then another year to give him a game lasting longer than five minutes. I was getting on to it, though, I could give Benny a pretty good game now as long as he spotted me a piece or two. So I called him; it was near on eleven thirty by then, the perfect time to get him as he never went to bed before four or five.

Somewhere earlier I mentioned I was occasionally a two-man agency; Benny was the occasional. Once upon a Hollywood dream I'd almost married his Aunt Jessica. When we split up, by some malevolent prank of Fate I wound up with custody of him. Benny was one of the earth's most successful hustlers and I don't say that lightly as I've met more than a few in my time, heard about a lot more and read about a lot more than that. He had so much nerve he made Sergeant York look like a sissy. He hustled his mother playing casino and his sisters playing fish, he hustled loco, drunk-inflamed Mexicans in all-Mexican bars in East LA playing eight-ball. He hustled airlines (lost luggage), car rentals (false ID and a speedy drive to Tijuana), camera stores and carpeterías. When they'd finished bringing in the sheaves up in Humboldt County he dealt superior grass to a select clientele. He owned four and a half houses in Anaheim, one of which he had rented for the past six months to Narcs who were using it for surveillance of an apartment block across the street where they suspected drugs were being sold. He liked to ski but most of the time his fabulously expensive ski equipment was hidden away as he'd reported it stolen and was waiting for the insurance on it to come through. There is a ruse adopted by some big-city dwellers to foil muggers – they carry two wallets, a fancy one with a little money in it to hand over if necessary and another one stowed away with the real wad in it. Benny had two safes in his apartment, working on the same principle.

I told him my sad, sad story.

He laughed.

I told him what I wanted and when I wanted it.

He laughed.

I told him why I wanted it, then hung up while I was still a hit. Then I made a wee call of a real-estate nature. Then I made another call of a real-estate nature, one to my landlord, something I'd been putting off because I didn't exactly have the kind of news a landlord is dying to get on a Sunday morning.

The landlord was watching the Raiders–Chargers game, I could hear it in the background.

'Guess who,' I said.

'My main man!' he said. 'Hang on til I turn the sound down.' I hung on. 'How's the burnt-out case?'

'Considerably peeved,' I said. 'How'd you hear about it?'

'Fire marshal, closely followed by a Señor Gregor Amoyan,' he said.

'Is that his first name, I never knew.'

'Lotsa things you don't know, my man,' the landlord said with great cheer. 'Pause for a toke.' He took a toke and held it in for about a quarter of an hour. I was glad he was stoned, he was a good landlord at the worst of times but a wonderfully tolerant one when smashed. His name was Elroy and he was twenty-two. Both of his parents and a couple of uncles had been killed by a drunk crossing the central divider on the 405 just after Christmas and he, king o' the drop-outs, prince of pot-heads, planetary commander of the space cadets, had inherited not only the development that included what was left of my office but two more like it, all in the neighborhood, plus a warehouse or two plus the odd house. He drove a De Lorean, carried a huge wad of singles which he handed out during the day to the needy (mainly the thirsty needy) and spent maybe a total of $3.50 a year on his wardrobe of T-shirts and flip-flops. In other words he was rich enough to ignore the mundane preoccupations of us mere mortals but then again he always had. But that didn't include business, that he took care of, twice a week he went to night classes at UCLA to learn accounting and tax laws and the like.

'So what are some of these lots of things I don't know?' I asked him.

'You don't know zilch,' he said. 'You no sabe nada. You don't comprende I had Sam board up your suite this morning.' Sam was a lugubrious black handyman who both worked for Elroy and was his connection. 'He says none of the walls went, the bathroom's fine, so is what he called dat strongbox of yours but the roof's done gone but it's just that cheap asbestos board anyway so he's doin' that today and I'll have those Armenian folk-dancing fools in by tomorrow afternoon and what color rug do you want, you're getting, wait for it, tundra, my dear, my darling, mi corazón. I have insurance that covers earthquakes, arson, tidal waves, termites, whale damage and the invasion of the bodysnatchers, that's one of the two things I learned from my old man.'

I stopped his flow long enough to ask, 'What was the second?'

'I forget,' Elroy said. 'I think it had something to do with girls.'

'Thanks, mate,' I said.

'Baby, anytime for my main man,' he said. He paused for another monster drag. 'Sam told me about the guy who was killed, shit.'

'Timmy,' I said.

'Yeah,' he said. 'What was his story?'

I told him what little I knew of Timmy's story.

'What was he doing in there, for God's sake? Stupid clot.'

I told him the stupid clot was more than likely in there trying to get this stupid clot out. Then he said something about the funeral, I said I'd take care of it if no family showed up. Then he said something else I didn't catch and hung up. I was wondering what had happened to Timmy's body and reminded myself to ask the lieutenant the next time I saw him where it would have been taken and what the procedure was now.

The nurse came in with something on a tray she called lunch. I'm no gourmet but you could have fooled me. When she departed I had a small debate with myself. Was this an emergency or wasn't it? I decided it was and telephoned Miss Shirley at her home.

CHAPTER NINE

Miss Shirley was in.

Actually she was out in the back of her place planting tomato seedlings at the bottom of her garden, she told me, but she also told me she had a new cordless telephone she was just wild about so she was using it and was actually talking to me and watering her plants at the same time and what did I think of that?

I thought it was pretty hot stuff and a triumph of modern communications and I told her so, then I mentioned my recent adventures and the sorry state to which they had brought me. Miss Shirley was so appalled she almost flooded one whole row of seedlings or so I like to think. When she'd finished finding out if I was really all right she wanted to know if I thought the arson had any connection with what I was doing at her school.

'No way,' I told her, but with my fingers crossed. 'I think I've convinced the police of it too, at least for the time being.'

'Well, that's something, anyway,' she said.

I agreed. 'Will you pass on the news to your boss for me and tell him not to visit me, also not to worry, it's not his fault and I'll get back on the job as soon as possible, about which I've had a couple of, if I do say so myself, brilliant ideas.'

'Of course,' said Miss Shirley. 'It's the least I can do.'

'There is one other little thing,' I said. 'I want you to come by for a visit tonight, and bring a friend.'

She wanted to know who and why. I told her who but told her I couldn't tell her why but if she was a good girl I could tell her why I couldn't tell her why.

'Tell me anyway,' she said.

'Because if you know you might have to pretend you didn't and despite popular belief women are terrible liars, especially beautiful ones. Fat, ugly ones are better but I do not want to speculate at this time on the reasons why.'

'Me neither,' she said. 'Men are the worst liars of all, especially huge, overweight ones.'

'Well, I'm not lying about this,' I said. 'There are two kinds of accessories, one kind is a matching glove and purse set, the other a legal term for a party who helps, or merely knows in advance of, an illegal act. Not that I'm planning anything of the kind, of course.'

'Of course. Perish the thought. Tiny little law-abiding you?'

After a bit more welcome badinage of this sort Miss Shirley went back to her gardening and I tried to take a nap. It wasn't easy as my head was positively awhirl with ideas, plans, and, in the case of a certain salad-grower, fantasies, but I finally did manage to drop off for a snooze just in time for Florence to wake me up and get me pretty for the doctor. He came in shortly thereafter trailed by several of those cringing, servile types who spend most of their lives following closely on the heels of medics. I think it has something to do with money. One of the retinue was pushing a trolley laden with the unpleasant implements of his trade.

The doctor was a tired-looking elderly man wearing a short white jacket over his civvies. He said, 'Good afternoon, I'm Doctor Franklin.'

I said, 'Good afternoon, I'm Victor Daniel and I hurt.'

He took the clipboard from the bottom of the bed, glanced at it, handed it to Florence, then picked up a pair of blunt-ended scissors and neatly cut through the loose-fitting gauze on my once proud Apollo-like legs. Then he gently eased the sticky bandages away from the burnt patches. His whole gang crowded around for a closer look.

'Good,' said the doctor. 'Will you bend your legs a little, please.'

I raised my knees very carefully. It hurt some but nothing fell off. He saw the knife scar on my inner thigh.

'What's that from?'

'The war.' I got the line from a book I once read.

'Which war?'

'Last month's,' I said.

'And what war's that from?' he asked, poking the old entry wound above the right knee.

'I forget,' I said. 'I think it was the war between the sexes.'

'I see,' he said. Then he unwound my turban. Everyone peered in again.

'I think we can dispense with the headgear from now on, Nurse,' he said.

'Yes, Doctor,' she said. Too bad, I quite liked the effect.

'Continue the something-o-benzocaine every four hours, with fresh dressings,' he said, 'and I'm starting him on a course of antibiotics.' The nurse made a note on the clipboard.

'What's something-o-benzocaine, if you don't mind me asking,' I asked.

'Fluoro,' he said. 'Antiseptic, analgesic, moisturizing and keeps the air out. I want you to keep bending those legs, too, even though they might be tender.'

'Forget the might,' I said. 'How about some pain pills while you're at it?'

'You can give him all the anacin he wants, within reason,' he told the nurse.

'Thanks for nothing,' I said.

'Tomorrow you could walk around a little,' he said. 'Good afternoon.'

'And a good afternoon to all of you,' I said. The doctor led his entourage out. Florence took a tube from the trolley and gingerly applied what's-its-name to the crinkly bits, then wrapped my legs up again in fresh gauze. Then she daubed some ointment on my aching head, upper right side, and adhesive-taped a pad over it. Then she shook out three anacins, if they were even that, from a large bottle and gave me two caps that I presumed were the antibiotics from a small bottle and made sure I took them. Hell, I would have anyway just on the long shot that maybe someone somewhere had made a mistake and put in some real dope.

The afternoon passed, as afternoons eventually do, even afternoons on the third floor of Kaiser.

I had a call from a worried Mr Lowenstein to whom I said all the right things, and put in a call to Mae to whom I said most of the right things. She blistered my ear for ten minutes while I said 'Don't blame me' and 'I didn't do nothing' and 'I was framed' and generally protested my absolute innocence. She finally hung up, miffed. Or is it in a huff? 'Ah the ladies, ah the ladies, they are sweeter than sweet,' my pop used to sing. 'Ah the ladies, ah the ladies, they make life so complete.'

Benny manifested himself in my room about seven thirty that evening, just at that time when Happy Hour in the Valley's many dark, cool and welcoming hostelries regretfully comes to an end. Perfect – I'd already had 'supper' – tinned tomato soup, crackers, hamburger steak, creamed spinach, Jello with bananas in it – and it gave us a half hour by ourselves before Miss Shirley and Friend were due.

Benny. Benny my buddy. He came into the room with the calm, ruddy-cheeked innocence of the truly amoral. With him the choirboy look was always in. Neatly trimmed ginger beard. Thinning (thinned) ginger hair that was mostly part, and he but a youth still in his early thirties. Unneeded wire-rimmed glasses. Harris tweed jacket, gray flannel slacks with cuffs, dark green (tundra?) turtleneck, black loafers with tassles. In one hand a bunch of flowers, in the other a smallish canvas suitcase.

'Am I glad to see you,' I said. 'That is you, isn't it?'

'The boy himself.' He turned around in a slow circle so I could get the full effect.

'A veritable fugitive from *Esquire*,' I said.

'So how're you doing, Uncle?'

'Don't call me that!' I told him for the millionth time. I didn't really give a fig if he called me uncle, aunt or granny but I knew he'd be disappointed if he didn't get the expected reaction. 'OK. Start unpacking, we haven't got all night. Did you find a way out of here?'

'End of the hall,' he said. He began taking bottles and tubes and assorted other goods from his case and laying them out neatly on the other bed. 'Firedoor, firestairs, emergency exit two flights down leads out into the back of the parking lot. Got it?'

I said I got it. Then he took out a white doctor's jacket and held it up against his puny chest. 'H'ummm, nice. Oh, I brought something.'

'Yeah, I saw, many thanks for the petunias.'

'Not the petunias.' He fished in his pocket and tossed over a tube of Demerols.

'About time,' I said ungratefully, popping two of them immediately and stashing the rest under the mattress. Then we began setting the stage for our eight o'clock visitors.

Miss Shirley arrived promptly on the hour as requested, with Dev, also as requested. She looked fetching as all get out in white, bell-bottomed slacks, blue blazer and matching blue sailor's cap worn at a rakish tilt. He looked less fetching in chinos and a red zip-up windbreaker. I looked least fetching of all, in fact I looked like I was at death's door and the door was wide open. The portable screen almost surrounded my bed; through one carefully left gap the shocked visitors peered in at what was left of poor me. One rubber tube taped to my arm led to the IV bottle hanging from its stand, another came out of my nose and disappeared into the darkness under the bed. A third red tube gave the impression it was emerging from my water works under the covers; it led under the bed to a highly visible bedpan. Most of my dome was swathed in gauze. I had one hand bandaged as well. Just the one, one didn't want to overdo it. The lowered lights gave an appropriately somber look to the whole set-up.

Outside the door Benny stood sentry, ready to tell Florence or anyone else who chanced by that I was with my girl and would be deeply grateful for a few stolen moments of privacy.

'How're you doing, Vic?' Dev asked softly after taking in the scene.

'Is . . . is that you, Dev?'

'And Miss Shirley,' he said. 'How're you getting on?'

'Ah, I'll be out of here in no time,' I bluffed.

'You poor dear!' said Miss Shirley. If she had any suspicions she kept them to herself. She moved closer and laid her cool palm against my cheek. Could I smell just a trace of freshly turned loam, of sweet, sun-ripened tomatoes and perhaps just a hint of, an elusive trace of, Johnson's baby cream? Not really.

'You're burning!' she said.

'Fires do that,' I said gently. 'By the way, we think we know who the bad guys were.'

'Oh yeah?' said Dev Devlin.

'Yeah.' I told them briefly about my little contretemps, which is a polite way of saying attempted castration, at the Oasis way out Ventura Boulevard and mentioned I thought I'd seen one of the emotionally disturbed youngsters, which is a polite way of saying spaced-out creep, in front of my office Saturday morning just before it happened.

'Those bastards,' he said. 'Saturday morning. Wish I'd been around instead of kicking out beer drinkers at the soccer game.'

'Me too.' I said. 'Listen, Dev, the reason I asked you to drop by, for which by the way many thanks, is that I won't be much use for a while according to the specialist so maybe you could do me a favor.'

'Sure, Vic,' he said. 'Name it.'

'Keep your eye on the storerooms for me, will you? My face, or what's left of it, might be in the papers tomorrow and someone from the school might start putting two and two together, you get me? I'm talking about maybe another fire, to cover up any shortages, maybe someone with computer access getting at the records, all right? Just keep the lid on for a couple of days.' Dev wasn't the only one in town with fancy footwork.

'You got it,' he said.

'Miss Shirley,' I said, 'and I want to thank you too for coming, is there any way you can cue the computer so you'll know if anyone mucks about with it who's not supposed to?'

She shrugged. 'I'm not an expert but I can try.' I wished she'd touch my cheek again or even my foot through the blankets.

Business being concluded I got them out of there before Flo or the mobile library or anyone else poked his or her head in. The business I refer to was of course letting Dev get a good look at me in my completely immobile, incapacitated and altogether pathetic state, à la chicken soup dope who couldn't possibly have moved but did.

Benny popped back as soon as they left and within five minutes we had the room and me back to normal, the screen and IV stand back where they belonged, tubes and bottles packed away, head-dressing off, lights up. Then he took off for a bite to eat and a bit of business involving two gross of Ray-Ban sunglasses. He left the suitcase as it had a few items in it I'd need later.

Later meant after Florence tucked me in for the night, that was about ten o'clock. I gave it another hour, helped myself to two more Demerols, allowed them time to dig in and start radiating their message that happy days were here again, then somewhat cautiously bestirred myself. Benny had brought some dark clothes more or less my size, dark sneakers ditto, dark toque to cover any head bandages and the white doctor's coat to go over everything in case I got caught sneaking out or sneaking back.

I didn't get caught sneaking out, anyway, but walking was murder, best I could manage was a sort of stiff, Frankenstein monster lurch. I propped the emergency door on the ground floor open with a wad of folded paper so it wouldn't lock behind me, climbed into Benny's waiting Ford and off we went to blow up things. Well, one thing in particular to start with, a certain B & B's (now Art's) hamburger stand. Art himself would come later.

CHAPTER TEN

The drive was pleasant, the Demerols uplifting, the legs bearable and Benny an amusing companion, as always. Well, as most of the time.

'A pleasant evening,' I observed.

'Indeed. How're you feeling, Uncle?' We cruised down the north slopes of Laurel Canyon Drive, then leveled off into the Valley Where Lilies Grew Not.

'I been worse,' I admitted. 'Thank God for pharmaceuticals that do their job and then some.'

'A-men,' he said. 'You will notice I'm driving very sedately on purpose but it would help my purpose if I knew where the hell we were going.'

'Turn right,' I said. 'And do me a favor, it's not a lot to ask, don't call me Uncle!'

He smiled and peered virtuously at me through his round granny glasses.

'Benny, you're a widely traveled individual, you get around, tell me about drugs. Drugs in LA.'

'Illegal drugs?'

'No, the cod liver oil war.'

'Now, now,' he said. 'It's embarrassing when a man your size uses sarcasm. Guy called Reese . . .'

'Tootie Reese?'

'Tootie Reese, ran most of the action in south-central LA til he not so brilliantly peddled some coke and smack to some DEA types; they reckon he'll get twenty to life next month when he comes up. So his action is up for grabs, you're talking maybe a hundred, a hundred and fifty houses so you can imagine what's going down.'

I said I could indeed.

'Guy called Whitey because he's blacker than the legendary Toby's bum at midnight in a coal mine, worked for Tootie, he's out on bail, I think it's a hundred grand, over that shoot-out in the pizza parlor downtown somewhere?'

'Last January,' I said. 'I remember. I was courting, if that's the word, your fey, if that's the word, Aunt Jessica at the time.'

'So you were, so you were. So you got something called Whitey's Enterprises and a bunch of ex-cons, very heavy, called Third World cutting up the LA market.'

'Next left,' I said. 'You know any of these dubious characters?'

'I see one or two of them around,' Benny said. 'I have, and I blush to admit it, even been known to do a little business with them.'

'You should blush,' I said.

'But they are not merely dubious, ol' buddy mio, they are killers. You have to figure twenty, thirty, forty murders this year alone between them and it's only May. They kill over who owns the turf, they kill rip-off merchants, they get killed trying to rip off themselves, they simply adore killing welshers and they love to kill driving by, it's like their trademark.'

'Next left,' I said.

'A gang of kids is having a party, they're out in the front yard to show how cool they are instead of being safe, or safer, anyway, out back or inside. A car drives by and starts shooting, they don't care who else gets hit.'

'You're talking kids now.'

'I'm talking kids now, hundreds of them, dealing on the streets. One kid I knew down on West 54th, they called him Gonzo, never had a job in his life. When he got hit he had four grand plus change in his pocket, his mother couldn't believe it. Some of them have gang tattoos, the smarter ones don't. They try and put the fear of God into other gangs by giving themselves names like "The Bloods", "The Crips", "The Schoolyard Crips" is a good one. Then you've got your

"Piru Killers". I personally like the "Van Ness Gangsters",
no hyperbole, just a simple statement of fact.'

'Turn right,' I said. 'How many gangs are there, would
you say?'

'Quién sabe, forty, fifty? How many kids are involved,
quién sabe, hundreds. And hundreds. You know how much
one house, which is like a wholesaler, will do in one day
down there? Twenty grand. I'm just talking coke, you understand, and maybe a little PCP for native use.'

We'd turned off Laredo by then and were heading at a
conservative pace along Del Mara, past the old railroad
station where no train had stopped for forty years. A couple
of bums sitting in the weeds along a siding were passing a
bottle back and forth. If they were waiting for the midnight
special to San Diego they'd better pick up another bottle or
two.

'Tell me about the houses,' I said.

'They're called rock houses because they sell mainly rock
coke which the kids push in baggies for a quarter up to
maybe forty dollars if they can get it. Lumps or rocks in coke
are thought to be a sign that it's stronger because the crystals
are intact, it's a complete scam. Anything'll crystalize pretty
much if you dampen it, especially that milk sugar stuff they
cut it with. So, woman moves in, respectable looking, a couple
of babies, and rents a house. She moves out pronto and the
dudes move in and commence their number, steel doors,
shatter-proof windows, fire-proof stashes, pay-offs to the
neighbors, you name it. Some of them have a sort of cubicle,
like a booth, in the hall or the living room where you put
your money in a revolving door or a turntable, then back
comes your goods. It's unbelievable now that I come to think
about it, I mean the size of the action and how public it all is,
a total stranger could score a grand's worth of coke in this
town in ten minutes. Five if he asked a cop for directions.'

'Grass?'

'It seems to be handled mainly by what *Variety* calls indie distributors although there are a lot of low-level groups involved. Mexican, Puerto Rican, your friendly Cubanos, but most of your real heavy muthas is black. Here endeth the first lesson.'

'Slow down, Benny boy, we are almost there,' I said. He slowed down; we turned into Greenview Avenue, the street on which Art sold his mediocre franks. 'Let's just drive casually past once, then go round the block.'

'Yes, let's just,' said Benny, 'and let's just tell Benny just what Benny is doing here and why.'

I told him as we cruised slowly down the quiet, tree-lined street.

'It used to be,' said I, 'in the dear dead days gone by, the days of *Liberty* and the *Saturday Evening Post*, the Mellow-Roll and the three-cent newspaper, it used to be the kindly old fart in the local candy store or soda fountain who had profitable sidelines, dirty comics . . .'

'"Mutt & Jeff in Tijuana",' Benny reminisced. 'That was a beaut.'

'So was "Popeye In Olive Oyl",' I said. 'Also numbers, he'd take your bet on the horses, sell contraceptives, sell cigarettes to kids, this and that. Where do the kids go now, you ask.'

'Where do the kids go now?'

'Drive-ins, my boy, and they got a lot more money than they used to. That crummy hamburger joint we just passed is run by a guy called Art. Art's got a nice new car with a phone, nothing flashy but new. He's also got a license for a camper. Also his wife has a car, nothing flashy, no phone, but new. I got his last name from his city permit and had my brother check him out with the DMV. Art's home address is a condo just this side of Griffith Park, heavens, they got horses and everything up there, I know cause I phoned them this afternoon, and you can imagine how much he takes in a week selling his sixty percent meat hotdogs.'

'I'm starting to get the picture,' said Benny.

'Good!' I said. 'Art, whose last name is Wetmore, by the way, also has a record and I don't mean the Bee-Gees. One GBH, one drug bust two years ago at which he turned state's evidence and got off on parole. Then he turned up at the emergency ward at UCLA a while later missing two fingers. He wouldn't say how it happened but the doc thought they had been cut off like with sheet-metal cutters so he filed a police report on him. Now what does all that sound like to you?' We pulled in and parked on a side street about twenty yards down from the back of Art's.

'It sounds like he was lucky they didn't kill him,' Benny said.

'Also my neighbor Mr Amoyan saw him. I remembered in the hospital. He said, "Red face, kid's car." He was sitting on his bench watching the girls when it happened.'

'What's a kid's car?'

'I dunno, but I bet he borrowed it from the school parking lot. Probably festooned with pennants, coon tails and fur dice.'

Benny whistled, then looked around.

'Let's do it,' he said. 'The coast is clear.'

'Not you,' I said. 'You stay here looking innocent.'

'What if you need some help?'

'No way,' I said. 'Piece of cake, I checked it out when I was getting a toothpick. Nice, well-built structure, airtight and cozy. Gas grills. Standard-issue lock, no alarms. No sign of a dog bowl or dog food. Back in a second.'

'Abyssinia,' said Benny. 'Oh. The key, silly me.' He passed me several keys on a Mickey Mouse key chain. 'Oh. Silly me, the gloves.' He passed me a pair of cheap work gloves which I took without comment and put on. The white coat was already folded up on the back seat. I took the toque from the glove compartment and put that on. We looked up and down the street; all was quiet.

'Well, go if you're going, Jesus,' said Benny. He rarely swore. I went.

It turned out to take more than a second but not a lot more; it does help when a chap's breaking and entering if he knows in advance what type of lock he'll have to open because then someone like Benny can get him a key for it. Picking locks is not as easy as popular literature would have you believe, nor is opening one with a credit card or similar bit of stiff plastic. I had three keys to choose from; the second one worked and I was in like Flynn. I took a quick peek around with the tiny flashlight that came with the keyring, then blew out all the pilot lights under the grill and the frier, leaving on only the one under the warmer.

A car came towards us up Greenview. I turned the flashlight off; it went right on by. I'd arranged with Benny to give a discreet toot on the horn if anyone approached from the back where I couldn't see, but so far so good. I turned the light back on and with my justly famous Swiss Army knife unloosened the clamp where the rubber tube of the gas supply was connected to the back of the grill and slipped the tube free. I didn't want to leave any of the gas jets on, they might survive the (devoutly hoped for) cataclysmic blast and get themselves noticed. Then I took my leave, locking up behind me like a model citizen, and Benny and I sedately got the hell out of there. A dog barked goodbye at us from the adjoining yard.

As we were making tracks I took the keys off the ring, tucked them down inside one of the gloves, then did the same with a set of picklocks Benny had brought along just in case; we hadn't wanted to break in as it was all supposed to look like an accident, which is no doubt fairly obvious by now. There was a heavy manila envelope in the glove compartment that was already stamped and addressed to yours truly at home; in went the gloves and hardware and at the first mailbox we came to, in went the envelope. The toque I took off gratefully and chucked under the back seat.

You never know, someone once said. I think it was Oedipus. Cops love to do their thing. All we needed was for one of the car's rear lights to be out or to be sideswiped by some lush or maybe even pass a savage, i.e., eager police rookie with an arrest book to fill up and we'd have a bit of a job explaining away a professional set of picks. I gave a small sigh of relief as soon as I had dumped the envelope, it looked like we were if not home free at least on our way.

'Phew,' I said. 'Turn left.'

'I know,' said Benny. After a while he said, 'How're you doing, Uncle?'

I told him I was doing pretty good. I was, too. I'd been worried some innocent might get hurt when she blew but there was a chain across Art's parking lot so no late-night neckers could get in and also he was set far enough back from the side road and Greenview so that if anyone was walking by they should be all right, I hoped. I also hoped the dog next door wouldn't get too freaked out.

Pretty good? Hell, I was doing terrific. All I needed to feel even more terrific was to hear from somewhere behind us the satisfying sound of a loud explosion. In a truly benevolent world the explosion would even blow a few large T-bones over into the barking dog's dinner bowl.

We drove a bit. I was hungry, I was thirsty and I was as hopped up as a road-runner on speed. I forget which he-man writer said, if you want to get your adrenaline pumpin', pal, bomb the shit out of someone. However it didn't seem too bright to stop for a drink and a nine-course meal as there was an outside chance – as in one in a million – that some angel of mercy at the hospital might actually look in my room to see if I was still alive, so we headed at a conservative velocity back toward Kaiser.

'Couple of things,' I said as we waited for a light to change. 'I suppose I owe you some money.'

'Always welcome,' said Benny. 'But no hurry, tomorrow's fine. I'll let you know what I laid out, the pills and the expert chauffeuring are on me. And the petunias.'

I told him I thought that was jolly nice of him.

'Heck, you're family, Unk,' he said.

'Benny, when you were a kid, what did you do in washrooms besides taking a leak?'

'Turned on,' he said. 'Still do.'

'And if the washroom smells like a chlorine factory, does that make you more suspicious or less suspicious?'

'Next question,' he said.

'Why would a girl, a cute girl, a cute girl who doesn't put catsup on her hamburger or French fries, steal the extra catsup packets?'

'Because they are free,' he said. 'A well-known corollary of Murphy's Law is, "If it can be stolen, it will be, irregardless of value or lack of it." What kind of question was that?'

'Just small talk,' I said. 'Why would a guy give an alibi when it wasn't asked for?'

'Who did you have in mind?'

'Guy called Dev.'

There was a pause.

'That's it?'

'Sworn to secrecy,' I said in a confidential manner. 'Jesus, I feel good.'

'I'm feeling all right myself,' said Benny. 'Well, in answer to your last question, he's either guilty of something and wants you to think he's innocent, or more likely he's innocent and wants you to think he's innocent but he isn't that innocent or why did he bring it up in the first place?'

'Exactly,' I said. 'Right on, cuz.'

We turned into the rear of the hospital parking lot; Benny pulled up but kept the motor idling. I got back into the white coat. We waited til a nurse going off duty pulled away in one of those new little Buicks, then I got out without trying to look inconspicuous, waved goodbye to Benny and walked stiffly over to the emergency door which I was pleased to see was still open a crack. In, up the stairs with some difficulty, into my room. Clothes off, clothes into suitcase, me into hospital gown, me into bed. Me sigh happily and take one more Demerol and a long drink of stale water. I wondered where hospitals got their stale water from, no one else ever seems to have it. Then me smile at Benny's flowers which were I don't know what but sure weren't petunias that Florence had arranged earlier in a vase on the bedside table.

I felt like phoning someone up for a good gossip but couldn't think of anyone who really wanted a lengthy cat-session at one thirty of the wee small hours.

I felt like phoning room service for a toasted club sandwich, side of onion rings and a cherry Coke.

I wished I had a dog sleeping on the bottom of the bed, crowding my poor old legs.

CHAPTER ELEVEN

I'm no cynic, despite what some may think. Show me a pimp who's really a nice, regular guy underneath it all and I'll believe it can happen. Show me a twenty-piastre Greek hooker with a heart of pure gold and I'll believe that can happen. Show me a miracle and I'll believe in miracles for ever and ever.

Monday morning started with one of the latter, a miracle, or at least as close to one as this unbeliever will likely ever see. What happened was that somehow by some administrative foul-up they let me sleep until almost seven o'clock. (And while I slept, Art's burned, or so I hoped.) When I did wake up Florence was rattling open the venetian blinds and humming to herself. This was a new-model Florence, a small black one with huge pink glasses and knobby ankles. She saw me watching her and came over to the bed to grin at me.

'What are you so cheerful about?' I asked her.

'Looking at you,' she said. 'Makes me warm all over. I hope you feel better than you look.'

'Tell you in a minute,' I said. 'I haven't heard from some of the outlying ganglions yet.' Actually, I felt awful. She took out a thermometer that was clipped to her breast pocket, looked at it, shook it like they always do, popped it in my waiting mouth, then left, taking with her the water carafe. I hoped she'd done gone to get me a gallon of coffee and a couple of warm Danish with extra butter, instead she reappeared a minute later with some fresh stale water and a trayful of things to hurt me with. She took the thermometer out, looked at it, made a note on the case sheet, hung it back on the foot of the bed, shook her thermometer and put it away.

'How's our temperature?' I asked her.

'Above normal,' she said, 'but I don't think we'll have to book the operating room yet. If you want to wash up now I'll do your bed.'

I got my groggy self up and taking it steadily made it to the small washroom to the right of the door, and washed the parts I could reach that weren't covered with bandages. Then, although I knew it wasn't a good idea, I couldn't resist one peek at myself in the mirror. The glass didn't crack but that was about all. I needed a shave but most of all a shower, and that promised to be a test of ingenuity. My legs weren't too bad, however, perhaps some of the painkiller was still working . . . oh, oh, my pills. I hied it back to the bed, but too late.

'Guess what I found when I was turning the mattress?' said Flo.

'Bed-bugs?'

'These.' She held up the vial of Demerols.

'Ah, those,' I said. 'Good, I thought I'd lost the little devils.'

'What are they?'

'Calcium,' I said, trying to take them from her. 'You know, for the bones?'

'Yes, I do know calcium is for the bones, among other things,' Flo said. 'What I don't know is whether or not these are calcium because these are in capsule form and calcium is usually in large tablets.'

'Ah,' I said. 'Multi-vitamins?'

She laughed and plumped the pillows; only nurses and mothers plump pillows. I've never plumped one in my life.

'Vitamin Demerol,' she said. She tossed them to me. 'Get back to bed and I'll change your dressings.'

I got; she changed, making a grimace of sympathetic pain as she ever-so-carefully eased the sticky bandages off instead of ripping them off in one go, something all nurses seemed to learn their first day at school. I decided I loved her. Our marriage would be a shock to Mom, I knew, but too bad. Flo started putting fresh, cool guck on; it felt like heaven.

'The night nurse left a note for me,' she said after a while.

'Oh, yes?'

'Yes.'

'She want you to double date with her sometime?' I asked after another while.

'No, she said you weren't here when she made her midnight rounds.'

Well, I was waiting for that one, wasn't I, I mean you don't mouse-trap ol' Vic too often, so I said, 'Did she look under the covers?'

Flo nodded. She was as cute as a Dallas Cowboys cheerleader. Maybe she was a Cowboys cheerleader moonlighting.

'All the way under,' she said. 'Where were you, sport? And make it good, because I have to decide whether or not to report it.'

She bundled up the nasty old dressings and put them in a small paper garbage bag, like an airline gag-bag.

'I was merely trying to get some chicken soup from the machine,' I said. 'I read recently it was good for burns as well as everything else. In *Cosmo*, I think it was.'

She nodded as if she was completely satisfied with the explanation, and why not?

'Breakfast tray'll be around soon,' she said. 'Rye toast or croissants?'

'Crumpets, please,' I said. 'With buckwheat honey.'

She picked up the torture instruments and headed for the door.

'Doctor at ten. Anything else you need?'

'A razor. TV. Something to read.'

'I'll send the porter. By the way, sport, our machines have coffee, tea, cocoa and tomato soup. No chicken.'

'Yeah,' I said. 'I found out. I was heartbroken. I hate tomato. We used to get it three times a week, made with water.' I didn't tell her where we used to get it.

The little darling left. I decided Yucatán would be the perfect spot for our honeymoon. We could go to Chichen

Itzá and watch them sacrifice virgins, although Dios knows where they got them from these days.

Well, there I was, all dressed up and nowhere to go, and it was already seven fifteen. Breakfast came and went, unlovely as a wallflower at an Odd-Fellows' dance. About an hour later an ebony porter in a long blue housecoat wheeled in a TV, plugged it in, tossed the remote control on the foot of the bed where I couldn't reach it, did likewise with a couple of tattered magazines and a throwaway razor in a tiny plastic bag, then left without saying a word, let alone singing a worksong or two. I wondered what his problem was, but not for long, because I knew what mine were and they were far more interesting.

I got the TV working but couldn't find anything on the early news about a mysterious explosion in the Valley, a leveled hamburger stand or strange, ominous sightings of flying meat patties, so I switched it off again and picked up the magazines. One was *Needlecraft for Today*, one was *Vegetarianism is Fun, and Cheap, Too!* but the last one turned out to be a rare, three-year-old copy of *Mechanix Illustrated*; that was more like it.

The morning passed almost as slowly as prison time although I didn't really mind, I was getting a good rest, flushing the drink out of my filters and there was plenty to think about, like Jalisco sunsets, the perfect car, getting old.

The doctor came and went and said I could leave tomorrow; I was leaving tomorrow anyway. I was deeply into a fascinating article on fretwork when two porters talking about football wheeled in a sleeping roomie for me; they unloaded him neatly into the spare bed, then put the screen around him. As one of them went by the TV on the way out, he pointed at the sleeper, shook his head and unplugged the set. Well, fuck you, Charlie, I wasn't even watching it anyway. And they have invented earphones.

I went back to my fretwork. Wouldn't Mae be surprised when I gave her fretwork everything for Christmas! I hoped to God Art's had gone up the way it was supposed to, I didn't want to go through all that again, I wasn't sure I could. No, not because I was chicken but maybe it wasn't such a good idea after all, maybe it was just as stupid and potentially lethal as firing my place had been and, even more horrible thought, maybe Art had had nothing to do with it in the first place. Unfortunately, in LA the serving of mediocre franks isn't in itself sufficient motivation to level a joint.

Anyway, it seemed that reality, which is a great place to visit but I wouldn't care to live there, was sneaking back into my life despite all my efforts to keep it at bay. And, as an example of that very thing, right then the phone rang, and there's nothing realer than that except maybe getting your foreskin caught in the zipper. It didn't ring, actually, it flashed, so it wouldn't disturb anyone else in the room, but it amounts to the same thing. Reality is reality whether it rings or it flashes, and if you want to know who said that, I did.

It was Benny.

'Kaput,' he whispered dramatically. 'Demolished. Flat as a pancake. Creamed.'

'You're up early,' I said. 'How do you know?'

'I looked,' he said.

'Benny . . .'

'I didn't stop, I didn't even slow down. I too know that old myth about felons returning to the scene of their crimes.'

'Some myth you turned out to be,' I said.

'I didn't even use my own car,' he said righteously.

I didn't bother asking him what car he did use.

'Any other damage?' I kept my voice down in case the sleeper was really a wide-awake police spy recording everything.

'A tree or two,' he said. 'Bit of the parking lot. Bit of a fence. One parked car. Sure hope he's insured, he's going to have half the world suing him.'

'Too bad,' I said. 'I wonder how much a forty-foot oak costs in these inflationary times.'

We wondered about that for a minute, then Benny said he had to go talk to a guy about buying some money, and he hung up. I took a snooze. When my brother phoned later I told him not to bother coming by, I'd be out the next day. I had sort of hoped that Juanita Morales might drop in with a mariachi band and a care package of piña coladas, but there you go.

The next day, I went home. Never did get to meet my roomie, he slept the whole time, unless he was dead and nobody noticed. Doctor Franklin came by before I left. He said all my legs needed was air and time.

'How about the spring of youth?' I said.

'And keep them dry,' he said. 'And don't be afraid to take as many anacin as you need while they're healing.'

I said I wouldn't and winked at Flo.

I'd told Benny when he phoned earlier that I'd hop a cab back to the office where my car was, I hoped, but he came by anyway about eleven and even insisted on carrying the suitcase. I left the petunias for my bride-to-be.

Benny had a copy of that morning's *Herald Examiner* with him in the car; there was a bit about V. Daniel in it and a short item about Art's. The bit about me said the police were investigating a case of possible arson by fire-bombing. I enjoyed the 'possible' – I would have called the arson quod erat mucho demonstrated, it was like suggesting that Adolph had a possible bias against the Hebrew persuasion or it was possible a Son of Erin from County Clare might take a drink on St Paddy's Day if you twisted his arm. I did learn Timmy's last name was Flexner, and he had a mother who owned a house on St Agnes, a short street a few blocks west of my office. I hoped Mae hadn't seen the paper, Christ, she'd shit a brick all over again. I know my brother would keep it from Mom in case she was having one of her rare good days when things sunk in and when she reacted normally.

The item in the *Herald* about Art's said the fire marshal's office was inspecting a possible gas leak; I enjoyed that 'possible' more than the last one.

It seemed to be business as usual on the corner of Victory and Orange, I was glad to see. I was also glad to see my car, water-streaked but otherwise OK. Benny let me out right beside it.

'Want some money?' I asked him.

'Wouldn't say no,' he said.

'What's it come to?'

'Ah, fifty for the clothes and stuff, another fifty to borrow the keys off a girl I know. You might let me have the suitcase back sometime, I borrowed it from my sister.'

I gave him five twenties from my wallet and, when he leaned over to take them, a couple of pats on his bald spot.

'See you next time you want to get violent, Unk,' he said. 'Knowing you, that won't be long.' He gave a toot-toot and took off. Mrs Morales was looking out her window at us; I gave her my customary wave. She waved back but a little half-heartedly, I thought. Maybe it was guilt. Maybe it was time I crossed her off my shortlist is what it was maybe, God knows I'd given her enough chances.

My office was still boarded up but the door was open. The explosion had luckily blown it ajar so the locks were still good. All it needed was a sanding and a new paint job. Who didn't? I said 'Knock, knock' and went in.

The decorators, or Armenian folk-dancing fools, if you will, were in the front corner of the office finishing up the carpet, using one of those strange stretching tools that work so well if you know what you're doing but are knuckle-busters if you don't. 'Tundra', as I suspected, being moderately literate, having read a book or two in my time, paperbacks I admit, was a dark green.

'Um-hum!' I enthused. 'Terrific, boys.' The walls had all been done, new plasterboard underneath, I surmised, and then repainted in the off-white they were before. I took a look out back; what was left of the charred furniture was piled against the wall awaiting collection. The cat from next door was sitting on its butt licking its tummy and looking particularly foolish. The washroom hadn't been touched; I opened up the safe and everything inside looked fine. Who's a lucky boy – a hundred bucks' worth of second-hand furniture, a visit from Ma Bell and I was back in business.

When I came out of the washroom one of the decorators, the elder one, was politely waiting for me.

'Sam said new glass goes in tomorrow,' he said. 'Safety glass, you know? The kind with a metal screen in it?'

I said I knew.

'Sam said electrician comes tomorrow,' he said. 'Telephone, too.'

'God bless Sam,' I said. 'And you two folk-dancing fools for getting it all done so quickly.'

'Aw,' he said. I took out a twenty and passed it over.

'You might like to buy a present for your children.'

'That lazy, good-for-nothing helping me is my children,' he said, 'and the only present he'd like is a bottle of Haig's Pinch.' He put the bill away in an old-fashioned change purse. I told him to just pull the doors shut when he left, the spring locks would catch.

'That's what we did yesterday,' he said, then shouted at his boy to stop goofing off and to start getting some work done around here. The kid looked up at me and grinned. What the hell – I grinned back. I looked at the pile of mail by the front door and decided to leave it where it was.

The week-old kitty-litter aroma of new paint was getting to me so I was glad to get out into what Los Angelenos have to make do with for air. The car started right up; it had only been standing three days and it had a battery that could turn over a Centurion tank. I backed it up in front of Mr Amoyan's and left it running while I popped in for a quick word. He was at the sander buffing down the edges of a new half-sole; he switched off when he saw me.

'How's by you?' he wanted to know, shaking hands with me.

I told him things were fine by me, thanked him for all his

help, refused his offer of some liquid Armenian poison, shook hands again, took my leave, got back in the car and headed for home sweet home and a large, cold brandy and ginger and then another brandy and ginger and then without a doubt in this world another brandy and ginger. Then take my lumps from Mae and then another . . . maybe if I got drunk enough I could figure out a way to take a shower without getting my legs wet. Some sort of harness, perhaps, or waterproof tights.

I'd gone about a block or two on my way to that first brandy and ginger when I had a better idea – to go and see Timmy's mother. I'd remembered the street she lived on, St Agnes, but not the address, so I stopped for a paper at a 7-11 and looked up the story again while sipping an Orange Crush through two straws.

I've always been a two-straws man. Was it my imagination that it didn't have as much flavor as it used to or was it that nothing had as much flavor as it used to? – I hoped it was Orange Crush's fault. I bought a couple of Baby Ruths for the bedside table, gave a panhandling wino a quarter, then hit the drugstore to fill the prescription for antibiotics the doc had given me.

Mrs Flexner's house turned out to be a large stucco affair probably fifty years old set well back from the street. The window frames needed repainting. The front yard had a high, wire-mesh fence around it, for animals, I thought. Wrongly, I soon found out. The gate was tricky to open but with my professional skills I managed it. The lady who answered the door was large, frizzy-haired, angry and black. She had a hefty-looking child in one arm and there were two more holding on to her legs and peeking up at me.

'Is Mrs Flexner in?'

'She's in. What's it about?'

'Her son,' I said. 'I'm Victor Daniel. He died in my office.'

'You better come on in then.' She led me into a shabby front room where another, older, child was lying on the floor cutting things out of colored paper.

'Sit yourself down somewheres.'

'Thank you.' I sat myself down on a plastic-covered sofa beside a huge, bald doll that was missing one leg. A mutt with an erection and a red ribbon tied around its neck wandered in from the hall and came over to smell my shoes. I smelled it right back. It sat on one of my feet, looked up and wagged its stump of a tail hopefully. I obliged with a scratch behind the ear. In gratitude it let out a terrific fart which no one seemed to notice but me.

'Mary-Lou, get the man a drink,' the lady said. One of the girls who was entwined around her legs detached herself reluctantly, then ran out.

'I'm her,' the lady said, sitting heavily down into an ancient lounging chair. The child on the floor snuck up one hand and turned on a switch in the chair's armrest; the chair began vibrating gently. The woman aimed a mock slap at the child and turned it off again.

'I know I don't look like her but I'm her. Children, remove yourselves. Elmira, you take Donald.' She passed over the baby. 'And keep the gate closed, you hear me loud and clear?'

The children removed themselves. Mary-Lou came back carrying carefully a glass of Kool-Ade in one hand, which she offered me shyly.

'Elmira made it,' she whispered. 'She never puts enough sugar in it.' Then she produced a vanilla sandwich biscuit from the other hand.

'Thank you, sweetheart,' I said.

'Welcome,' she said, and ran outside to join the others. I watched her go. I don't know. Sometimes you see a little girl who's so beautiful she gives you a brief surge of hope. Mrs Flexner closed her eyes for a moment; the flea-bag barked excitedly from the yard.

'Nice kids.' I took a sip of my Kool-Ade. It was lime, not my favorite, but with Kool-Ade I had no favorite.

'Nice enough,' agreed Mrs Flexner. 'That Kool-Ade OK? Don't care for it much myself.' I said it was fine and ate my cookie.

'Mrs Flexner, do you know what Timmy was doing when he died?'

'Not exactly,' she said. 'Something crazy.'

'Someone fire-bombed my place. Timmy saw the fire and thought I was inside and went in to try and help me. He thought of me as a friend because I got him that job down at the liquor store.'

'Well, he didn't have many of those, friends or jobs, and that's the truth, poor soul,' she said. We sat in silence for a minute. Out in the yard Mary-Lou was whispering something into the mutt's ear. Then Mrs Flexner said, 'He was my best friend's child, she lived two doors up, she never had no husband, it got to be too much for her, she just left one day. Never heard a word from her in sixteen years. So I adopted him. Adopted six so far. Got those four monsters left.'

'Mrs Flexner, is there anything I can do to help? I don't want to embarrass you but if there's going to be a service, maybe I could pay for that if you'll let me.'

'No thank you,' she said shortly. 'We'll manage ourselves.' She took another look out the window to check on the children. 'I don't know how that dog puts up with it.'

'Why did he wheel all his things around with him all the time?'

'I dunno,' she said. 'He was just a kid. Maybe he was afraid they wouldn't be there when he got back. Maybe he was showing off.' She told me when and where the service for Timmy was to be held; I said I'd try and make it.

'Well, there won't be no crowd,' she said. 'Us and the kids, one or two more.'

I finished up the Kool-Ade and got up with some difficulty.

'You get hurt too?' she asked. 'Aside from your face?'

'Nothing much, I was lucky. I got out the back just as Timmy must have been going in the front. It was a brave thing to do.'

'It's nice to think so,' she said tiredly. She saw me to the door. We shook hands. I waved goodbye to the kids and the mutt and drove off.

CHAPTER TWELVE

I don't think the driving helped my legs any but at least I could manage to do it. When I arrived home I pulled into the driveway and parked behind the rented truck. Feeb – landlady, blue hair, bottom apartment – was waiting for me at the door.

'What happened, what happened?' she wanted to know.

I didn't know what to say to her. What if she wanted us out? I couldn't blame her – who was to say it wouldn't be her house that got fried the next time or maybe one of our cars in the driveway? However I got a reprieve, she didn't mention the fire.

'Where's Lillian, wasn't she coming Sunday?'

Lillian is my mother's name; the old girls got on pretty well together. Once Feeb took Mom to a Kings hockey game at the Forum but they had a spot of bother in the third period when the Kings were grimly hanging on to a 6–2 deficit and Mom couldn't get to the bathroom in time so they never went again. Feeb had season tickets, I guess she must have known someone.

I told her some story about my brother wanting a free week later during his holidays so he was keeping Lillian an extra week now. God knows what I was going to tell Feeb when she read the paper or when one of her kindly neighbors broke the news to her about my office.

'Oh, shoot,' she said. 'Gotta run, got a macaroni cass' in the microwave. Want some?'

I said no. I hate macaroni, especially in a casserole with potato chips and especially especially in a casserole with potato chips and mushroom soup.

We went our separate ways. I could hear my phone ringing

as I labored up the stairs but took my time, only partly because of my weary legs, I couldn't think of any good news it might be. Except Miss Shirley, wondering how her big boy was, with a spare two-pound T-bone sizzling on her backyard barbecue . . . I moved my ass. Ain't love wonderful?

It was Mae. She didn't have a spare T-bone sizzling on her barbecue, she had a full head of steam sizzling and let me have it right between the eyes. I couldn't help wondering why she was doing such a number.

Did I know how worried she was?

I knew.

Did I know how stupid I was?

I knew.

Did I know I could have been killed?

I knew.

Why didn't I call her to let her know I was getting out?

That I didn't know, except maybe I did. She finally hung up and I could get myself a drink. It is nice to have someone worry about you, I guess; it does mean they care for you, I guess. After all, nagging is a form of caring. I guess.

The drink was delicious. I silently toasted Mr Papanikolas and wondered what he would do without Timmy. Maybe put one of his clan up in the hot-seat, or offer all potential troublemakers a slice of his Aunt Fat'ma's halvah.

After a while I phoned the car rental and told them I hadn't stolen their truck, I'd bring it back mañana, and gave them a credit-card number to keep them quiet. I noticed my glass was empty again – always a problem in the Valley, evaporation, ask any fruit farmer. So I made another one with that good, slightly rough Christian Bros brandy. Brandy and ginger ale can be a trifle sweet for some and a trifle pukkah sahib for others but I've never had any trouble with it. Frankly, I can't think of all that many drinks I have had trouble with.

After another while I wandered into the bedroom to put away the candy bars, they belonged in the same drawer of the bedside table as the second of my .38 Police Positives. I was pointing it at myself in the mirror when I got a phone call from the vice-principal of St Stephen's.

'Are you receiving?'

'Barely,' I said.

'See you in ten,' he said, and hung up forcibly. I put the gun away again, I didn't quite know why I got it out in the first place. I knew it was there, because it always was; I knew it was clean, for the same reason, and I knew it was loaded, ditto. I had four of them altogether. The one in the office, the one by the bed and the one taped underneath the driver's seat in the car. I know that only makes three. My brother got them for me one Christmas, under duress. There is a lot of philosophy written and talked about guns. I thought they smelled nice, like a garage or a woodworking shop. Strangely enough, in this lawless, violent, crazed and gun-mad frontier called California I am allowed to have a weapon in my place of work, my residence and my vehicle but not about my valuable person, even in the course of my dangerous duties, without a special permit, one I did not have and could not easily obtain. What I did normally carry about my person when I hadn't stupidly left it behind like that midnight at the Oasis was a leather bag of ball-bearings. It was a pouch, really, about as long as a hotdog and twice as big around, held closed by a leather thong that was long enough to hang around your neck or to tie from a belt. It had some sort of fake American Indian motif painted on it; hippies used to use them for cigarettes and lighters and their stash. It was the invention of a girl I used to know – I suppose I still know her, I just don't know where she is – but she was in Sacramento then, studying to be a forest ranger. Hers was full of BBs but the V. Daniel modification Mark 2 utilized ball-bearings instead for greater heft. It served nicely as a paperweight when I wasn't lugging it around.

The doorbell downstairs rang; I peeked out the front window and there was Mr Lowenstein, paper bag in hand. I went down and let him in. He didn't say anything as we trudged upstairs, then he said,

'Got any mayo?' I went to the kitchen and brought him back a jar of Best Foods, a knife and a plate.

'Lunch hour,' he said, taking two thick sandwiches out of the bag. 'Tuna and bean sprout on whole wheat. Want some?'

'No. Want a drink?'

He allowed he might take a beer so I got him a bottle of Corona and a glass. He ate, I sipped. I figured I could wait him out without too much trouble, he had only an hour for lunch, I had what was left of a lifetime. He took a swallow of beer, burped none too delicately, then said,

'Was it you?'

'No.'

'No?'

'No. Whatever it was.'

'I don't see how it could have been, from what Miss Shirley told me about the state you were in, but I still think it was you because if not you, who?'

'Not me,' I said firmly, looking him right in the eye. He spread an incredible amount of mayonnaise on the second sandwich.

'Better than Art's,' he said slyly. I looked innocent.

He sighed. 'Do I or do I not remember a contract in which the party of the second part, you, agreed to tell the party of the first part, me, underline "all" of your activities, nefarious or otherwise?'

'No, sir,' I said firmly. 'Not all, remember? Also, Mr Lowenstein, I don't know what you're talking about.'

He sighed. 'All right, Mr Daniel, all right,' he said, licking a finger. 'I will take it that your motives are pure as the driven snow and that you know what you are doing because if I didn't take it that way this whole mess would be even worse than it already is and God knows it's already bad enough. But please, please, on bended knee I implore, don't tell me some ghost from your dim past just happened to destroy your office the day after I hired you, even the luscious Evonne didn't believe that.'

'Evonne?'

'Miss Shirley to you.' Well, I knew from her employment record her initials were E. B., but Evonne . . .

'Then two days later,' he went on, interrupting ruthlessly the train of thought I'd embarked on which was getting pleasanter by the second, 'a mere two days later, up goes Art's, or down goes Art's would be more like it, or atomized into toothpicks would be even more like it. Don't tell little ol' me they're not connected, connected by much larger you.'

'No need to get personal,' I said. 'Also I plead the Fifth for the same reason I pleaded it – or is it "pled" it – God, I've got to read more, with Evonne, Miss Shirley to me, so as not to incriminate the innocent.'

'Goodness, I figured out that much all by myself,' said the Vice, 'or I wouldn't be here at all and you'd be reading the want-ads. What I want to know is, what next? Does it escalate? Is someone going to blow up the whole darn school?'

'Not a chance,' I said confidently. 'You don't shove a stick of TNT up the ass of the goose that lays the golden egg, do you?'

'Vividly put,' said Mr Lowenstein. 'But only vaguely reassuring.'

'Mr Lowenstein,' I said, 'you got a moment?'

He looked at his watch.

'Yes I have a moment, just about.'

I told him the highlights or maybe lowlights of Benny's estimation of the present scale of drug traffic in and around LA and added a bit of book-learning of my own. I said out of his enrollment of just under 900 students he could expect a quarter to a half of those fifteen years old and up to be using some king of drugs more or less regularly. With the dear, sweet, backward thirteen- and fourteen-year-olds, maybe only one or two in ten. Or three.

'Facts of life as it is being lived in the Valley in 1984, Vice,' I said. 'Someone is pulling a grand, a grand and a half, every week out of your establishment of learning, which is not a fortune by the time it gets split up but it's not greasy kid stuff either. Of course that's nothing compared to what goes on downtown. But our options are limited. There's no way we can remove the source or the sources unless we find a way to remove both greed and the greedy from the world, and better men than me even have tried that. Now we can, temporarily, remove a middleman from the chain, say, for example, hypothetically, just running a name up the flagpole . . .'

'Art,' said Mr Lowenstein, 'there's a name.'

'Why, what an idea!' I said. 'And that may quiet things down for a week or two, but that's all, folks, then word gets around as word does that the man to see is perhaps good old Fred down at your friendly neighborhood car wash.'

'Satisfaction guaranteed or your dirt back,' said Mr Lowenstein. 'I saw that sign on one of them once.'

'Me, too,' I said. 'So, taking it as read that we can't clean up the world, where does that leave us?'

'We clean up what we can clean up, obviously.' He finished off his beer. 'Good stuff. But can we even do that is what I'm starting to wonder.'

'It's been done before,' I said.

'By you?'

'Well, not exactly by me,' I had to admit. 'But I know the theory.'

'You know the theory,' he said. 'God almighty.' He shook his head. 'It's heartbreaking when a school hits the skids. It happened to me once before, in Inglewood, I was head of the so-called science department, suddenly it all fell apart. Kids were joining gangs instead of teams, average attendance went down to nothing, we had eight armed security guards on duty at all times and they couldn't do anything, no one could do anything, the good students left and the good teachers left . . . ah, hell, I feel sick about the whole thing.'

'I don't,' I said. 'I think we can clean it up and keep the lid on pretty much, but it will take action. Have you got the power to lower the boom when you have to?'

'Like what?'

'Like bust ass, kick kids out, replace teachers, maybe close up for a few days.'

'With cause,' he said.

'Oh, you'll have that,' I said. 'You'll have plenty of that.'

'Oh?' He perked up a bit and raised his eyebrows at me.

The doorbell rang.

'Expecting anyone?' I asked him.

'Yes,' he said morosely. 'With you around, the bomb disposal squad.'

I went to the window and looked out. There in the yard, strutting and fretting in his peacock finery, was Lieutenant Conyers.

'Close,' I said. 'It's the fuzz.'

'Well, isn't that sauce for the gander,' said the vice-principal of St Stephen's.

CHAPTER THIRTEEN

Someone once told me that movie sets, especially Western sets, are all built only nine tenths life size so as to make the hero appear more masterful; what Lieutenant Conyers needed was a world about seven tenths life size. Mr Lowenstein joined me at the window and looked down into the yard.

'Him?'

'Him.'

'What do we do?'

'We go downstairs, we say goodbye, you leave, and if you're parked close you walk away and come back for your car when he's not watching. Then I see what he wants.'

'Sheesh,' said Mr Lowenstein. 'Just like in the movies.'

We exited left; I pocketed his check on the way out. It wouldn't be terribly clever to let little Big Eyes get a look at a draft for $750 made out to me and drawn on a St Stephen's High School account. St Stephen's High School, you will remember, is just across the street from Art's, where not only the burgers are char-broiled.

We could hear through Feeb's door that she was watching one of the midday soaps, a harmless enough pastime, I suppose, if you like taking your downers electronically.

I opened the front door and said 'So long' to the Vice. He said 'So long' back and strode off down the street.

'Who was that?' the lieutenant asked casually.

'Old school friend. Go on up.'

I followed him up the stairs, which gave me plenty of time to admire his two-tone, basket-weave shoes. In the apartment, I took the dirty dishes from the table out to the kitchen while he looked around with great interest, as if he'd never seen a furnished apartment before. When I came back he was perusing a photograph on the end table next to the TV; it had been taken one long-ago summer when me and my brother were kids, we were sitting on the grass in front of a tourist cabin on Lake Kiwana, in northern Minnesota. My mother and father, arms around each other, both in shorts, stood behind us. Tony was proudly holding up the world's smallest fish.

'And where does the time go, answer me that,' said the lieutenant, shaking his head dolefully.

'You got me there, pal,' I said, shaking mine just as dolefully. 'Sit down, make yourself comfortable. That chair there by the window should be small enough if you don't lean back.'

He gave me a look, sat on the arm of the leatherette sofa, took out his yellow notebook, flipped through it until he found the page he wanted, then sighed deeply, making a sort of whistling noise. Then he flexed his foot a couple of times, straightened his already straight slim-line chocolate-brown tie, favored me with another of his aimless whistling noises. I heard a car start up from outside the house and hoped it was Teach making his getaway.

'Well, Lieutenant, if you need me for anything, I'll be in the kitchen washing up,' I said finally.

'We found those guys,' he said.

'What guys?' As if I didn't know.

'Those guys,' he said. 'Those guys that were mean to you. At least we think we did. They tried to knock over another bar last night, no, I tell a lie, it was the night before.' He consulted his notebook again. 'You ever heard of the Elbow Room, 11873 San Vicente?'

'No.'

'Me neither. I'm not a drinking man myself, really, I mean I take a drop from time to time but I have to watch it, too much alcohol seems to do something peculiar to my metabolism. How about you?' He smiled at me in a friendly and disarming way.

'I confess I take a drop from time to time too, Lieutenant,' I said. 'Usually with Mother at Christmas.' He nodded politely. 'One sherry.'

'You see, I have had a busy schedule this weekend, Mr Daniel,' he leaned forward to tell me. 'Not for me the suburban pleasures of barbecues and cocktails on the patio, nor the joys of camping in our great outdoors or even a quiet Sunday reading the papers and watching sports, my loving children sprawled at my feet squabbling over the funny pages . . .'

That'll be the day, I thought.

'So! After our chat at the hospital, and may I say on behalf of the entire West Valley Police Department we are delighted to see you up and about?'

'You may,' I said. 'You may also get on with it.'

'Why oh why are you always so aggressive, Mr Daniel?' he said in a hurt tone.

'Gee, I dunno,' I said. 'Maybe you bring out the beast in me.'

He looked at me reproachfully.

'Get on with it, yes. After our chat I took the time to look up the descriptions you gave to Officer Lyam O'Ryan, I believe it was, of those two juves who tried to shake down the Oasis. Imagine my surprise and delight when, the following morning, bright and early, I saw on my cluttered desk those same descriptions again, almost word for word. And on an arrest sheet, too.'

I could imagine, all right. What I didn't want to imagine was the trouble I was in if it really was the same two juves. It went something like this: say it was the same two. One of them, the white kid, I'd positively identified as being outside my office Saturday morning as I never thought there was a hope in hell the law would ever catch up with him. Sure as God made death and taxes he'd turn out to have been in bed that morning, with twenty members of his immediate family and a couple of visiting Mormons to swear to it, and where did that leave me? With my foot in my mouth is where. Arson is taken moderately seriously these days, let alone when there's an accompanying fatality; remove the kid as a suspect and that midget clothes-horse, or in his case, Shetland pony, would want a few answers. I wouldn't give them. Before I could say 'I wuz framed' he'd be knee-deep in my tapes and disks and unfortunately they weren't on self-destruct like the ones in whatever that boring series was called.

On the other hand, if it was the same two and I said it wasn't, they might well get off on the attempted robbery charge of the Oasis and they would certainly get off on the charge of assaulting me because if the chap who almost had his scrotum sawn off couldn't recognize the guy trying to do it, who could? A fine mess I'd gotten myself into this time, as Tricia Nixon used to say. It seemed my only hope was maybe it wasn't the same two fun-lovers after all or that Lieutenant Conyers would suddenly have a petit-mal seizure and keel over on my sofa.

'Quite a rare case,' they'd say at the autopsy. 'He died from being too short.'

'So who collared them?' I asked before the pause between him talking and me answering got any longer; long pauses are considered by policemen, Customs agents, tax inspectors and others of their know-it-all ilk like shrinks or proctologists to be highly suspicious, and in my case at least, rightly so.

'They ran right into, and bounced off of, six Albanians who work at the yogurt factory . . .' and here he consulted his notebook again, 'at 11871 San Vicente.'

'I didn't know there was a yogurt factory at 11871 San Vicente,' I said.

'Oh, yes,' he said. 'They also make sour cream, ice cream, yogurt ice cream and buttermilk.'

'Fancy that,' I said. 'I worked on a farm once that used to make buttermilk. It was awful. Watery.'

'Fancy that,' he said.

'Anyway, what a break, eh?' I said, trying to sound

enthusiastic. 'Let me ask you this – did you get a report from the fire marshal's office yet, like maybe with a set of prints on a piece of the bottle?'

'Shore did,' he said happily. 'Got it yesterday, those guys are really on the ball over there. But alas fingerprints rarely survive temperatures above the boiling point, although freezing temperatures help preserve them, did you know that?'

I said I didn't but it wasn't really the point anyway, was it, as the kid hadn't touched anything in my deep freezer as far as I knew and anyway I didn't have a deep freezer.

'We do,' said the lieutenant. 'It's out on the back porch, empty. My wife uses it to store paint.'

'Fancy that,' I said.

There was a pause. Then I said, 'Anyone else from the Oasis identify the kid yet?'

He shook his head.

'I imagine you'd like me to have a look at him, right?'

'Right.'

'Well, let's go,' I said. 'I'd hate to keep the little bastards waiting.' I got up stiffly from the armchair and straightened my leg gingerly. The lieutenant looked on sympathetically.

'I burnt myself once setting off a roman candle,' he said. 'Boy, did it hurt. My parents made me watch the next firecracker night from my room.' I knew where I'd like to insert and set off a Roman candle and I could guarantee him it would hurt a lot more.

'Coming?' I said.

'No hurry,' he said, looking vaguely embarrassed for some reason. I sat down again with the first faint glimmering that mayhap Fate was going to spare me yet again as it had with Feeb. Still, I wondered what was coming next with the same fascination you open a letter from your wife's divorce lawyer.

'That your truck I saw?' he asked. 'In the driveway?'

'Rental,' I said. 'Helping a pal move.'

'Your school pal?'

'Nah,' I said. 'A work pal.'

'Your school pal,' he said. 'Where did you say he was a pal from?'

'School,' I said. 'Back East.' Tricky little beggar. I thought he was just fishing but he was still a tricky little beggar.

'Does he have a car?'

'Everyone's got a car, Louie,' I said. 'You know that, you're a detective.'

'My son doesn't,' he said. 'I took it away from him. You know what he did?'

'Before or after you took it away from him?'

'Before, before,' he said. 'The reason why.'

'I give up,' I said.

'He forgot to empty the ashtray.'

'Ah, well,' I said, 'can't have that.'

'He didn't empty the ashtray and there were two roaches in it.' He gave me a broad smile. Or anyway a smile as broad as he could give with a mouth the size of a snake's guess what. 'Know what was in the roaches?'

'I give up,' I said. 'Grass?'

'Grass with little white specks,' he said.

'I can guess what the little white specks were,' I said.

'A policeman's lot is not a happy one,' he recited.

'Look,' I said. 'I don't want to sound unsympathetic but I've got a few problems of my own so can we go if we're going?'

'We're not,' he said. 'I made it all up.'

I positively gaped. 'All of it? The Elbow Room, the six Albanians?'

'No, just the IDs,' he said. 'No one could make up six Albanian yogurt makers. It was two blacks they caught.'

'Why? Why bother?'

'The generation gap, that's the rub. Chucking molotov cocktails about, well, OK, for your race riots and politicals, but it's out of date, you take my point, it has an old-fashioned feel to it, almost an innocence.'

'Like the St Valentine's Day massacre,' I said. 'Old-fashioned, innocent. From a bygone era like high button shoes and heart-shaped boxes of chocolates.'

'Exactly.' He sighed deeply, as if pining for a better, gentler world. 'So I conjectured that perhaps it wasn't the younger generation that made a bonfire out of your office after all, which got me wondering who it was, which got me thinking it was probably something you were presently involved with and that I might be able to find out about. All this of course only if you started getting jumpy about identifying the kid.'

'Luckily I'm a truthful and genuinely helpful citizen,' I said.

'Yeah,' he said. He looked at a watch the size of a lady's discus, then got to his feet. 'Well, I can't sit around here all day chatting with you, pleasant though it's been, would you believe I got another fire to go to? A shoe store down on Cranston and I don't like the look of that one either. A neighbor saw a lot of action out back the night before the fire. Stock going in, stock coming out.'

'Expensive lines coming out, cheap schlock going in.'

'And a little sweetener to the insurance investigator, if he even bothers to look closely. Ah, well.' He moved to the door. 'TTFN. Know what that means?'

'No.'

'Ta ta for now.'

He finally left, thank heavens; he was not only short, he was nuts, I was beginning to think. I took one of Benny's pills and a couple of aspirin and my daily dose of antibiotics, although I was supposed to take one before every meal, and before long I figured I could manage a bath if I dangled my legs over the side so I manufactured another weak brandy and ginger and gave it a try. Once I was in, it felt just fine, as the bishop said to the actress or the choirboy. Steam rose; I dozed. The phone rang while I was soaking; I let it ring, I cared not.

'I build my castles in the sky, they turn to smoke, but what care I?' my pop used to say, blowing smoke rings to amuse his boys. He died when I was sixteen and Tony fourteen; I wonder what he'd say if he saw us today. Probably the same thing.

CHAPTER FOURTEEN

I took the truck to work the next morning. I took my hangover, too. I like hangovers – mild ones, anyway. They shift your head sideways into a devil-may-care, goofy space where non sequiturs roam and witty phrases dance and sing.

I stopped on the way at Blumenfeld's Office Supplies, New 'n' Used, which is on Magnolia about at Colfax, where a hustler name of Syd was thrilled to unload on me a one-owner desk and swivel chair, a spare chair, a filing cabinet and a card file. He offered me the price of a lifetime on a large, framed, 3-D photograph of Reagan seated in the Oval Office but I managed to curb myself. Syd and I loaded the junk in the truck, then money changed hands.

Next stop was Mrs Martel's store next to the post office. I needed everything, she was delighted to hear, new personalized stationery and envelopes, something to be getting on with until they were printed, memo pads, pens and filing cards, all the impedimenta of the upwardly mobile businessman. I made a mental note to ask my landlord how much of all this crap was covered by his insurance. Mrs Martel offered me a sensational deal on a thousand personalized ballpoints but again I somehow managed to curb my lust.

'Will there be anything . . . else?' she asked me in a stage whisper when she handed me my change. 'Anything . . . special? Will you be writing any more letters for the Department of Immigration or the California Parks and Wildlife Commission or the Highway Department, Orange County Branch?' I blushed becomingly, scuffed my feet and told her I'd let her know. Then it was next door for stamps. I like standing in line at the post office, it makes me feel humble.

My office was empty; I opened up and began unloading. I

didn't see Mrs Morales but to hell with her anyway. Quite frankly, now that I was upwardly mobile, she'd be nothing but a handicap at events like Rotary Club picnics and Young Businessmen lunches. My place still had that ammoniacal smell of cheap whitewash, but was otherwise neat and clean, rug down, painting finished. I placed the new old furniture where the old old furniture had been, arranged the bits and pieces on the desk, opened the back door to air the room out, picked up the pile of mail from inside the front door, sat down in my new old swivel chair and began to go through my correspondence. I left Betsy and the typewriter where they were in case I didn't need them.

Top of the pile was a note from the decorators. It said, 'Don't forget!!! Phone & electric and glass & lights tomorrow,' which was today. I hadn't forgot. Underneath that it said, 'Gave cat milk. Thank you!' Should have given it a hit of that Haig's Pinch, I thought, that's more its style.

There was a note from the messenger service saying that they had called with a delivery Monday and Tuesday but would not call again until they heard from me, the addressee, regarding my future whereabouts. Well shet ma mouf. I went to the pay phone outside the Nus' and gave the service a call. They said they were on their way. Then I popped in next door for a spot of business with the Nus' enterprising cousin, Nyom Pnung; I was never sure if that was his name or where he came from, or both. I waited while he sold a couple of hard-core home videos to a middle-aged lady in shorts. Then, after exchanging pleasantries, I asked him if he happened to have any telephones.

'What color, you care?'

'No, me no care.' He let me have a bright red, lightweight, touch-tone for a ludicrously low price and threw in a twelve-foot lead. He tried to tempt me with a telephone answering machine that did everything but write home to Mother, but for the third time that day, and it was still early, I was strong. Anyway, I hated those things even more than I hated water-picks, electric carving knives and glass-frosters.

Back I strolled through the noon haze to the office and the waiting pile of mail. Out went something from the *Reader's Digest* that might have made me a very rich man. Out went something from Johnny Carson's stooge, ditto. Out went something beginning 'The Curse of Rameses Will Follow You Forever If You Break The Chain'. Out went an insulting leaflet beginning 'Your name has been given to us as one of the 24,000,000 American men who have some sort of problem with hair loss'. Out went 'Dear Neighbor, America's foremost painter of clowns has just printed a limited edition ...' Mental note – buy a wastepaper basket.

John D., Valley Bowl, had sent me what I'd asked him for – employment records on the three girls and his receipts from the past month. I looked them over to see if any lightning would strike. The ladies' names, in no particular order were Maria Cintron, single, Barbara Herbert, single, and (Mrs) Martha F. Nazarof. Their respective ages were nineteen, twenty-four and twenty-seven. They lived, respectively, in East LA, Van Nuys and La Crescenta. They all had Social Security numbers. They all had car license numbers. They had been slave labor for John D. for, (respectively), three weeks, nine weeks and three and a half years. Ah so.

Back to the phone booth. My brother was off duty but I got on to a co-worker of his, not Morrie the weird this time but a morose older man called Larry I'd met a couple of times, once at the station downtown and another time at the funeral of a trainee policewoman, a good friend of Tony's and mine, hell, it must have been three years ago already. Larry grumbled a bit as usual but came through as usual – Maria owned a ten-year-old Ford, home address the same, four moving violations, traffic class attended. Barbara had an ancient Bug, home address the same, no violations. Martha was driving a newish Toyota, registered in her husband's name, home address correct, no violations.

'Anything else?' he said sarcastically. 'God knows I got

nothing else to do. There hasn't been any crime at all in LA for weeks.'

'No, thanks, Larry,' I said.

'Take care of yourself, stupid,' he said, then hung up. 'Stupid' – I guess my brother had been singing my praises at his office again.

The receipts John D. had sent were in groups of five slips stapled together, one group for each day. There were sub-totals from the bar, the snack bowl, the lanes and any sales of merchandise, and on the fifth slip the total was entered. Once every two weeks there were additional entries from the pinball and video machine share-outs and once a month payments from some of the leagues that paid that way. No help there that I could see.

I looked over the cards again in case I'd missed any clues, like, Hobbies: buying expensive jewelry or raising afghan puppies or keeping younger men; no such luck. Well, all things being equal, or almost equal, I thought I'd start with Barbara Herbert, twenty-four, single, from the nearby residential horror of Van Nuys.

My legs were itching like crazy so I got up to distract myself. I did have some spray for them but I'd cleverly left it at home. That bloody cat was sitting just inside the back door peeking out at a bird that was hopping around the garbage; I told it to get out and stay out, or else. It got out, taking its own sweet time about it. The molting mouser belonged to an aging hippy who lived with his girlfriend in a dilapidated loft across the back alley from me. All his window boxes were planted with huge pot bushes that he had slyly disguised as tomato plants by festooning them with round, red Christmas-tree ornaments; I suppose a blind Narc might be fooled for a couple of seconds.

The glass man cameth about then and I rubber-necked while he and his lady associate installed my new shatter-proof front window in something under ten minutes, laughing hysterically at nothing that I could make out all the while. Then

Sparks showed up and started on the rewiring. Then laughing boy and his girlfriend helped me carry the now superfluous boarding that had been covering the window area out back for the cat and his gang to play on, then they pissed off. Then the man from Ma Bell, or I suppose it was now Pacific Bell, made an appearance. He wasn't laughing hysterically, in fact he wasn't laughing at all; he did what he had to do, presented me with an illustrated folder on the use and care of the telephone, adding a poorly printed pamphlet on Being Born Again, then took his leave. Mental note – an even larger wastepaper basket.

I plugged in my new phone and heard the comforting sound of the dial tone. When I was younger I used to listen to it at night sometimes, feeling a sense of wonder and latent adventure that was as long gone as the flavor in Orange Crush.

I looked over the pamphlet on Being Born Again as a Christian. Could a private eye be born again, I wondered briefly. Would one want to? If that were only my main worry today.

All right. Back to the mail. Photo-Date was after me again. Cal Edison wanted their monthly pittance. The May Co. was having a summer sale of ladies' separates, super! Someone in Ohio wanted to know if I was satisfied with my present cost of automobile insurance. Was anyone? The last item was an announcement from a specialty house in Pasadena of a sale in electronic protection hardware; I glanced through the five-page list that was enclosed until I got discouraged, which didn't take long. Out.

The boy from the messenger service putt-putted up on his underpowered bike; he entered, I signed, he left, I opened. It was as expected the regular weekly payment from Mr Seburn, cuckold, but this time he had added a note taking me up on my suggestion that we try and get a statement from Mr Universe who worked the desk at the health club. He also mentioned that any more photos of an incriminating nature would be useful as he was planning to bring the affair, no pun intended, to a close, if possible by the end of the month. The news made me glad and sorry; glad because I'd had nine weeks at $82.50 per, sorry because there wouldn't be any more such paydays. But I was pleased to have a chore to do, I like keeping busy, it's good for the complexion, someone said. I had not repeat not forgotten St Stephen's and all the complications thereof, au contraire, if I may show off my learnin', every itch was a constant reminder, but didn't someone else once say all life was a question of timing? I figured I'd give the simmering pot of cupidity at the school one more stir in the next day or so, then leave it to simmer again for a short while. Then, look out.

'Don't get me mad!' my pop used to say. 'Just don't get me mad!' He would say this of course in a voice that suggested it was all he could do to control his total rage. Well, I was mad already. It might be claimed that I'd been mad since I was sixteen, mostly at myself, the rest at Tony. And Pop.

The messenger boy, having made a brief pit stop at Mrs Morales', was just pulling out of the parking lot when a customer walked in through my newly painted front door. I didn't know she was a customer at first as I'd never before had one with lime-green and orange hair styled in a Mohawk and I'd also never before had a customer with a whole string of safety pins hanging from one ear. However, what am I if not adaptable, who am I if not tolerant of all the minority elements in society, including freaks? And I did sort of dig the Day-Glo underwear which I could spy through a jagged tear in her purple gauchos. Her eyes, undoubtedly so bloodshot they were solid crimson, were hidden behind wrap-around sunglasses, one lens of which was badly cracked.

'Hey, man, what happened to you?' she whispered after looking me up and down.

'I was born,' I whispered back. 'What's your excuse?'

'You know Elroy?' she then whispered.

'I know Elroy,' I admitted. 'He's my landlord. I like Elroy. I was late with my rent once and he just laughed and laughed while he broke both my legs.'

'Jesus, man, what stinks in here? This is all his idea,' she said in almost a normal voice. She was still hovering by the door, jumpy as a zebra who can smell the lions but can't see them yet.

'Look,' I said. 'Let's pretend. Ever play that? Let's pretend we are both level-headed, sensible types and go about this in a sensible, businesslike way. You come in. You sit down. You tell me about it, whatever it is, then I'll tell you if I can help or not.'

She thought it over, closed the door and finally sat down across from me in my new old spare chair and immediately lit up one of those long, thin, fake cigars girls smoke these days. Mental note – steal new ashtray.

Slowly her story emerged; it took a while but I had a while. Her name was Sara Silvetti but that wasn't her real name, it was her adopted name, she didn't know her real name. She was a poet. She was an amazing poet, actually, considering her lack of experience. She lived with her adoptive parents in one of Elroy's apartment buildings, the same one he lived in, in Sherman Oaks, on Huston, near the park. She was eighteen and had just been thrown out of Pepperdine College, not that she gave a good Goddamn about it. She told me she didn't give a good Goddamn about anything. I told her she must give a Goddamn about something or what was she doing talking to me. She owned that, OK, maybe she did give a Goddamn about something.

'Like what?'

'Elroy thinks I should find out who my real mother is,' she said. 'He thinks not knowing is helping to screw me up.'

'What do you think?'

'I think he's full of shit,' she said.

'Yeah, well,' I said, 'you could be right and he could still be right.'

She sighed and looked around for something to do with her cigarette ash. I got her the top of a Bromo-Seltzer bottle from the bathroom. She looked it over.

'I like classy guys,' she said, deadpan. 'So what do we do?'

'So what have you done so far, have you talked it over with your adoptive parents?'

'Is he nuts?' she said to the ceiling. 'Is he completely out of his bird? I got enough problems already at home.'

I could well imagine.

'Have you ever seen the adoption papers?'

'No.'

'Do you know where they are?'

'No.'

It was my turn to sigh. I did so, deeply. 'Sara, do you know anything at all about the facts of life?'

She threw me a look that was half contemptuous and half, if you only knew.

'Not those facts of life, Mata Hari. Your adoptive parents have rights, both legal and otherwise. Now I don't need their permission to try and find out who your real parents are but I sure as hell wouldn't start looking without at least telling them what's going on, it's called consideration or politeness or both. Also, they could obviously be a lot of help. They know what agency you came from, or through, or what stork brought you, they know when, it's even possible they know who your real mother was, they might even have met her. And they may also know that laws have changed, today the child has certain rights; in some cases agencies can be obliged to make their adoption records public. In any case, we need something to start with; that is, if we do decide to go on with it and I for one am not exactly thrilled by the whole idea.'

'I got something,' she said quickly. 'I know when and I know where I was left.'

'Left?'

'Yeah, left,' she said. 'As in deposited. Abandoned. Deserted. Chucked out with the bath water. Get the picture?'

'Yeah, I get it,' I said.

'Not that I really care,' she said.

'Of course not,' I said.

She glared at me suspiciously. I felt like giving her the heave. What a dope, with her stupid hair and stupider torn clothes and even stupider safety pins and black nail polish except for the nails that were yellow. Next thing I'd be inviting that mange-infested cat in for cocotte de chicken livers and chilled Chateau Carnation.

Sara lit up another one of her foot-long specials.

'Well?' she said.

'Your folks have got to know,' I said, 'the sooner the better.' She had shoes on that didn't match, in fact one was a boot. I know, I know, she had another pair at home exactly the same.

'Well, they don't want to know,' she said. 'And they don't want me to know. And they are not going to help me find out anything about my mother, my real one.'

'How do you know that?'

'I listened,' she said. 'I used to listen a lot. Then it got boring.'

'Why do you think they won't help?'

'Who knows?' she said.

'Do you think it's remotely possible they love you and don't want to lose you, silly as it may sound?'

'Me?' She thought it over for a moment.

'You.'

'That'll be the day,' she said. 'That will be the bright new dawn.'

I raised the one eyebrow I had left at her.

'Listen,' she said, leaning forward. 'I been thinking. What if you did find out who my mother was and where she is and I got in touch with her, then it would be too late to stop me, they'd have to face up to it then, wouldn't they?'

'What about you facing up to it?' I said. 'What about that?'

'Facing up to what, that cat of yours?' She pointed behind me.

'That'll be the bright new dawn,' I said, 'the day that cat is mine. Beat it!' I chased it out and closed the back door.

'Facing up to a lot of things,' I said when I came back. 'We may never find out who your mother was; probably we won't. The records may not exist; if they do, you may not be able to afford the potential litigation involved. Sad but true. Your mother may be dead, Sara. She may be alive and not want to meet you.'

'I can't see that,' she said.

'Look in a mirror,' I said. 'What if you were the result of a rape? What if you were illegitimate and it would harm your mother's life now if it all came out? What if she met you and didn't like you? What if you didn't like her?'

'What if I don't like you?' she said. 'What difference does it make? You going to help me or not? Elroy said you would. I said why should you.'

'That's what I say too. However, ever heard of money? Bread? People will do a lot of foolish things for bread.'

'Well, I haven't got any,' she said. 'They don't give me any. Well, they give me some but I spend it. On clothes, mostly.'

She looked at me carefully; when she saw I wasn't going to rise to the bait, no matter how tempting, she went on. 'My mother will give me some when I find her and I can pay you then.'

I had to laugh. Santa Claus hadn't really forgotten that Red Ryder air rifle I asked for a few decades ago, he was just a little behind on his deliveries.

'OK, OK,' I said. 'Don't break my heart. Let me try it the easy way first. If that doesn't work and you want to go on, we'll try the hard way.'

'Like what?'

'Like injunctions and subpoenas and a lot of money from you or a nice long chat with your adoptive parents, or both. For now, just tell me where and when you were left.'

'On 22 March, outside St Mary's Hospital, Davis, California.'

'Any particular year?'

'Nineteen sixty-six. You ever been to Davis, California?'

'Never,' I said with a shudder. 'Unless I was left there too and Mummy never told me. However, I am going to talk to Davis, California, as soon as you give me your address and phone number.'

She provided me with the information, stood up, stretched, lit another stogie, then offered me one. I took it to clinch the deal and said I'd save it for supper if she didn't mind.

'I don't care if you save it for your next Tupperware party,' she said. 'Can I help?'

'Help what?'

'Help you, whatever you're going to do.'

'No,' I said firmly. 'Go home and write some poetry or tear your clothes or something.'

'Why not?'

I sighed surprisingly gently, considering the provocation.

'There isn't anything for you to do right now, that's why not. There is something for me to do and I'm going to start doing it as soon as you buzz off.'

'Well, why can't I do it?'

'Because you don't even know what it is!' I said. 'Now beat it.'

'You could tell me,' she said, 'then I could do it.'

'By the time I tell you I could do it myself,' I said. 'Go away, will you? I know you want to help, I do get it, but some things are just one-man jobs.'

'If you do get a two-man job, can I help, I mean, if it concerns me?'

'Of course!' I said warmly. 'You'll be the first person I think of, I promise. Now go home and sit by the phone.'

'You big liar,' she said. She took a Walkman out of a shoulder-bag that looked like a WWII ammunition holder, then slouched out. I hate Walkmans, too. Jesus Christ, you know you're getting old when there are more things you hate than like. I picked up her present, took it to the back door and chucked it out for the cat. Then I checked the time –

there was plenty of it, as usual. I got through to Information in Davis and Information in Davis didn't know if there was a Davis daily paper but did know that everyone in town took the *Sacramento Bee*. Shortly thereafter I was talking to a Miss Spencer who worked in the *Bee*'s advertising department. She helped me frame an ad to run daily for three days in their personal columns to the effect that a substantial reward would be paid for any information about a Caucasian baby girl who had been chucked out with the bath water on to the steps of St Mary's all those years ago. Complete confidentiality assured, this is in the child's best interest and at her bequest. Call collect, etc. Miss Spencer also rented me a box number and said the ad would be inserted as soon as they had received my check for $17.50. I said it was practically on its way. She said any mail I received at my new box number would be forwarded to me within twenty-four hours but this service would be discontinued two weeks after the date of the insertion of the first ad. I said I fully understood, wished Miss Spencer a happy day up there in dear old Davis, and rang off. I figured with the cost of the phone call, Miss Lobotomy was already into me for over nineteen big ones but what the hell, you can't always put money first, there is such a thing as altruism, is there not? Still, after making out a check for the *Bee* and sending it off, I did make out a bill for the peanut-head just in case she ever did get a proper job or maybe her foster parents might even cough up.

Then I had a quick visit from the Nus and their cousin Mr Nu. They just popped in to see if I was all right, they said. I was all right, I said. Mr Nu took in the new wall to wall and made a Vietnamese gesture with one hand that I think meant, mighty classy, but then I'm not exactly an expert on one-handed Vietnamese gestures.

They had no sooner bowed their way out than Mr Amoyan bowed his way in, on more or less the same errand. After he had assured himself that I was still in the land of the living, he too took in the new carpeting and then rolled his eyes heavenwards in what I interpreted as an old Armenian gesture of deep contempt. Mr Amoyan had kindly, as an office warming (ha ha) present, brought me a new calendar to replace the one he'd given me last Christmas. It was from some Armenian garage down on Pico and featured a brightly hued picture of a gypsy-looking lady being serenaded by a gypsy-looking gaucho type in front of a backdrop of gypsy-looking mountains.

I said, thanks very much, it was just what I needed, and then rolled my orbs skyward.

He left.

I finally managed to get out of there before anyone else dropped by, took the truck back to the rental office as it seemed clear my days disguised as a gay house painter were through, caught a cab back home and began looking in the clothes closet for something suitable to wear to a funeral. If there was such a thing. If it made any difference. If anyone was really watching.

CHAPTER FIFTEEN

Mrs Flexner turned out to be correct, there weren't many of us at Timmy's last rites.

The service was held in a small room off the main hall of the Angel Baptist Funeral Home way out on Chandler Boulevard, Reverend Jimmy Barson, Officiant. I was a little late getting there; the other mourners were already seated. Piped organ music coming from somewhere wafted over us. The ceiling was a dark blue with tiny lights scattered in it, giving a cut-rate impression of a starry sky at night. All but the youngest of the kids were there, on their best behavior, the girls wearing white gloves, the boy a dark blue suit. Then there was Mrs Flexner and two of her friends, then there was me.

The usher, a black man in a black suit, handed me a . . . I don't know what you call it, a 'program' sounds like we were at a concert. Anyway, it had four pages, with a picture of Timmy in an oval on the back. A large black lady in a robe sang 'Sleep and Dream', then she sang the Lord's Prayer. Then the Reverend Officiant delivered a short eulogy, which was followed by a reading from the Scripture. Psalms, if anyone's interested. All the kids were crying by then; I was sick and angry.

Then we had a remembrance from Mrs Flexner, then a spirited rendition of 'Goin' Up Yonda' by the singer. A final prayer from the Reverend Jimmy, then something devastating called the Recessional, when those who wanted to filed past the coffin. I passed.

The family left first, then the friends, and then myself. We all met up in the hall outside. Mrs Flexner was sitting on a bench weeping. One of her friends and one of her children were comforting her. I was going to say something but didn't know what, so I left. It seemed particularly incongruous to step outside into the heat and sun and palm trees. A sign on a bar across the street said 'Fri – Sat – Girls'. Dying and going to heaven was a relief and a blessing and a time for joy, the Reverend Jimmy had said. Well, don't believe everything you hear is what I say.

To cheer myself up, on the way home I stopped at Blumenfeld's and let Syd sell me a wastepaper basket that had English hunting scenes painted on it. That did the trick. It cheered me up so much I thought I'd stop at the Two-Two-Two to celebrate. I was still celebrating three hours, seven brandy and gingers and a half a dozen games of pool later. I thought maybe Mae would like to come out and help me celebrate. What a brilliant idea. We could play doubles. We could lick any mixed pool team in the Valley, heck, maybe the world.

Mae was out. Her obnoxious roommate was in.

'She'll probably be out a lot from now on,' I was informed. 'Especially to some.'

'What does that mean, Charlene?'

'Oh, didn't she tell you? She's engaged. To a terrific guy who sells condos.'

'Sure, sure,' I lied. 'Just called to wish her the best. Just called to see if silver would be appropriate for a wedding present. I don't think you can ever go wrong with a nice piece of silver, do you?'

Charlene wasn't sure. Charlene wasn't even sure if it was the male or the female stork who delivered the babies. Anyway.

I hung up and went back into the bar to continue celebrating. Maybe that was why Mae had been so mad at me the last couple of times we'd talked. Funny, though – she gets engaged, and she's the one who's mad at me. Wouldn't it make more sense the other way around?

I posed this riddle to my ol' pal, my ol' compadre Jim the barman. Good old Jim, he was your original heart of gold, as long as you had the price of a drink and didn't try and put the make too hard on his insanely yummy bar girl Lotus.

'The way I see it,' Jim said thoughtfully, pouring out a few more stale pretzels into the freebie bowl on the bar, 'is like Israel invading Egypt before Egypt invades Israel.'

Ah – the unexpected wisdom of the common man – yet another reason for celebration.

Thursday morning. Bits and pieces. I awoke in my own bed, which was a relief. Alone, another relief, I guess. I didn't seem to be bleeding anywhere, except through the pupils, another relief. My legs were hot and itchy but the doc had said that was good, it meant they were getting better, there was good pain and bad pain, you know. Well, I didn't know. I thought good pain was as unlikely as the Baptists' rosy afterlife – nice work if you can get it.

Anyway, up and at 'em – a busy day ahead in the fascinating life of aging but still mean V. Daniel, Valley private eye. I felt something under my pillow – my God, I thought, the Tooth Fairy – she didn't forget! It turned out to be a large plastic ashtray from the Crow's Nest. On it was a picture of two crows having a cocktail. The male crow was singing to the female crow, 'Come fly with me.' Perfection in schlock.

I cleaned up, drank a quart of loathsome instant coffee, took my pills, sprayed my burns, grabbed the ashtray, snuck out without seeing Feeb, drove with great concentration to the office, and opened up. Mere moments later I had Betsy set up on my new old desk and was getting up to date with the files, a chore I rather liked, it made me seem businesslike, mobile, contemporary. I had the material from John to enter, a new file to enter on Sara, the Orphan of the Storm, and the latest in the thrilling Seburn case to type in. Into the monthly accounts went the deposits from Messrs Seburn and Lowenstein, out of it the payment to Cal Edison. Also out of it debits for the truck rental, furniture, stationery, stamps, telephone, wastepaper basket and Haig's Pinch, a legitimate business expense if ever I saw one. New balance – could be worse.

Bits and pieces. Did I ever mention my life was naught but a shower of assorted bits and pieces that never quite fit? If I didn't, remind me to do so some time as it's a fascinating topic.

Clear screen. I typed in 'Schedule for today, Thursday, 21 May 1984', and up it came in clear, soothing, green print right before my very eyes just as quick as all get out. Good old reliable Betsy. She did everything she was told to immediately, faster than immediately, and you try and find help like that today. 'Schedule for today: buy cat trap, preferably the highly illegal, jagged-tooth, 100-pound spring pressure type. See (at home? Work? Neutral place?) Barbara Herbert, single, 24. Call brother re mother. Call Elroy re insurance. Call Evonne (!) re St Stephen's. Bloody mary at Corner Bar. Afternoon: Lucy Seburn. Evening: frighten the freckles off as yet unselected student at St Stephen's. Later in evening: curl up with good dirty book.'

I was on the phone having a word with brother Tony when the Valley's only pygmy policeman, a stunning vision in heliotrope, strolled in without bothering to knock. I told Tony I'd get back to him, cleared the screen, and said, 'Now what?' to Lieutenant Conyers.

'And a good, good, top o' the morn to you,' he said. 'I was passing by, thought I'd just pop in.'

'Try not to make it a habit,' I said. All in all I preferred the cat.

'Feeling better, are we?' he asked, looking around brightly.

'We are.'

'Busy, are we?'

'We are.'

'Anything interesting?' He wandered out back to snoop some more.

'Nah,' I said. 'Domestic quarrels, insurance claims, same old stuff. How're the Albanian yogurt stirrers?'

'Aren't you the one,' he said. I looked modest. 'How's your old school friend?'

'OK,' I said. 'How's your son?' He didn't like that one; he stopped by the desk and looked daggers, as they say, at me.

'You know your problem, boyo?'

'Yes,' I said.

'You don't ask the right questions,' he said. 'You're too busy being funny. Why don't you ask me if we found the mysterious fire-bomber who destroyed your elegant office and almost managed to destroy you?'

'And who did manage to destroy Timmy Flexner,' I said. 'By the way, we missed you at the funeral. But, OK, have you caught him?'

'Guess,' he said.

'I guess no,' I said. 'Otherwise you wouldn't be sneaking around here with your trick questions.'

'I do not particularly care for you, Mr Daniel,' he said, picking an almost invisible piece of lint off his padded shoulder.

'Gee, I'm sorry,' I said. 'I could use a few friends right now. Neat shoes.' They were burgundy loafers. 'I admire a classy dresser.' Sara wasn't the only deadpan comic in the world. All right, it was childish, but is there not some of the child left in every man? Also he got on my nerves, I thought his technique was obvious and his wardrobe a disaster in pastels, but who knows what stresses the very small live under?

'And I don't like the insinuation that I don't care if the people responsible aren't caught and strung up by the balls,' I told him. 'A lot of people get killed in this part of the world, in fact in every part of the world, but I rarely know any of them or have been involved with any of them. I live a dull, humdrum life, Lieutenant. Once in a while I follow somebody and maybe take a picture or two. You're the cop, it's your job, not mine. Insurance claims, runaways, stolen pets, bounced checks, that's my job.'

'You know what I hope?' Lieutenant Conyers asked me. 'You know what I hope deeply?'

'Yes,' I said. 'To be born again as tall as me.'

'I hope you need me sometime.'

He walked out on his toes, got into his Dodge, and began to drive away.

'I hope I don't is what I hope,' I called after him. I could just see the top of his head through the rear window and that was with two cushions under his clenched little butt.

It was too early to call Elroy and much too early for John D. so I was forced to call Evonne. Miss Shirley to me, so far, but I can dream, can't I, as Jung used to remark so amusingly.

Miss Shirley was in. How was I? I was fine, but busy. How was she? She was fine, but busy. How was Mr Lowenstein? He was fine. Was he busy too? He was always busy. Did I want to talk to him? No, I wanted to talk to her. So talk.

'Miss Shirley, are you capable of discreetly finding out something for me without asking any questions and then keeping it to yourself afterwards? I know you're capable of it, but will you?'

'How've I done so far, Pablo?'

'Ah,' I said. 'Ah. Are you referring to the other night?'

'If you mean the night Dev and I visited you in the hospital and there you were, helpless and wan, battered and bruised, yes I am. Have I even asked you one question what that was all about, as if I couldn't guess, and by the way, I've got good news for you, they think they can save one of the trees.'

'That is good news,' I said. 'And I mean that sincerely.' For a terrible moment I thought I saw Timmy going by the window but it wasn't him, it didn't even look like him.

'Well, then,' she said. 'Out with it, mister, I got work to do. Have you ever done a payroll for a staff of forty-two?'

'Big deal,' I said. 'The computer does it all. What I want to know is does Dev have any regular dates or appointments or jobs off the school grounds and after school hours Thursday or Friday?'

'Gotcha,' she said. 'Anything else?'

I said no. She said, 'Later,' and hung up. I hung up too,

then straightened my new ashtray. Then I straightened the phone. Some girls always bring out the domestic in me.

By then it was a little after ten and I didn't seem to have anything to do for a bit. Mind you I could have found something but the doc had said that walking was good for me so I switched off Betsy and walked. Although it was but mid-morning, it was already warming up nicely in the Valley. There was another smog alert but it was only stage two which meant you could see a good hundred yards in all directions except up, which was more than enough for me.

I walked. Strange place, the Valley. Dirty movies and chi-chi kitchenware stores, movie studios and eerie shopping malls where Valley girls wandered lost and forlorn, wondering whatever happened to their fleeting moment of fame. Car lots and health-food stores, bridle paths along the dried-up Los Angeles River and wide, never-ending boulevards lined with those tall, skinny palms that have all the action at the very top, like Wilt Chamberlain in an afro. Hopeful vendors of tropical fish, second-hand bookstores, foreign car garages and 'For Sale' real-estate signs. Booze stores and orange trees, cut-rate drugs, tans and sirens.

I wound up at Don's Deli, on Ventura, dawdled over some rye toast with cream cheese and a glass of milk, then strolled back to the office. On the way I stopped in at Mendleson's Family Jewelers and bought Mae a sterling silver cake dish and a matching cake knife, to be gift-wrapped and delivered. What the hell. Once a sport, always a sport.

Back at my place of business I gave Elroy a call on my new red phone. He was up, if you call lying on your back in a hammock on a balcony eating granola bars being up. I asked about his insurance; no sweat, my man, he said, keep a list. Then I thanked him effusively for sending me such an eye-catching, let alone affluent, client as Sara Silvetti. He laughed, then choked on his breakfast. Served him right. I tried John D. but he wasn't about yet. Then I broke a rule; I punched up the file on St Stephen's, made a note of a few names, addresses and phone numbers, then packed everything away, got in the car and headed west on the Ventura Freeway towards Manhattan Beach, there was a guy I wanted to talk about boats, but I never did find him. I didn't try all that hard.

It was too early in the year to swim but not too early to sit in the sun and to stroll out the pier and watch the fishermen and try to relax. Mae says I worry too much. I say there is no too much. I bought a slice of pizza for lunch and watched some girls playing volleyball. A small boy learning to roller-skate ran into me. A chap all dressed in black and a white, powdered face, was pretending he was a robot. Another chap was inside a large cardboard box that was decorated like a jukebox and if you put a quarter in the slot, a flap in the front dropped and he sang you a song. Another chap was playing with great aplomb and many flourishes a stringless guitar. And I thought that I had problems.

I came back to town late in the afternoon against the traffic and by five thirty was where I was supposed to be – on Rivera Street, around the corner from the Seburns' house in bustling, suburban Burbank. A quarter of an hour later, same old routine – south to the freeway, off at La Cienega, her car into the health-club parking lot, mine into Moe's. I had to give her a few minutes to start doing whatever it was she did so I had a couple of hotdogs and was just about to get out of the car and go over to open negotiations with Mr Universe at the front desk when lo and behold if Mrs Seburn didn't come out of the club with another woman.

And lo and behold even more if they didn't cross Ventura and walk right up to Yours Truly, Taken Aback.

CHAPTER SIXTEEN

Yes, taken well aback. Nonplussed. Good-looking woman, Mrs Seburn – late thirties, I suppose, tanned, expensive, low-heeled half boots, short skirt, full-sleeved, collarless cotton shirt. Her friend was younger, also attractive, permed blond hair in an all-over frizz, silver sandals, silver jumpsuit festooned with a lot of decorative zippers. They came right up to me and looked in the car window.

'You've got mustard on your mouth,' Mrs Seburn said.

'Thank you,' I said, wiping it off.

'Nice wheels,' her friend said.

'Thank you,' I said. I switched the radio off.

'I don't know, Pam,' Mrs Seburn said. 'I'm not sure.'

'I am,' her friend said. Mrs Seburn took a deep breath.

'I can't do it through a car window,' she said. While I was getting out, her friend said, 'My God, how do you fit in that thing?'

'I fold,' I said, getting out the rest of the way. Then we all went and perched on stools on the shady side of Moe's. Son of Moe came over to see if we wanted anything. I said I didn't. Lucy and Pam said they didn't. Then I changed my mind and asked for a coffee. Then the ladies changed their minds and a few minutes later, there we were, on the shady side of Moe's, all sipping terrible coffee.

'Well, ladies?' I finally said.

'Look, Mr Whoever-You-Are,' Lucy Seburn said, 'is it too much to ask you to tell us the truth?'

'Try me,' I said with my disarming, little-boy grin.

'Have you been following me?'

'Yes.'

'I told you it was him,' Pam said.

'Every Thursday?'

'Yes. What put you on to me?' I was curious. I mean I know I'm not the world's best when it comes to following people but I had taken certain precautions, especially as both me and my car are somewhat noticeable. After the first time, when I knew the route, there were always plenty of cars between us and I always parked out of sight both from the Seburn house and the club.

The ladies look at each other.

'Not fair just me being truthful,' I said.

'My husband's secretary,' Lucy said, looking away. 'She found out and phoned me up. God, what awful coffee.'

'Why?' I asked.

'Why?'

'Yes, why. I don't want to be coarse but what's in it for her?'

'She's a woman,' said Pam, as if that explained all. Maybe it did.

'Do you know my husband?' Lucy asked me.

'No, I never met him. But we write a lot.'

'He's a nice man. I like him a lot. I don't want to hurt him any more than I have to, can you believe that?'

'Pass,' I said. 'You're right, it is awful.'

'Look,' Pam said, taking her friend's hand and giving it a squeeze. 'We're lovers, OK?'

'OK by me,' I said, having just figured it out for myself.

'Bob, her husband, is going to have enough problems anyway without finding out his wife has left him for a dyke, as he would put it. We want to leave him something.'

'He's a nice guy,' Lucy said again. 'He's a personal manager for athletes, a couple of Dodgers, a couple of Lakers, a whole bunch of golfers. He's a complete sports freak himself, plays football, softball, golf, hangs out with the guys, one of the boys, you know?'

I nodded.

'Look,' Pam said. 'Lucy just wants out. No money, no house, nothing that isn't hers. Right, Lucy?'

Lucy grinned. 'Right, I guess,' she said. 'Just kidding, Pam, but it is a little scary. I'm not a spring chicken any more and all I've done for ten years is go on diets and spend his money. A lot of lovely money,' she said a bit wistfully. 'There's a lot of beautiful places in the world when you've got a lot of money.'

'And they do say travel broadens,' I said. 'So what's the plan, then?' A thought struck me. 'Has it anything to do with that good-looking young hunk who I hate who walks you to your car and then gives you a big smooch for the benefit of any prying eyes?'

'Give that man a cee-gar,' said Pam, pointing one finger at me. 'Look. You snap some nice clean dirty pictures of him and Lucy in flagrante delicto, otherwise known as on the job. Ah, the old story – neglected wife of un âge certain meets young, gorgeous iron-pumper – something any husband can relate to. He can also if he wants to relate the sad tale to his friends so they can all relate to it too in their macho ways.'

'Ain't men just the worst,' I said.

'So Bob gets très, très angry, which will help him over the pain of separation and loss and he can justifiably, more or less, and without guilt, or too much, anyway, cut her off without a cent, little knowing she doesn't want a cent anyway.'

'I guess,' said Lucy. 'Just kidding, Pam.'

'Maybe, but it isn't funny, Lucy,' said Pam. 'So quit it. So everyone winds up happy. Well, if not happy, at least as little unhappy as possible.' She swung her nice legs up to the horizontal a couple of times.

'Nifty plan,' I said. 'All I have to do is fake evidence and lie a lot. What about the secretary?'

'What about the secretary?' they both said together, then smiled at each other.

'Does she know your master plan?'

'Are you kidding?' said Lucy. 'How would she know? All she knows is Bob thinks I'm playing around, having the occasional quickie on the side.' The ladies smiled at each other again.

'There is one other little thing I might mention here,' Pam said.

'Yes, I think you might mention it,' Lucy said.

'I don't want you to think in any way that we're trying to bribe you . . .'

'God forbid,' I said.

'. . . but it did strike me that you might have to bill Bob, that sounds funny, doesn't it, bill Bob, for the considerable extra expense involved in getting the clean dirty pictures. After all, he is loaded, and he is getting out of it fairly easily, all things considered.'

'I don't know about that,' I said. 'I never had a wife but I almost had one and there was nothing at all easy about losing her. I'm getting over it, of course, hell, in another five years the pain'll probably die down to a dull ache.'

'Yeah but facts is facts,' said Pam. 'And the fact is he's going to lose her anyway. And the fact is he's lost her already. You think he hasn't been humping every cheerleader west of the Pecos? You don't think we could hit him with that? Hell, his secretary gave Lucy a list a mile long and that was without thinking.'

'There is that,' I said. I thought for a moment. Awful coffee doesn't get better when it's cold, I thought. On the other hand it doesn't get any worse. I thought Pam was one smart cookie. Tough, too. Gorgeous too, damn it. And I thought she was probably correct, her way was the best for all including my client, whose rights I was morally if not legally committed to protect. And I didn't see how it could hurt his position, although it might wreak havoc with his feelings, to have some 8 × 10 glossies of his wife playing doctor.

'I just happen to have my camera with me,' I said, 'so if Lover Boy's available, let's get it on. I suppose you've already worked out all the details like where and how I just happened to be there with my trusty Baby Brownie.'

And they had, they had. I paid Son of Moe, then got my Canon from the glove compartment. We waited for a break in the traffic, then jay-walked across the boulevard and entered the club. The style was open plan – on the left was the gray and red metallic reception desk where Mr Universe held sway; opposite it were innumerable complex machines designed to do wonderful things to flab. Behind the desk area was a half-sized boxing ring with a green Astroturf track circling it. After that was a small, health-food snack bar. I must go back and eat there sometime, I heard the aubergine cutlets were unforgettable. The sauna, steam room, changing rooms and medical offices were in a row at the back. There were two black girls working out side by side who were so beautiful I felt like hitting someone.

Pam waved to Mr Universe and led us down a hall at the back that led to a small storeroom, along one side of which was a waist-high pile of padded, white gymnasts' mats that made a spiffy bed. A strong, bare bulb hung from an overhead fixture and the door, which was almost at the foot of the mats, opened inward. Pam and Lucy seemed to know the place well but that was none of my business, was it? Pam went off to get the hunk while I fussed professionally with my camera which had not, by the by, come from the Nus' cousin, it was a birthday present from Benny from a few years back. Of course where he had obtained it from one did not inquire but it was noticeable that the neck strap had been slightly worn when he gave it to me.

Pam came back with Lucy's friend. She didn't introduce us but she called him Joseph. He was an overpowering stack of rippling muscles and glistening health tanned to perfection, maybe six foot five, wearing a black leather cock-sock tied at the back with a thong and a matching black leather headband; the rest was skin. I would have hated him on sight if I hadn't already loathed every square inch of him.

Joseph thought the whole thing an absolute and total lark.

'Ready when you are, Mr de Mille,' was the first thing he said to me.

'Call me Cecil,' was the first thing I said to him. Then he looked at my shirt and shuddered.

'I had the worst time in Hawaii last year,' he said, as if it was my fault. Maybe it was.

We got down to business. Pam, giggling, directed. I lurked by the door. Lucy stripped down to her yellow panties. Joseph kept saying helpful things like 'Places, please' and 'Quiet on the set' and 'Makeup! Makeup!'

I must say it wasn't really all that much fun, in fact it was depressing, especially for Lucy; I had to admire Pam and Joseph for doing their best to keep it all light. Pam had decided that what we needed were shots of naked torsos in which Lucy's face was completely recognizable, without any full frontals, despite Joseph's more than willingness. When the two were posed to everyone's satisfaction I went out into the hall and shot off a quick roll through the door which had been left carefully ajar; the theory was the lovers had been so engrossed in their passion they hadn't noticed me. I suppose the theory was also that they either didn't mind the bare 100-watt bulb hanging right over them or they liked it that way. I've heard there are people who enjoy making love in blinding light, it's supposed to be quite fashionable these modern times, share everything, hide nothing. I say nerts to that, like my pop before me.

It didn't take long; soon we were out in the heat and haze again. Pam had a quick word with Mr Universe on the way out; I never did find out what arrangements she had made with him. Maybe they did it for friendship; I suppose it's remotely possible that someone could have all the muscles in the world and still be nice.

I walked the girls to their cars.

'Well, TTFN,' I said. 'All the best. Mr Seburn should have the prints tomorrow afternoon sometime so get your act together in the highly unlikely chance you haven't already.'

Lucy stood up on tiptoe and kissed me firmly on one cheek, then Pam kissed me noisily on the other. I crossed Ventura and made my way back to Moe's and perched on a stool on the sunny side for a change. When Moe brought me over a medium root beer, he gave me that kind of look that says, what a sly dog you turned out to be. I gave him right back the kind of look that says, if you only knew, pal.

I sipped my soda and swung my heels. I watched a dog take a pee on one of my white-walls. I saw a cat go up and inspect what was left of a dead gull in the far corner of Moe's parking lot. I saw two flies playing piggyback. Amazing what the observant naturalist can find in a big city.

I wondered how much I could hit good ol' Bob, the man's man, for, in what would more than likely be his final tab. Let's see . . . there was the hefty bribe to Mr Universe at the desk, the ditto to the janitor who kept the coast clear and perhaps unlocked the door for me . . . were hotdogs and root beers legitimate expenses? . . . the cost of the film, of course, nothing but the best, then the special one-day processing . . . how about if Lover Boy had caught me, there was a scuffle and I lost a couple of teeth . . . how about if he chased me to my car and picked up a handy 2 × 4 and started smashing it up . . .?

Oh yes, there was plenty to think about as I made my way westward along the freeway toward the Valley Bowl and Barbara Herbert, single, age twenty-four. When I was twenty-four I was already about thirty. I was in southern Louisiana learning what a fool's mate was.

CHAPTER SEVENTEEN

'Oh, Barbara? She's got the night off, she'll be in Friday,' Mrs Martha F. Nazaroff, twenty-seven, from La Crescenta, told me chirpily. 'Aren't you something to do with security?'

'Right on,' I said. That didn't seem to frighten her at all. 'Is Barbara a good friend of yours?'

'Pretty good, considering she's only been here a while. Should I tell her you're looking for her?'

'That might be a good idea,' I said. In fact I thought it a splendid idea, then Babs could spend the next twenty-four hours or so shivering her timbers from fright so she'd be a nervous wreck and ready to confess all when I did catch up with her. If it was her in the first place, of course.

'Should I give her a hint what it's all about?' Mrs Nazaroff asked with unashamed curiosity.

'She'll know,' I said mysteriously. I thanked Mrs Nazaroff and ambled off to the bank of public phones; Big Sally blew me a kiss as I passed the snack bowl. I looked shocked.

Miss Shirley answered the phone almost before it started to ring. Ah, just awaitin' my call, was she, just hopin' against hope.

'It's me,' I said chirpily.

'I'm busy,' she said distantly. 'What do you want?'

'Dev.'

'Oh. Friday nights he gets tanked up at some veterans' organization. V F W? The Legion? In Glendale.'

'Sure?'

'Sure I'm sure, I found out from Frank.'

'Who's Frank?'

'Frank! He's one of the other guards, they go together, Dev picks him up about seven forty-five. Goodbye.' She hung up.

'TTFN,' I said to the dial tone and hung up too. Moody things, women, who can figure them? Maybe it was her biorhythms. Sure. I took out the list of names I'd made at the office and propped it up in front of me. I called Robert Shenley, student president of the St Stephen's Rifle Club. Robert was at the movies, his mother told me, was it anything important?

I said no.

I called Robert Santee, secretary of the St Stephen's Rifle Club. A young girl, his sister, I deduced, asked me politely to wait a minute, then shouted, 'It's for you, rat! Bobby!'

After a minute and after what sounded like your normal friendly scuffle between siblings, Bobby said, 'Hello?'

'Robert Santee?'

'Yes.'

'My name is Richard Morse; your vice-principal Mr Lowenstein suggested I have a word with you.'

'What about?'

'I don't want to alarm you, Robert,' I said, wanting to alarm him out of his socks, 'but I'm an investigator of sorts. Let me say right now that what I am interested in has nothing whatsoever to do with you, your friends or your family, in fact, Mr Lowenstein only gave me your name because he considers you a decent and patriotic young man who would do his duty to his school and his country without question. Is he correct in that assumption, Robert?'

'I guess so, sure,' said the boy uncertainly. 'But what's it about?'

'I'd rather not tell you over the phone for obvious reasons,' I said, lowering my voice. 'But let me say only at this time that if you have any doubts whatsoever about meeting me later tonight, please give Mr Lowenstein a call at his home immediately, and I have the number right here. If he's not in, you might try his secretary Miss Shirley.' I hoped if Bobby did call anyone it would be Miss Shirley, and she'd be interrupted in the middle of something romantic and get in a snit.

But it was unlikely. As all door-to-door salesmen will have appreciated by now, it was the old 'if you have any doubts' routine: if you have any doubts, madam, please telephone the Chamber of Commerce at this number and they will tell you I'm not only fully licensed but our work (or delivery of product) is fully insured by the state. A total lie, of course, but no one ever phones except the occasional paranoid bag who's not going to buy anything in the first place.

Not that it would be the end of the world if Bobby did give one of them a call; as soon as they said no, never heard of the guy, then I'd just have to get on to them and explain why I wasn't using my own name and then explain the same thing to Bobby. But I didn't want to do all that. Firstly, it was tiresome. Secondly, and more important, I'd gone to great lengths with Dev to conceal my part in the highly successful demolition of Art's; not only couldn't it have been me who did it physically but I'd mentioned to him I worked alone, without a partner. Now it was time for Mr X the phantom bomber to strike again, and I hoped my cleverness would serve the dual purpose of keeping me, my property and my friends out of the firing line and also suggesting that there were other dangerous and aggressive parties involved.

And Bobby would likely tell all, immediately, even if he had sworn to a clean-cut FBI agent (me) that his lips would remain for ever sealed. He was human, and suddenly involved in important and mysterious events, and D. Devlin was not only the head of his marvelous rifle club but probably his idol, too. In fact, if I was really clever, and I know I've unfortunately, due to circumstances beyond my control, over-reached myself in this area before, but say for once I was really clever, then not only could I ensure that Bobby spilled the beans to Dev but that they would be the wrong beans. Sometimes I don't think it's fully appreciated that we investigators need a blazing intelligence as well as a robust physique.

So I told the kid I'd be driving by his building at exactly

seven thirty and would buzz his apartment three short ones. Then he would come down and we'd go for a drive, fifteen minutes should do it. Would his parents let him out on a school night?

'Are you kidding?' he said. 'Anyway, they're not even home.'

'Was that your sister I spoke with?'

'That was one of them.'

'Please, not a word to her or to anyone else until you get clearance from us.' I hung up, more than satisfied with my low-keyed but intense performance.

I needed to borrow a car, my own being obviously unsuitable for the task in hand, so I tracked down John D. without too much trouble, he was in the first place I checked, the bar. He was sipping a fruit juice and charming the bulging pants off a tableful of lady bowlers, all of whom had 'The Overpass, Vallejo, CA' on the backs of their blue and silver bowling shirts and their names in flowing script over their front pockets. The girls were feeling no pain; it seemed they were celebrating their first-ever victory over their hated rivals from Darlene's Hair Salon. They let John D. out of their clutches but with screams of protest.

'It's all right for some,' I said as soon as we got to the comparative quiet of the long bar. '"John D., don't leave us!" "Do you think I need a heavier ball, John D.?"' I shook my head in disgust.

He grinned. 'It's a living. Buy you a drink?'

'A Coke,' I said to Phil the barman. 'Hold the maraschino. By the way, John D., don't happen to know a Mr Lowenstein, do you? Comes here with his family? Tall chap? Gray hair? One might call him an educator?'

He grinned again.

'Sounds like you got together. What's that word for a matchmaker? In Yiddish?'

'Hello, Dolly,' I said. 'Yes, we did get together, and that is for your cauliflower ears only, which is why I need to borrow your car for an hour or so.' He drove a nice ordinary one-year-old Ford sedan. He dug out the keys and tossed them over.

'Thanks, pal.'

He waved it off. 'Get that stuff I sent?'

'I got it.'

'Who done it?'

'I could know tomorrow,' I told him. He leaned towards me, looking at my head in the dim light.

'Burn?'

'Like crazy.' Actually, it was coming along, I forgot about it most of the time.

'How does one burn one's head one wonders,' he said. There was a burst of ribald laughter from the Overpass ladies. 'Singeing off those split ends again?'

I told him the main points, he hadn't heard about any of it. He wanted to know if there was anything he could do. I told him I'd keep him in mind if I ever needed anyone's head creased with a heavy, round object that had finger holes in it. The girls squealed again and it was all very pleasant but it wasn't getting a lot done so I made my adieus and took off in John D.'s clunker, heading for home and my Junior G-Man disguise kit.

Laugh, fools, laugh, but it did come in handy once in a while. It wasn't a kit per se, just an old potato-chip carton on the floor in the clothes cupboard that contained a collection of odds and ends, bits and pieces, hats, glasses, some TV makeup, the kind you put on with a sponge, a couple of ratty wigs, a twist of crepe hair, glue, some stale cigars, some GI aftershave, an assortment of lodge pins.

Back home, with still no sign of Feeb, thank God, I got it out and started making myself look like what I thought Bobby thought an FBI agent would look like. I applied a nice tan, a straight leading-man mustache, a pair of square-framed, slightly tinted glasses, gray fedora to cover the hair and burnt forehead, gray suit to cover me, white shirt and boring tie, small knot. Sensible shoes. Wallet with suitable enclosures.

Holster with suitable enclosure. As a final touch I added an unnecessary Band-Aid to one cheek. Perfect, as long as the lights were dim and so was he. Not that it really mattered if he saw through my handiwork, all he'd think was I was an FBI type who was bad at disguises.

Bobby didn't live that far away, which made sense, as the school was fairly near to me and, as a student, fairly near to him. Still, I was a few minutes late when I pulled up in front of his high-rise on Lemon Farm Drive, right on the border of Studio City and Sherman Oaks. I gave his buzzer the agreed-on three shorts; a few minutes later he came out of the front door and looked around. I was back in the car by then, slouching in the seat to try and look shorter; good luck. I gave him a wave, he slipped in beside me and we took off.

I was looking for a poorly lit stretch of road where I could park, and found one around the corner on Celito. I switched off, turned to him, and gave him my best FBI seriously im-personal gaze. He gave me a seriously frightened one back.

Bobby was endeavoring to cultivate a mustache. He was wearing a new pair of jeans, clean sneakers, and a Michael Jackson 'Victory Tour' T-shirt. On one wrist he had an expensive-looking black chronometer with a hinged cap on it to protect the dial.

'Robert, I appreciate this,' I told him sincerely. I took his hand and shook it firmly, then showed him some phony FBI ID in the name I'd given him, Richard Morse. He peered at it in the gloom; I wanted him to get a good look at it so I lit it up for him briefly with a small penlight I had clipped in my breast pocket. When I put my wallet away I made sure the gun in my hip holster showed.

'What's up, Mr Morse?' he asked nervously. 'I don't have too long, Mom and Dad are just up the street at a friend's. Is there anything wrong?'

'There's a lot wrong, I'm afraid, Robert, at your school, so we've been called in. What was the name of that boy who got stabbed a while back?'

'Stabbed? Oh. That was Carlos. He plays baseball. He's back at school already.'

'Do you know why he was cut?'

'Well,' said Bobby, 'not really.'

'Suppose you had to make a guess, Robert?'

'A girl?'

'Guess again, Robert.'

'Gee, I dunno,' he said. 'Drugs?'

'Drugs,' I said with impersonal loathing. 'How do you feel about drugs, Robert?'

'I don't know any,' he said. 'I mean I don't know much about them. I don't know anything about them.'

'You must know something, Robert,' I said gently. 'Everyone knows something.' I took an empty pipe out of my pocket and sucked at it noisily. 'Sure wish they'd let us smoke on the job, but there you go.'

'Yeah,' he said.

'Drugs are in the paper every day, Robert. They're all around us. In good homes and bad, good schools and bad. They're all around St Stephen's, aren't they, Robert?'

'I guess so,' he admitted.

'Robert, in a minute I'm going to ask you to do a difficult thing. But first let me ask you this, do you love your sisters?'

'Course.'

'Your parents, the United States of America?'

He nodded vigorously.

'And a girl, is there some lucky girl you care for?'

He squirmed a bit.

'Yes, well,' I said understandingly, 'I was young once too, believe it or not.' We both laughed falsely. The aftershave I'd put on was getting to me so I opened the window a couple of inches.

'Robert, you're secretary of the rifle club, are you not?'

'Yes, sir!' A passing car lit up his face; he'd be a good-looking boy when he got rid of that fungus.

'Yes, sir,' I repeated slowly, as if the words had great

significance. 'Yes, sir. Robert, can I treat you as a man, not a child, a man who will make the right choices when difficult choices have to be made?'

'Yes, sir!' he said again.

I looked into the empty bowl of the pipe as if I was trying to make my mind up about something. What I was trying to make my mind up about was how much longer I should go on shooting the shit before putting it to him. Should I let him have five low-keyed but hair-raising minutes on drug addiction and addicts I have known? The wasted speed-freaks listening to static on their ghetto-blasters and finding detailed instructions therein. The all-bone meth-heads on the floors of cold-water crash pads. And some of the runaway kids . . . ah, the hell with it. He already knew, anyway, everyone knew, everyone'd seen the pictures and read the book. Who cared, though, but thee and me? That was another story.

It did take a little more priming but finally Robert rolled over and delivered like the good, patriotic, gun-loving American boy he was, which is why I looked up the cadet corps and rifle club members in the first place as they are more likely to have these occasionally helpful qualities than those in the Drug of the Month Club or the St Stephen's Chapter of the Hell's Angels. And what he delivered was the names of some half a dozen of the school's bad boys, including the one who did the cutting, which was an open secret to all concerned except the authorities. He gave me the smokers and the dealers, the truants and the car stealers, the ones he knew with juvenile records, the ones the worst stories were told about, the one he knew who kept a .22 in his locker.

I thanked him deeply and sincerely.

I could have approached the whole problem differently, I suppose, I could have run the whole male population of the school through the police computer's juvenile files except there were too many of the little bastards and also juvenile files aren't the easiest to get into as they are supposed to be secret and a lot more would have been required than one friendly call to the long-suffering Larry and I don't like to call on my brother too often for help as it makes him feel superior.

During the short drive back to Bobby's I told him that unfortunately it wasn't our policy to issue letters of commendation to civilians, so his good deed for the day might never be known to anyone but us. Tough, but there it was. And he obviously couldn't go around telling everybody about our undercover work and means of operation or they wouldn't be undercover any more, would they. Of course not.

When we were drawing up in front of his place I asked him what he thought of Mr Devlin. He thought he was terrific. You should see him shoot. I hoped I never had the pleasure. I told Bobby I felt bad going behind Mr Devlin's back this way; on the face of it it would seem that he would have been the likely person to approach for inside information but we had a hard and fast rule never to involve local law-enforcement personnel unless absolutely necessary as they had to go on working in their communities afterwards and any connection between them and such as us might well undercut the trust and loyalty they and their communities had mutually built up. Sometimes I don't know where I get it all from, but, as I perhaps mentioned, I do read a lot.

I did tell him however he might just pay our respects to Mr Devlin, whose good work we of course knew about, but to leave it at that. He said he would. We shook hands man to man, then he got out and headed for home and kid sisters and Mom and Dad and bedtime stories, secure in the knowledge that out there in the steamy, predatory jungle called the Big City determined and decent men like me were watching over him and his.

Dev would pump him dry, of course, Dev the ex-army military man, especially about the details I had gone to such trouble to get right. The ID card had the photo in the upper left corner and it had been correctly signed over the raised

Department of Justice seal. Both card and badge numbers were on it. The ID was always displayed using the left hand to keep the strong, or gun hand, free. With me being a lefty, it should have been the other way round, but who's to notice? Guns were these days worn in hip holsters, never shoulder. Car, nondescript. Manner, polite. No alcohol on breath. Stars and Stripes flying atop the mast at all times.

OK so far, I thought on my way back to the Valley Bowl. Dev wouldn't know what the hell was going on. He'd tell Art and that would make two of them who didn't have a clue. And Art would have to pass the word on to his supplier, ripples in a cesspool, who knew what might get stirred up?

I switched cars at the Valley Bowl, gave John D. his keys back and bought him a thank-you drink, then drove home. When I parked in the driveway, I could see through the front window that Feeb was in, watching television. My conscience had been gnawing at me about you know what, so I told her all about it.

'Shoot, I already knew,' she said, keeping one eye on the screen. 'I figured you kept it to yourself so's I wouldn't worry.'

'You're a living doll,' I said. 'Look, I've just put in considerable time and energy into trying to make sure it won't happen again, but there's always an outside chance, I have to tell you.'

'Listen, life is tough, then you die,' she said. 'I should worry. Lillian coming Sunday?'

I told her she was and let her get back to the TV. She was watching a roller derby on Channel 56. I went upstairs, took my pills, sprayed myself, got into an old bathrobe a girl had once made for me from a couple of heavy towels, and watched the local news.

After a few minutes I switched over to the roller derby too, where the violence was only make-believe. There were times I wished everything was.

CHAPTER EIGHTEEN

Bright and early, as they say, although it was really fuzzy and not that early, the following morning, I took the roll of film to Wade's garage out on Domingo, near the turn-off for the Burbank Airport. Actually it was his brother and sister-in-law's garage but Wade had requisitioned it to set up a film lab. He did pretty good, the kid, he'd paid off all the equipment inside of nine months or so, mostly doing sub-contracting work for other developing services. I told him to make up a proof sheet of the twenty-four shots on the roll, then to choose a half a dozen of the best and print up two 3 × 5s of each of them.

'Well, I wonder,' he said, stroking his goatee dreamily. He was lying in a Mexican hammock which he had strung up beside the garage. A dog of some kind was zonked out in the patch of shade beneath him. A cat of some kind was sharing the hammock with Wade.

'I'll have to think about it,' he said. 'A man's got to think about things if he's going to get ahead.'

'A man's got to work if he's going to get ahead,' I said.

'An hour,' he said finally. 'Big job like that, be a good hour.'

I spent the time having three poached eggs, bacon, side of rye toast and coffee in a greasy spoon around the corner, and reading a morning paper someone had kindly left. There was an article on the front page about a raid on a rock house in East L A the night before. One man killed, one wounded. The police had to use explosives to blow the front door open and some sort of armored bulldozer to break in the back and it still took them ten minutes to get in. I'd had a vague idea of more or less trying the same thing myself but after reading the article forgot about it.

I picked up the prints and proofs, paid Wade, and headed for the office. One nice thing about the kid, he never commented on the subject matter of the films he handled but he'd go on for ever about the technical side of it if you let him. Being a considerate sort of bloke myself, once in a while I did let him, about once every five years.

The office was hot and still smelled of new paint. After calling up the messenger service to request one of their slaves I typed up a beauty of a bill for Mr Seburn, as padded as a teenager's bra, put it and copies of all the photos in a well-sealed envelope, then handed it over to the boy when he came.

All right. That took care of that, it seemed. There was nothing to be done for the nonce about Barbara Herbert, twenty-four, single. There was nothing to be done until that evening about Dev Devlin and St Stephen's. And there was nothing to be done about Sara for a couple of days, at least. Another check-up at John D.'s wasn't due for a while. I had a similar contract with a huge used-car lot out on Victory but they weren't due a visit for another couple of weeks either. It was too early for the mail. I could always bring the records up to date or learn a new program but I could also go shooting instead. I decided to go shooting, it was more sociable.

For a couple of years I'd forked out two hundred dollars per to belong to a gun club in the hills just the other side of South Pasadena and I used to go out there and practice once in a while. Then I met a guy who had a small orchard up north near Magic Mountain. He was getting pressured to sell his place to a developer but God had told him not to, so he wouldn't. When the pressure had escalated from the typical nuisance level like dumping a truckload of garbage on his herb garden to running over two of his short-haired samoyeds, or whatever they were, he came to see me. It wasn't hard to find out who was behind it, as there was a big sign with the guy's name on it at the front of the property next door. So I found out where he lived and ran over one of his kids' bicycles and peace reigned thereafter and I had free shooting. The man who talked to God was a friend of Benny's – who wasn't? Benny . . . did I not remember Benny, the last time we talked, saying something about going to see a man to buy some money? By God, I did remember, it was when he phoned up to say he'd driven by Art's to see what was left of it, if anything. Well. I gave the lad a call. I could always find a use for some money, depending on how cheap it was.

'Money, Benny, money,' I said, getting him at the third attempt after two misconnections. 'You were going to buy some money, what was that all about?'

'This guy had some money,' Benny said around a yawn. 'I heard. Twenties. Absolutely beautiful. Do you know it's the middle of the night?'

'Local guy?'

'Out of town guy.'

'Has he done any business yet?'

'How do I know?' said Benny. 'Not last I heard, he was looking to unload in large chunks and he's not too well connected out here or the guy I got it from would never have heard about it.'

'What was he asking?'

'Five.'

'Beautiful?'

'Gorgeous.'

'Pass a scanner?'

'Not that gorgeous. But gorgeous.'

'Do you think he might sell you a mere couple of grand's worth if you did him a favor?'

'What favor?'

'The favor,' I said, 'would be putting him together with someone who would take a large chunk.'

'Yeah? Like who?'

'Like me.'

There was a pause. Then Benny said, 'If you want a large chunk, why do you want a small chunk too?'

'I don't really want a large chunk, Benny,' I said patiently. 'I just want him to think I do so he'll sell you a small chunk as a favor.'

'Ah,' said Benny. 'Ah ha. Aren't we being clever today? He's going to be edgy, though, I mean it is against the law.'

'Really?' I said. 'God forbid you should get mixed up in anything illegal. Come on, Benny, give him a call.'

'I can but try,' Benny said. 'Stay where you are, I'll get back to you.'

He hung up. I stayed where I was. A few moments later he rang back.

'We got lucky,' he said. 'He needs walking-around money. I can get two grand today if I sit on it for a week so as to give him time to move the rest.'

'Well, you're going to sit on it, aren't you? You're going to give it to me, that's the same thing as sitting on it, isn't it?'

'OK, OK. I'll lay out the five hundred and pick it up from you later. Now can I go back to sleep?'

'Sweetest of dreams,' I said. I'd no sooner hung up than I thought of something, and called him right back.

'Yoo hoo, it's me again. Benny, could a stranger get into a rock house and make a buy?'

'Depends on the stranger. You, no.'

'How about a black stranger? A kid. Obviously not the heat.'

'Why not, if he's got the bread.'

'Oh, he'll have the bread,' I said. I hung up again, satisfied; I seemed to be progressing. I called up Evonne; I had to arrange either to get into her school that evening sometime or to get in earlier, and stay on. The Apple of the Teacher's Eye, and mine too, if truth be told, was in, and working.

'Hope I didn't interrupt anything important the other night when I phoned,' I said shamelessly.

'You did, but not what you think,' she said.

'How do you know what I think?' I said.

'Easy,' she said. 'I just pretend you're a large, he-man type whose hormones are still working. And what can St Stephen's do for you today?'

I told her. She thought the best plan was to come in the front way when school was getting out because Dev would be out back in the parking lot keeping his beady eyes on the kids. Then Mr Lowenstein could lock me in his office, for which he had the only key, and there I could idle away the hours until the coast was clear. Maybe brush up on my spelling. Did I know that a common denominator of most eccentrics and oddballs was poor spelling?

'No, I did not,' I said. 'Anyway, my spelling's excellent. It's that damn geometry. Miss Shirley, there's something I've been meaning to ask you. Do you have any prejudice against men who are just that little bit taller, just a soupçon more manly, than your average American male?'

'Yes,' she said. 'I feel sorry for them. Especially in movies. People behind them keep asking them to take their hat off and it isn't a hat, it's their head.' And she hung up. Well, it wasn't exactly the answer I'd hoped for but it wasn't bad, for a girl. I wondered what she'd be like in the prone position – firing at a target a hundred and fifty yards away down wind, I of course mean. Maybe she'd like to come with me someday and talk to the man who talked to God, the innocent I hoped to be talking to in about half an hour from then.

But I never did get to go shooting. I was just locking up when an elderly gentleman walked up to me and asked me if I was Victor Daniel.

I owned up.

He said he was Raymond Millington, of St Charles, New Mexico, the one with the missing daughter Ethel, did I remember?

I remembered. Ethel Ann, age fifteen, last seen at the Taos bus station early in February. I'd written him the week before taking myself off the case as it was hopeless.

'Can we go inside?'

'Of course.' I unlocked the one lock I'd had time to lock and in we went.

'Are you busy right now, is this a bad time for you, sir?'

I said, no, sir, it was fine, I had some time.

We sat down and took each other in. You know more or less what he took in, a sort of Stewart Granger type who, as the hayseeds put it, looked like he'd been rode too hard and left out wet too often. What I took in was a tired, fifty-plus and looking it, man in his best blue suit, tie still done up despite the heat, with old, well-polished black boots and a black cowboy hat which he took off and carefully placed on the desk between us.

'I'm not here to complain,' he said, 'in fact, I appreciated your being honest with me in your last letter, but I just couldn't leave it at that. My wife says it's only me being stubborn again and she could be right, it's been known to happen.'

'Her being right or you being stubborn?'

'Both,' he said. 'But it's terrible not being able to do anything, especially when you're used to doing most things by yourself. I thought at least I could come out here and see for myself.'

'See what?'

'I don't know,' he sighed. 'See you. See if you did everything you said you did and charged me for. See Los Angeles, see why she wanted to come here. See if it's hopeless, get it out of my system. I got the time, I took it off. I got the John Deere agency back home, it can look after itself for a few days. It's not like the car business which I used to be in once, you don't get customers coming in saying I need a twelve-foot disk harrow and I aim to drive it out of here today.'

He smiled briefly; so did I. There was a pause.

'I don't know what to tell you, Mr Millington,' I said finally. 'As far as finding your daughter goes I can't think of anything else to do. Maybe there isn't anything else to do but wait, hard as that is. Usually kids do get back in touch with their parents, often at Christmas or their birthdays, if that's any help. As far as the work I did for you, or claimed I did for you, I don't know what to do about that, either. I could show you my files but you've already had a copy of everything in them. You could call my brother, he's a cop, he could tell you I'm honest – but who'd believe a cop, let alone a brother?'

He looked at me for a moment, then offered me a stick of what looked like cinnamon gum. I declined with thanks. He helped himself to two sticks, then crumpled up the wrappers and put them neatly in my new ashtray. Then he said, 'You said, usually they get in touch with their parents, or something like that. Is that from your own experience or is it just something you say?'

'Experience, statistics,' I said. 'It's true all right, although I might have said it anyway.'

'You do a lot of this sort of thing?'

'I used to do more,' I said, 'and could do a lot more now if I wanted to.' I didn't tell him the reason I didn't want to was because it was more often than not a waste of time – mine – and money – some desperate poor parent's. But he wasn't dumb; he got the message.

'What do you do these days, then?' he asked a little bitterly. 'Solve murder mysteries?'

I understood his bitterness.

'Hell, I don't usually see a mystery from one year to another,' I told him. 'Not what you'd call a real mystery, like a puzzle. People keep doing things that are a mystery to me why they do them, but that's about it.'

'Well, it's a mystery to me where my girl is,' he said. 'We're not even sure why she left. Her mother and I aren't monsters, we're ordinary people living in an ordinary town and we do what people like us do . . .' He took off his glasses, then put them back on again. I thought he'd already given me three good reasons for leaving.

'Look, Mr Millington, I know you're going crazy with

worry about your girl,' I said, 'but like I said, I can't think of anything else to do that might help. You want your money back, you can have it. If you'd like me to suggest another agency, a larger one, just say the word. If you'd like to talk to someone in the police who's involved with this sort of work, no problem.'

He waved one hand.

'I don't mean to take it out on you,' he said, 'it just came out that way. I guess I don't know what I want, aside from a miracle.'

'I got an idea,' I said. 'You want to see something of LA, see why she wanted to come here, maybe wander around where kids hang out. Just because it's one in a million against your spotting her on some street corner doesn't mean you won't feel better if you have a look.'

He shrugged, then rubbed his face.

'Why not?'

'I'll see if I can get you a guide. Got a car?'

'I rented one at the airport. Needs a tune-up but it works all right.'

I got the Silvetti number from information and dialed it. The twerp answered.

'Yeah?'

'It's your old pal the private eye.'

'Oh God,' she said.

'What are you doing?'

'Writing, what do you think I'm doing, making cookies? What are you doing? Is there any news?'

'I'm detecting, what do you think I'm doing, roasting marshmallows? And no, I'm sorry, no news about you yet. Anyway, want a job? Come to think of it, want two?'

'Doing what?'

'Get over here and you'll find out.'

'Do I get paid?'

'Of course!' I said. 'What do you think I am, an exploiter of child labor?'

'At least,' she said. 'O K, see ya when I get there.'

'Girl's coming over,' I told Mr Millington. 'Weird but bright. Very weird. She'd be better than me at taking you around. I know some places where kids go, she must know thousands.'

'Can't hurt,' he said. 'Thanks.' Then he told me if I had any work to do to get on with it, he'd sit quiet in the corner or go for a walk or something. I said, no, I'd be happy to chew the fat with him til Sara came.

'So what kind of work do you do exactly?' he asked me after adding a third stick of gum to his wad. I suspected he'd rather have a good chew of tobacco but was minding his manners in the big city. 'If you don't spend all your time solving murder mysteries of Hollywood stars in swimming pools after all. If you don't mind me asking. I never met anyone in your line of work before.'

'I don't mind,' I said. 'What do I do? I do what I did for you, or what I claimed I did.'

'Forget that,' he said.

'It doesn't look much on paper,' I said. 'I go places and look for things, mostly.'

'That's it?'

'Sometimes I go to other places and ask questions. Once a month I get to follow someone. I take pictures. Sometimes I guard people. I guard things a lot. It's like any business, a combination of knowing people, experience, telling lies, and knowing a good, cheap tax accountant.'

'What about danger?' he asked. 'What about helping people? What about shooting people? What about them things?'

'Oh, them,' I said. 'I never think about them.' I got another one of his thin smiles.

Sara came slouching in a little while later, after ten or fifteen minutes, when he was telling me some things about St Charles, New Mexico that didn't materially increase my desire to ever see the place. Mr Millington got up when she came in, I didn't. I introduced them; they shook hands.

As he took in her get-up I could hear him thinking that maybe his Ethel was wandering around town in a similar state, lost to him for ever to the land o' fruits and nuts. I thought Sara was looking pretty normal, all things considered, I liked her drawn-on, inch-long eyelashes, liked the gold and silver glitter stuck on each cheek, liked her bandanna halter top, liked her paisley bermudas and adored her green cork wedgies. As a purse she was using a Yogi-Bear tin lunch box.

She wanted to know what the score was pronto, otherwise she had work to do at home, she was in the middle of an epic about a surfboard that suddenly grew wings. I filled her in, briefly. I asked Mr Millington how long he was planning to be around. He said he had a return ticket for the following day but he didn't know for sure, it all depended. I asked him if he'd excuse us for a moment; he said, sure, and went outside and looked around without a lot of interest.

'Take him around,' I said. 'He wants to see L A. He wants to see his kid standing on some street corner.'

'Fat chance,' she said. 'Like my nailpolish?' It was white, except for the thumbs, which were orange.

'Hate it,' I said. 'Take him where kids go. V D clinics, police stations, riots. Burger-Queens.'

'Ha ha,' she said. 'What do I get paid?'

'About nineteen dollars,' I said.

'Where is it?'

'It's coming off your bill, which is about nineteen dollars so far,' I said.

'You cheap turd,' she said. 'What about expenses?'

'O K,' I said. 'You want expenses you got expenses, but that makes it official.'

I handed her over a five-dollar bill and counted off with pretended reluctance five additional singles.

'This is your first official duty as temporary, underline temporary, assistant to Victor Daniel, licensed private investigator for the State of California. I shall therefore want from you a written report of all your activities and, underline and, an itemized list of expenses by tomorrow afternoon at the latest.'

'Don't I get a badge, too?' she said, putting my hard-earned money away in her lunch box. 'I didn't know they piled cow pats so high til I met you.'

I patted her with mock fondness on the red side of her head; she jumped a foot.

'Run along now, child,' I said. 'Ol' Uncle Vic's got grown-ups' work to do.'

'What's the other job? You said there were two.'

I told her, at some length.

'That's more like it, man!' she said. Then she fluttered her eyelashes at me for some unfathomable reason, and went out in search of Mr Millington.

I hoped they'd be happy together.

CHAPTER NINETEEN

The following afternoon, someone, I don't know who, stuck a large, sealed envelope in through the mail slit in my door. Inside was Sara's report, neatly typed, with only two spelling mistakes. I insert it here as it seems to belong here:

CONFIDENTIAL

22 May
Report
From: Agent S.S.
To: V.D. ('V.D.' ha ha, never noticed that before)
(From notes taken in the field)

Found Old Fart staring into taco store window
Entered and ate two (2) burritos each, served by fat Mex
With too much lipstick. Bill $4.20. He paid.   Expenses: 00.00
Went looking for kids.
Found some at West Valley Clinic,
Sprawled on floor,
Waiting outside,
Several babies.
O.F. (Old Fart) found daughter's particulars typed on
File card thumbtacked to bulletin board among many
Others similar.
Suspected your work, V.D. (Ha ha).
O.F. talked briefly with young,
Mucho hung
Doctor about (a) anonymousness of patients
(b) privacy of files (c) heat.
Contribution to donation box on wall, $5.00 Expenses: 00.00
He paid.
Next stop: No-Name Hamburger hang-out on Riverside:

Too early, not much action, like, man,
Couple 'a pushers, couple 'a punks,
Couple 'a bikers,
One kid hooker with bandage on neck, strung out much?
Walking ad for herpes.
Two Cokes. $1.20. He paid.
Early, it was too early, where to go, brain, brain,
Get movin'! Venice!!
So next stop – Venice Beach, an' all the freaks were out,
Black freaks, white freaks, yellows, browns, reds and
    blues . . .
Dot dot dot
Not a winner in the bunch, says I to the O.F.
Cokes at Carlos Broasted Chicken, $1.80.
I paid.   Expenses: 01.80
Lotsa kids for the O.F. to oggle/goggle/break his heart over.
Kids on skates,
Kids on boards,
Kids on uppers,
Kids on downers,
Kids on the boardwalk,
Kids on the sand,
Kids playing volleyball,
And a one-man kid band.
We walked miles going nowhere,
Then miles to get back.
In the Beginning he kept seeing Ethel
Almost.
Once he almost had a fight when he went running across
The beach,
After a girl, after a girl,
But it wasn't her, natch.
I'm not even sure it was a girl.
Once he asked me searching questions about Youth Today
And you. I lied;
How I lied. I said we were both okay, tip top, old sport,

A-fuckin' number 1.
I said, do not be
Misled
By V.D.'s outré appearance, clothes aren't everything,
And in his case, not even that.
Ice cream, one (1) only, double strawberry, from
Tacky No-Name stand.
I paid $1.00.   Expenses: 01.00
Watched the Muscle Builders in their cage.
A cage is the right place for them.
O.F. said he'd wrestled in high school.
I said, me too, with boys behind the gym.
Needed new ballpoint pen.
I paid, 69 cents.   Expenses: 00.69
Coast Road, Ventura Freeway, V. Mall,
Lotsa kids. Not runaway kids, like his,
Or left kids, like me, but kids, boring, normal kids.
Kids with money. Yecch. Awesome. Gross.
Money begged from Daddy or gotten from Mummy
Who got it from Daddy for spoiled little Snookums.
Good old Daddy. Good old Mummy.
They make *you* look bright, Stoopid.

Across the Hills to H*O*L*L*Y*W*O*O*D*,
Drove up and down H*O*L*L*Y*W*O*O*D* Blvd.
Lotsa kids. Parked le car. He paid.   Expenses: 00.00
Looked in ripoff clothing stores & record stores.
Lotsa kids.
What's it called, Lengerie? Punk music joint near Western,
Closed. Two other clubs, closed,
All closed. Assorted bums outside, waitin' for the
Good Times.
Didn't know what else to do so we drove,
And drove,
And drove, sir.
Yes, sir.

Glendale, Silver Lake, Echo Park,
Eagle Rock, South Pasadena, Alhambra,
Monterrey Park, East Los Angeles,
Boyle Heights, Exposition Park,
Culver City, Inglewood and Lennox,
Santa Monica and West LA.
We drove looking,
Then not looking.
1,000,000s of people,
        ”   of houses,
        ”   of cars.
She could be in any one of them
Or none of them.
Or none.

It was gettin' on
By then
So I sed
What next, Pop?
How about San Diego?
San Francisco?
San Jose?
Santa Barbara or
San Clemente?
Maybe Nixon's home an' you could shoot the shit with him
For a while about farm prices.
He smiles and sez
Home, James, and don't spare the horses,
Whatever that means.
Rustic small talk, I guess . . . dot dot dot dot.

He drops me off
And shakes my hand
And says goodbye
And says thank you
And says to thank you too.

Got home in time for supper,

Campbell soup and hotdogs.

Total expenses:	$03.49
Out of:	$10.00
Balance:	$06.51

Emotional wear and tear from hanging out with

Old people:	$06.51
New balance:	$00.00

So tough shit to you.

Sez

Sara S.

Typical, I thought when I read it, so typical, so pathetically typical. I could tell that twerp a thing or two about emotional wear and tear. At least there wasn't anything in it about a flying surfboard.

CHAPTER TWENTY

Anyway, back to Friday.

After the world's worst poet had left, I noticed Mr Amoyan sunning himself in front of his shop so went over and joined him for a while. I was supposed to drop by the out-patients department at Kaiser sometime that afternoon for a check-up but what the hell, who needed to fight that crosstown traffic and it was pleasant where I was and I did have to conserve my strength for the evening's activities.

After a bit I worked on a presentation I was getting together for a large, independent grocery up on Magnolia, I'd met the owner one night at the Two-Two-Two. It was a fairly straight-forward security job but the man's wife wanted every detail down on paper beforehand, not unreasonably. Then, figuring it might be some time until my next meal, I had a late lunch at Mrs Morales', the combination platter with a side of guaca-mole and extra beans. I need hardly mention here that Mrs Morales was neither fat nor wearing too much lipstick; amaz-ing how bitchy girls can be sometimes.

Then, I put everything I thought I'd need, including the camera, in a canvas carrier bag, and then I locked up and drove over to St Stephen's. I parked a good ten-minute walk away from the school grounds so my car wouldn't be seen in the neighborhood. Unfortunately my route to the school didn't afford me the joy of getting a look at the hole in the ground that used to be Art's, as it was on the same side of the school as the parking lot which I was avoiding.

I timed it pretty good; I had only to lurk behind a laurel tree for a couple of moments before the first driblets of Ameri-can youth began oozing out into the still-hot afternoon sun. I nipped in the front door and made it to my favorite blond's office without seeing anyone but a lot of noisy kids. She was at her desk doing the crossword puzzle in the newspaper.

'Need any help?'

'Not from you,' she said. She was wearing a pale blue sweater and a string of pearls and had two red barrettes in her hair.

'Well, I need some from you,' I said.

She filled in a word, then asked the air, 'Can't a girl ever get a few moments to herself? Oh, well. What is it now?'

I told her what it was now, a master list of which student used which locker. She supposed it was somewhere around, made a call, said, 'Thanks, Fran', told me to mind the store, and left. I figured I'd fill in a few words in the puzzle for her but she'd done all the easy ones. I was never much good at them anyway, which always surprised me, given the level of readership they were aimed at.

Evonne was back in a few minutes with a Xerox of what I wanted. The names weren't in alphabetical order so it took me a while to find the ones I wanted, the half-dozen names I'd gotten from young Robert the night before, and jot down their locker numbers. I did this sitting on the edge of a spare desk in the corner of the office by the window but I still couldn't get a peek at where Art's used to be. I'd be able to from the vice-principal's room, though; I could hear him through the door dictating something.

Then Evonne checked her watch and said, 'OK, that's it for this girl.'

She got up, tossed me a ring of keys, opened the door to Mr Lowenstein's room and told him she was off.

'So goodbye,' he said. 'Is that what's-his-name I heard out there?'

'Who else,' she said. 'See you on Monday, boss.'

I was looking over the keys; there were four of them. The biggest one had 'Val-Alarm' stamped on it, which was no surprise, as I'd already seen several of their blue and white 'Valley Alarm Security Armed Patrols' signs around the school perimeter. What the big key did was turn off the whole alarm system; you used it in a box just inside the front door and then had thirty seconds to get out and lock the door behind you with one of the other keys. I didn't see why Dev's inside apartment door should be hooked up to the system, as all the doors leading to it were and also, why draw attention to yourself. But if it was I'd just have to try something else another time.

'The box is in a cupboard on the left as you go out,' Evonne said, giving her face a quick check in the mirror of her compact. 'The little one's for the cupboard. The boss's is a spring lock so just close it. He's got the only key; Dev might come by to try it but he can't get in, at least he's not supposed to be able.'

'That's all I need.' I said, 'him finding me in there.'

She put the compact away. I had a thought.

'The boss's phone doesn't get cut off automatically after hours by the switchboard, by any chance?'

'It does but just press "1",' she said.

'I think I can manage that,' I said.

'Well, happy exploding, or whatever it is you're going to do,' she said, and left.

I knocked on the VP's door and when he said, 'For Pete's sake, come in,' I went in and promptly made my way to the window that overlooked the parking lot. Without showing myself, I gazed down with great expectations and there it was, a beautiful, deeply satisfying nothing. There wasn't even a hole in the ground although there was a charred patch, all the force of the explosion must have been up and out. There was nothing, not even a pile of rubble, not a toothpick. Art's, formerly B & B's, had vanished as totally as, if I may wax poetic for the second and last time herein, the faded dreams of yesteryear. I wondered if that genius Arab on the banks of the Nile who had invented zero (o) in the first place had been as tickled with his nothing as I was. I hoped so. I always admired him.

'Be with you in a minute,' the VP muttered. He had stopped dictating and was now typing away furiously.

'No hurry,' I said.

'Is there anything as persistently stupid as the California Department of Education?' he growled after a while.

'I can think of something,' I said, 'but maybe you don't like Polish jokes.'

He finished what he was doing, turned the machine off, then ran a hand through his already ruffled hair.

'What are you looking for out there, friend, your misspent youth? I doubt you'll find it.'

'Actually, I'm looking at something else which isn't there,' I said. He gazed sourly at me.

'I'm worried,' he said. 'Worried, worried, worried. Who said "If I dealt in candles, the sun would never set"?'

'Mussolini?' I guessed.

'Come sit down, for heaven's sake,' he said. 'Stop gloating, if that's what you're doing.'

'Yes, teacher,' I said, and sat down meekly.

'Evonne says you want to stay in after school.'

I nodded.

'She didn't say why.'

I shrugged.

'Why?'

I shrugged again.

'She thinks you're going to do evil, hurtful things.'

'Well, you know girls,' I said.

'What are you going to do?'

'Clean the brushes,' I said.

'OK, OK,' he said irritably. 'It's for my own good, I know. Well to hell with you, friend. How are you, by the way?'

I said I was fine, thanks.

'I'm not. I'm old. I'm tired. I'm worried. I don't care anymore. I'm going home. Coffee machine works. Water in the cooler. Books in the corner. Don't forget to lock up if there's anything left to lock up.'

I said I wouldn't.

Mr Lowenstein turned his desk light out and went his weary way. I checked to see that '1' was pressed on the phone; it was. I checked to see if there was a dial tone; there was.

I had a few hours to put in so I made myself comfortable, put some coffee on to drip, wheeled the swivel chair over near the window, then went to investigate his library. There was nothing really up my alley so I settled for a tome by someone called *Maeterlinck* on bumble bees. Did you know that every once in a while all the male bees jump on the queen bee and smother her to death? What a way to go.

Gradually the last of the soccer fanatics and tennis players packed it in; gradually the parking lot emptied. At about six I watched Dev tug the movable bit of fence across the entrance and lock it for the night. I had another cup of coffee and went back to the library. This time I wound up with a paperback by one J. H. Fabre, wherein I found out something extremely unpleasant about the courtship of the praying mantis. I'd pray too if I knew my wife was going to turn cannibal, especially with me as the first course.

At seven thirty-five the phone rang. It was Sara.

'OK chief,' she said. 'He's done gone.'

'Thanks, kid.' I'd given her the task of rounding up some boyfriend with a car, then parking across from Dev's; I didn't know if he kept his car in the lot at the back of the school or, more conveniently for him, in front of his door. Also, wherever he kept it, I wanted to give him a few moments' grace after he left in case he forgot something and came back for it.

'He left about ten minutes ago, wearing a funny hat,' she went on.

'What were you guys doing while you were waiting, necking?'

'Yecch,' she said. 'You have a dirty mind, you know that?'

'Had it for years,' I said. 'OK, Sara, that's it. Buzz off. Where are you, anyway?'

'Nearest phone that works,' she said. 'About three blocks east, we tried it earlier.'

'Maybe you're not so dumb after all,' I said. 'Maybe. So long.'

'You creep,' she said. 'Aren't you gonna tell me what you're doing inside there?'

'No,' I said, and hung up. I put the book back on the shelf, the chair behind the desk, and got out of there.

I made for the boys' locker rooms first, clutching in one sweaty palm the list, in the other a small steel jimmy or prybar or hub-cap remover or whatever you want to call it. Tire iron? Why not. There was still plenty of light lingering about but I had the little flash from the Mickey Mouse keyring just in case.

A more sensitive individual might have found the empty corridors spooky, as large empty buildings at night tend to be, but I managed to make it to the lockers without my hair turning completely white. Once there, it took maybe ten minutes in all to rip open the six lockers I was interested in and go through them, tear up a few books, scatter clothes on the floor, rip off the pinups taped inside the doors and generally make a good, satisfying mess. I discovered soft drugs in four out of the six lockers, hard drugs in two, long-barreled .22 in one. Knives in two. A machete in one. A bottle of cheap bourbon in one which I felt like smashing against the wall, so I did. A stack of hardcore pornographic magazines in one; 'Blonds Have More Cum' looked like quite a good read. All the above except the bourbon went into my carrier bag.

Then, moving right along, I made tracks to the science wing. It was locked but the fourth of Evonne's keys opened it up smartly. I made my way down the hall where not a creature was stirring, thank God, although I could hear some rabbit and guinea-pig noises coming from one of the labs. Guinea pigs – remind me to read a book about them some time.

Dev's door looked harmless enough, a couple of locks but no tricky stuff that I could see. Of course if it was really tricky you wouldn't be able to see the tricks. I tried the jimmy but couldn't get enough bite so I stepped back and put the boot in right beside the bottom lock. I felt it give and did the same thing with the top lock, then shouldered my way in.

All right. One problem out of the way. Now the only problem left was I didn't know exactly what I was looking for but I figured I'd know it when I found it. If I found it. If it was there to be found. It's not as easy as people think, my line of work.

There are only so many places in which things can be hidden from Mother, as all small boys know. I started by taking a speedy look around the whole apartment in case anything jumped out at me – a piece of furniture in the wrong place, a picture that didn't belong, a bit of the wall-to-wall carpet loose along one edge, a crooked light fixture, books out of alignment, anything.

Dev had a half a dozen framed pictures in the front room and more in the small bedroom, all of Ireland, but none of them seemed to be less dusty on top than another, suggesting that none of them had been handled more than another, suggesting that nothing was hidden behind or in any of them.

All right. Time for some serious deduction. If anything was hidden it would have to be somewhere moderately easy to get to but well out of reach and sight of, say, a cleaning woman or window washer or curious girlfriend. I started looking closely at all the electrical outlets along the skirting boards and voilà, or eureka, as some say – in the kitchenette there was one outlet where repeated friction had worn the paint off the slot in the screw that held the plastic plate to the wall. So I loosened the screw with the appropriate gadget on my knife and sure enough, the space behind had been enlarged just sufficiently to hold a heavy plastic transparent baggie. Inside the baggie was a roll of money. Inside the baggie was also some horse. I found out later the money totaled $3750 and the heroin was worth about another grand. I remembered to shoot a few snaps of the operation as I went as I had done at the lockers, they might be useful if not as legal evidence, at least as illegal pressure.

Oh, Dev.

What a silly boy.

I didn't bother screwing the fixture back on, one look at the front door and he'd know anyway. Or at least he'd fear the worst and go right to it to check it out.

I departed the premises with as little trouble as I'd entered them: small key – cupboard; large key – time switch; medium key – front door. If Val-Alarm really did have armed patrols and it wasn't merely the usual bluff, none spotted me. But I spotted something, a disturbance of some kind up the street, there was a cop car double parked but I didn't think it too prudent to look into the matter too closely given the contents of my carrier bag, so I headed briskly but casually in the opposite direction back towards my clown car.

And that was about it for Friday evening; Saturday afternoon, all being well, it would be Art's turn again. I was looking forward to that.

As I drove away I found myself singing that little ditty of Pop's: 'Ah the ladies, ah the ladies, is the song meant for you? May seem silly, willy nilly, they make love's dreams come true.'

Silly is putting it mildly; if ladies didn't make love's dreams come true, who did?

CHAPTER TWENTY - ONE

I was at home, feet up, relaxing.

Brandy and ginger in one hand, $3750 of Dev's money scattered on the cocktail table in front of me, about ten grams of Dev's horse piled up in an empty nut dish beside it and a tape of Crystal Gayle playing softly in the background. The perfect picture of contemporary Valley Man at his leisure. I hooked the phone closer with my free hand and called Benny; although it was an unlikely time of the day to find him home.

'Benny. What are you doing home?'

'Nothing.'

'You scored yet?'

'That's why I'm home, I just got back.'

'Goddamn it anyway.'

'Why Goddamn it anyway?'

'Because I don't need it any more, at least not all of it, that's why.'

'Too bad,' he said. 'You got it. When are we going to get out of these wet clothes and into a nice, dry game of chess?'

'Soon,' I said.

'You're coming over anyway to pick up all this money you suddenly don't want, aren't you?'

'I guess so.'

'So?'

'So I'll see you later.'

I put the money and the heroin away in a supposedly fireproof steel box I kept locked on the top shelf in the cupboard, had a quick wash-up, took my pills like a good boy, had another drink like a bad boy, donned a sensational, gorgeous, pale yellow and blue Hawaiian shirt and was on my way out when the phone rang.

It was a very angry man.

'Mr Daniel, what the hell is going on?'

'I don't know.'

'You don't know. Well, who the hell does know?'

'May I inquire to whom I am talking?'

'You're talking to James R. Bolden, whose brand-new fucking 'Vette has just been smashed up, that's who you're talking to.'

'Oh,' I said. 'That James R. Bolden.' I'd never heard of the guy.

There was a brief argument on the other end of the line, then, 'Mr Daniel? Guess who.'

I guessed. 'What's going on, Sara?'

'Good question,' the little twerp said. Then, picking her words with unaccustomed care, she said, 'Eh, you know that official assignment I was on tonight?'

'This better be good.'

'It is, it is. I asked my friend Petey to help. Because of the seriousness of the assignment, he borrowed his father's car without permission.'

I was beginning to get the picture, or part of it.

'It wasn't a new 'Vette, by any chance?'

'The same,' she said. 'After you-know-who split, or rather departed, I had a feeling, you know?'

Did I not. I was getting a feeling too, in the toe of my kicking foot. But it turned out I underestimated her for the first time and no doubt the last.

'So we decided to stick around. And sure enough he came back.'

'He must have had a feeling, too,' I said. 'So what happened?'

'Acting on your instructions, we hit him.'

'You hit him.'

'Petey was marvelous. He pulled out as if he wasn't looking and ran into him. Guess what the cops found in his car?'

I guessed a gun.

'Right on, Dad. He had a license for it, though.'

'I hope they didn't find anything in your car,' I said. 'Like a million uppers.'

'Nah,' she said. 'You taught me always to be clean on a stake-out.'

'I did?'

'Mr Bolden wants a word. Here.'

'I'll bet he does.' Back on came the fire-breathing James R. Bolden, but I got in before he did.

'Mr Bolden, on behalf of an agency whose name I can't mention on the phone but it has three letters in it, I want to officially thank and commend your son Peter and Miss Silvetti. If it hadn't been for their prompt and decisive action one of our most valued agents might have been in great danger.' Yeah – me.

There was a pause while someone else was being taken aback for a change, then he said,

'Listen, I don't think it's right for you to use kids, whatever you were doing. They could have gotten hurt.' At least he'd gotten off the subject of his over-priced, plastic status-symbol.

I told him we very rarely used youngsters as few of them had the courage and intelligence shown by his boy and Sara, that took him aback even further. If his kid was the complete juvenile delinquent I figured he was, as (a) he'd used his old man's new car without permission and (b) he hung around with Sara, probably no one had had a good word to say about him since he got one gold star on his attendance record in grade six.

I buttered the father up a little more by informing him that of course we would be responsible for all repairs and that an official letter of thanks, even if couched ambiguously for security reasons, would be sent to his fine boy soonest. Note – visit Mrs Martel soonest re FBI-headed notepaper. Damn, another unclaimable expense.

'Well!' said the suddenly proud Mr Bolden. 'In that case . . .'

I thanked him for his cooperation and asked if I might have a final word with Miss Silvetti. He put her on.

'You is but a brainless clod,' I told her. 'You could have gotten wasted.'

'Look who's talking,' she said. 'I suppose you'll want a full report from me in the morning as per usual?'

'Get lost,' I said, and hung up. If there's one thing I've learned on the weary path of life it is that you can do nothing with a smart-ass.

So. I was on my way out again when the phone rang again. This time it was John D.

'Guess who didn't show up for work tonight?'

'I'm doing a lot of guessing all of a sudden,' I said. 'But, O K, Big Sal?'

'Nope.'

'Barbara Herbert, single, age twenty-four, from Van Nuys?'

'You got it. Was that your doing?'

I admitted modestly it was.

'How come, Brains?'

'Professional know-how,' I said. 'Tricks of the trade. Good undercover work.'

'I bet you guessed,' he said.

'I did not,' I said, hurt. 'It was length of employment, John. Martha's been with you, what, over three years, she likes it there. And what's her name, Maria something . . .'

'Cintron.'

'Right, she's only been there a couple of weeks, it's too obvious if she starts right off tapping the till, also it isn't that easy, she's got to have access to her own score sheets. No, I always liked Barbara. After a couple of months she knows her way around, she's more or less trusted and she knows your suppliers. So I put the word out to see what would happen.'

'I still think you guessed,' he said. 'It was only a one-in-three shot.'

'I'm too hurt to continue this conversation,' I said. 'Also I have more important things to do.'

'Me too,' he said. 'Guess who's filling in for her tonight, renting smelly shoes to drunk trouser suits?'

'Serves you right,' I said bitterly, and hung up.

Third time lucky; I made it out without any more interruptions and a scant twenty-five minutes later I was gazing fondly at a stack of money on Benny's cocktail table. Someone had done a beautiful job on those twenties, damned if I could find anything wrong with them and I had a good hard look. They were all in groups of ten held together by a band of brown sticky paper, just like you get them from the bank.

'How do you make new bills look old?' I asked my host, who was reclining opposite me in a huge lounging chair.

'Gee, I dunno,' he said. 'Carry them around in your wallet for a month? Walk on them? Put them under your arm? Wet them and dry them again in the oven? All of the above and a few more I'll think of in a minute.'

'We can but try,' I said. 'God, they're gorgeous, aren't they?'

So we dampened a few hundred dollars' worth and then put them in a low oven, then I tucked another hundred bucks' worth in each shoe.

'That'll limp them up if anything will,' said Benny.

Then I rolled up a further twenty bills into a wad and kept it clutched in my hand the rest of the evening while we played chess, shifting the outside bill to the inside whenever I remembered. As for the chess, I almost had him the second game but he forked my knight and bishop with his bloody knight when I got distracted by his getting up and noisily making himself another couple of banana daiquiris in his Goddamned blender. I was making progress, though, there was no doubt about that.

During the third game he picked his moment carefully and just before a key move of mine he casually inquired how Mae was. Truly, stranger than fiction is the compulsive need of some men to win at all costs, even in a harmless, un-competitive, friendly game between old pals. Well, two can play at that; just before one of his moves I tossed the small, glassine envelope I'd found hidden away at Dev's on to the board.

'What's that?' he asked without looking up.

'That's what I want to know.'

He opened it up, looked at it, then rubbed a bit on his gums.

'Smack. Very good, too. What they call Persian, not that dirty Mexican stuff.'

'What do you do with it?'

'Smoke it, when it's that good. Anything else you want to know?'

'Yeah, as a matter of fact. How about the address of a good, reliable rock house?'

He gave me an address down on West 56th.

'Anything else?'

'Yeah, while I think about it.' I wrote him a check for what he'd laid out for the funny money.

'Anything else?'

'Yeah. Can I use your phone?'

'Sure. I'm still going to beat you, you know, your queen's file is hopeless.'

'What else is new?' I dialed Sam the handyman's number, had a word with him, then one with his eldest son, Charles.

'You got it,' said Charles.

I took my leave of Benny's nondescript West Hollywood apartment around midnight more or less sober, as the following day, Saturday, promised to be a lively one. The bills in the oven had dried out nicely and looked passable, pun not only intended but worked hard for; the others would do in a pinch. Benny, polite as always, escorted me not only to the door but one flight down to the ground floor, past the pool and to my car.

'Take care, Unk,' he said.

'What else, Benny.'

I drove home without stopping in at either Dave's or the Two-Two-Two, both of which were on my direct route. Empires have been won by men with less strength of character than I often show.

As requested, Sam's eldest came by my place Saturday morning not too early, it was almost eleven. I'd just finished stuffing two thousand dollars, about a quarter of it fake, the rest of it Dev's money, into an envelope when I buzzed him up. He shuffled in lugubriously, took one look around, widened his eyes, then shook his head slowly and sadly like he was looking at what was left of the cotton crop in the south forty acres after the weevils had struck.

'It won't do,' he said. 'It jus' won't do.'

'What won't do, Charles? Want some coffee?'

'This pad, bro. It's like some old woman's place.'

'It is an old woman's place,' I said. 'I call her Mother.'

'Oh,' he said. There was a long pause. 'She heah?'

'No, she heah tomorrow, now do you want some coffee or not?'

He thought it over for about thirty seconds, then, 'Maybe.'

'Is that maybe yes or maybe no, Charles?'

'Dat's maybe later,' he said. I couldn't believe any son of Sam would be that thick so he had to be putting Whitey on. I didn't mind, I was having almost as good a time as he was.

'So what you want me to do for a hundred dollahs, bro?'

'Buy some coke.'

He peered at me suspiciously, then looked up at the ceiling. At what, I don't know.

'Dat's it?'

I nodded.

'From who?'

I told him who.

'Why?'

'Because I can't.'

'Why not?'

'Charles, what do I look like?'

He ambled over unnecessarily and looked closely at me.

'Mostly white.'

'Anything else?'

'Large.'

'If I came knocking at your door, would you sell me two grand's worth of coke?'

'No way,' he said. He shook his head a few times, then a few more times, then a few more times.

'Why not?'

'I don't have two grand's worth of coke.'

'If you did have it.'

'No way.'

'Why not?'

''Cause you could be de Man.'

'Ah ha,' I said.

'Well, why din' you say so 'stead of all this rigmarole?' he said. 'Where's de bread?'

I tossed him the envelope, it had the address of the rock house Benny had given me scribbled on it.

'Two grand in dere?'

I nodded. I didn't bother telling him part of it had been made in someone's basement, I've got a sense of humor too. Too bad I had to include so much real money but two grand in slightly used twenty-dollar bills would make anyone suspicious, let alone a coke dealer.

Charles took the money out and ripple-counted it as expertly as a Kurdish rug-seller.

'You wants all coke?'

I nodded.

'Then I gets a hundred from you?'

'And a good toot,' I said.

He brightened just perceptibly, stuffed the envelope in the hip pocket of his yellow flares, then, putting his feet down with exaggerated care, started towards the door. Halfway there he stopped and turned back.

'If dey asks, should I tell them who I is buying it for?' He gave me a look of earnest inquiry.

I sighed. 'Charles,' I said, 'I will admit you're the funniest thing since the invention of the whoopie cushion if you will just go and get the d-o-p-e, please.'

'Oh,' he said. 'De dope. Cool, bro, cool. Sure, boss. I'se done gone already.' He managed a couple more steps toward the door.

'Charles,' I said, 'if you turn around again for any reason whatsoever I'm going to kill you.'

'No need for violence, my man,' he said in a posh, upper-class English accent. Then he had the nerve to add, 'Enfin, la violence, c'est le signe toujours d'un clown, un pédéraste ou un colonial.'

With that brilliant parting thrust, whatever it meant, he left.

Big deal. Now he could steal cars in French.

CHAPTER TWENTY - TWO

I watched from the window as Charles wheeled his old red Caddie into a U-turn and took off. Bonne chance, mon ami. Then my brother called to see if I was still planning to pick up Mom the next day.

I said, 'Sure.'

He asked me how I was.

I said, 'Cool, bro, cool.'

I made another pot of coffee and was spreading some soft cream cheese on a couple of slices of raisin bread when the phone rang again. This time it was the VP.

'A fine mess you got me into now,' he said.

'Keep your cool, bro,' I said. 'Things are looking up.'

'Really?' He sounded incredulous. 'I had a phone call a few minutes ago from Devlin, he tells me some lockers were broken into during the night.'

'Tsk, tsk,' I said. 'Kids today.'

'Kids today, that's all you got to say to the man who is employing you, remember?'

'So what is Dev doing about it?'

'He's doing nothing until I get back to him is what he's doing.'

'Well, my suggestion to you, esteemed employer, is to tell him to go on doing nothing. We do not want the mess cleaned up, we do not want the police in, but we do want a half a dozen kids not to know what the hell is going on when they come in Monday morning.'

'Oh, do we?' the VP said.

'Dev didn't have any other news by any chance, did he?'

'Yes he did, by any chance. He mentioned he'd lost his keys and had to break into his own apartment.'

'Why didn't he get a locksmith?'

'He didn't say.'

'I like it,' I said. 'And you are going to like it too, Mr Lowenstein.'

'I hope,' he said grimly. 'Let me ask you this, friend. Do you think the day will ever come when you will live up to your contract and let me know what in God's name is going on around here?'

'Yes, I do,' I said. 'And that happy day will not be long a-coming.'

'It had better not be,' he said. There was some noise in the background. 'I've got to go, my daughter needs the phone for something vitally important that can't wait a second, it's life or death, the future of the entire civilized world seems to be at stake.'

'Wow,' I said.

'Yes, if she can't borrow her friend Susan's sweater tonight not only will she die but we'll all be sucked with her into some dreadful black hole to instantly perish.'

'Oh, Daddy,' I heard his daughter say in the background.

'Goodbye, then,' I said, and hung up. Poor old Daddy.

So I ate my lonely breakfast and waited for that goofball Charles to come back, not without a certain amount of apprehension. I suppose I could have told him that part of the cash was do-it-yourself but then he wouldn't have even considered making the buy because then he could wind up dead. And I didn't want Benny involved, it had to be a stranger on a one-off so they wouldn't know who to go looking for when they found out they'd been ripped off – as they would surely do, and soon. If the rock house was one of Whitey's it figured that they'd go looking, heavily armed, for the Third World. If it was a Third World house, vice versa. Actually, a nice, violent little war between the two factions was what I was hoping for. But I was a little worried, in that league anything could happen and usually did, and if anything happened to Charles I might as well leave Earth for good – and yesterday, if possible, because Sam and the rest of his family would be extremely angry at me.

By the time it was twelve thirty I was more than a little worried, I was a lot worried, and by the time it was twelve forty-five I was worried sick. But then I heard someone screech to a halt outside the house; I looked down and it was the great comic himself, stuffing the last of a Big Mac in his face, he'd only stopped for lunch on the way.

So I buzzed him up and in he came and after a bit more dialogue out of a zombie movie he took off again with his hundred and another fifty worth of coke up his nostrils, leaving me with two grand, less fifty, worth of cocaine in small, white, gram-size envelopes on the table in front of me. I hadn't given Charles four hefty lines only because I'm a good tipper, I also wanted to make sure it was what it was supposed to be, and it was that, all right, judging from Charles' reaction when he got the first rush.

'Hot damn!' he said, giving himself a couple of high fives. 'Dat's boss! Um hum! Ace, man!' And so on. I figured he could spend his time more usefully learning English instead of French.

One o'clock. It was time to call Art. The only trouble was I didn't have his home number, nor did the telephone book. It did list a business number for him, which I tried just to see what would happen, I'd never telephoned a void before. What happened was a recorded voice telling me that the number has been temporarily disconnected. You're telling me.

So then I called the Pacific Telephone Company Security Office and gave them my brother's code number, which allowed me to obtain any two unlisted numbers at one time. Art's was all I wanted.

He was out, his wife told me, but he was due home in a few minutes. Would I leave my number?

No, I'd call back, thanks.

Would I say who was calling?

An old pal.

While I waited for him to get back from wherever he was – maybe plotting new plots with Dev somewhere – I went into the kitchen to wrap him up a dainty present as a token of my affection. I borrowed an empty candy box from Mom's comprehensive collection of empty candy boxes, also a length of darling blue and silver ribbon. I filled the box with a few old newspapers to give it some weight, then thoughtfully added a paperback on chess for beginners, a book I'd long ago mastered, the perfect gift for someone who, if things went the way they were supposed to, would soon have a lot of spare time, as in seven to ten years.

I tied the box up neatly with the ribbon. I added a birthday greetings card with his name and address handwritten on it. I added a 'Fragile' sticker just for sheer devilment. Then I tried Art again; this time he was in.

'Hello, Art!' I said cordially. 'It's me.'

'Me who?'

'Me who blew your hamburger stand into the twilight zone.'

There was a pause.

'Do I know you?'

'We met briefly,' I said. 'I'd like to get to know you lots better.'

'Me too,' he said. 'Just say where and when, pal.'

'How about you moving your car down the street a bit from your place and being in it in about an hour, that way I can see you're alone and vice versa.'

'You know where I live?'

'I sure do. I wish I could afford an expensive place like that.'

'You know my car?'

'I sure do. Wish I could afford a new one.'

'How'd you get my phone number?'

'Looked it up in the book, Art.'

'Yeah,' he said. 'O K. I'll be there.' He hung up.

'Looking forward to it,' I said to the dead line. 'Enormously.'

I got on to the messenger service I use and told them to send over a fresh-faced, willing boy right away. They said he had just left. I put on an old safari jacket that I hated because it was so second-rate Hollywood but I needed the pockets; into one went the coke, into another an envelope with five of the counterfeit twenties, into the breast pocket my bean bag, then I typed up a little something on the portable and tucked that away in another envelope. I made sure I had a pen that worked. I made sure I had a gun that worked, the fourth of my Police Positives, actually, the unlicensed one.

I dialed the West Valley Police.

Was Lieutenant Conyers working Saturday?

Yep.

Was he in the office?

Yep.

Could I talk to him?

Yep.

'Shorty? It's me, your favorite PI.'

He hung up.

I dialed the West Valley Police.

Could I talk to Lieutenant Conyers, please?

Yep.

'Drugs, Shorty,' I said. 'You know how you hate drugs.'

'Go on,' he said after a moment.

'To make it short, pardon the expression, I got a dealer for you. If we do it right we'll get him with a couple of grand's worth of Bolivia's finest and a handful of play money and an unlicensed firearm and who knows what else. Of course, if you're not interested, if you're going to let personal feelings like jealousy get in the way . . .'

'Details, please,' he said.

The details I gave him. Some of them, anyway. Then he gave me his car radio's call sign. Then he said, 'No fuck-ups, Daniel,' and rang off before I could sneak in any more short jokes. Who knew, maybe he'd turn out to be a decent sort once he got his full growth.

It wasn't long after that when I heard the telltale putt-putt of the messenger's bike; I told him out the window to hang in there, I'd be right down. I grabbed the candy box, locked up, and down I went. The kid had taken his helmet off and was combing his long blond hair with a large plastic lady's comb, the kind with a foot-long handle. I checked the mailbox; there was one envelope, written on the front of which was 'Delivered By Hand'. Super-Punk strikes again.

'Are you a willing boy?' I asked the kid, pocketing my mail.

'Yes, sir,' he said. 'I would call myself a willing boy. As far as business goes, that is.'

'Jolly good,' I said. 'Willing boys are the kind who occasionally make a lot of money for doing very little.'

'Really?' he asked in mock surprise. 'Fancy that. But I don't want you to think I'm doing this job just to hustle a few fast bucks, I've always seen it as a chance to learn a useful trade.'

'God,' I said. 'If only this country had more willing lads like you it wouldn't be in the mess it is today.'

He hung his head modestly, then had to comb his locks all over again.

'To get right to it, willing boy,' I said, 'I have here a gift for an old and dear friend of mine. I wish you to deliver it to him. However, as it is a surprise, I will cleverly distract my old pal, in fact I'll be down the street in his car with him, while you deliver it to his lovely wife.'

'How thoughtful of you,' he said, taking the package and shaking it a trifle suspiciously.

'Nothing like that,' I said, 'and nothing illegal, either, otherwise I wouldn't be dealing out in the open directly with you like this and also I've been using your company for years and they know me well.'

'I take your point,' the kid said, tucking the parcel away in a saddle-bag after glancing at the address written on it. 'So all I have to do to get rich is to give this to the little woman?'

'There is one other minor thing,' I admitted.

'I have never been so unsurprised,' the kid said. I was getting to like him; maybe I could fix him up with Sara.

'Using all your youthful charms, see if the lady of the house will let you use the bathroom.'

'To do what?'

'To have a fifty-dollar leak in. Don't forget to leave it tidy after you.'

'That's it?'

'That's all she wrote.'

'And what if she says no? I mean, believe it or not it's happened once in a while, ladies have said no to me. Why, only last year . . .'

'I want you in that apartment somehow, by yourself preferably if only for a moment, even if it's only to get her to sign the delivery slip. Say your pen's broken so she has to go get one, say you have to phone in, anything. If you manage it, do something noticeable on the way out that I can see from the car. Got it?'

The kid nodded. 'Do I hear seventy-five dollars?'

'You do not,' I said firmly. 'You hear fifty.' I gave him half right then and told him I'd send the rest in a separate envelope addressed to him when I paid the service, then off we went in tandem into the unknown, or, more prosaically, towards Art's condo. And I mused. I don't often muse but that Saturday I mused. Maybe it was the lull before the storm. I wondered how Aunt Jessica was; she'd gone back East and I hadn't heard from her for over a year, not that there was anything much left to say. I mused briefly about Mae – too bad I didn't have a picture of her, I could have gone all dramatic and torn it up or turned it to the wall or something. Too bad I didn't have a picture of Miss Shirley – I could have kissed it goodnight before I went to sleep. I thought about a girl I used to know who ate mayonnaise sandwiches; I remember her telling me once that she had a cousin who ate vegetable sandwiches.

Funny that some illegalities you can not only accept, but practice, while others make you sooo mad! The idea of someone stealing from my friend John D. upset me but the idea of me buying questionable material from the Nus' cousin doesn't upset me at all. Padding expenses normally not only doesn't upset me, it's sheer pleasure, like cheating on your income tax, but why the difference between Mr Seburn and Mr Millington? Do they not both bleed? How do the lines get drawn? I've never seen a bullfight but I wouldn't mind. I've never seen a cock fight or a fox hunt but I would mind. Some people can fish but not hunt. Some people eat horses instead of cows, which is not a bad idea if the horse you're eating is the one you had a hundred bucks on and came last, but still. I read once that after a bullfight you can go around to the back and buy the bull's balls and fry them up for tea. See where too much musing gets you?

CHAPTER TWENTY - THREE

Art's condo was tucked into the north slopes of the Hollywood Hills, just over the ridge from the famous Hollywood sign. It was a fair way, but I stayed off the freeway as I wasn't sure the kid's putt-putt was allowed on it, which means we went east on Ventura then cut up into the hills below the reservoir. Right at the turn-off there was a hamburger stand where I used to go once in a while because the owner also sold tickets to the Dodgers games; I tooted a couple of times to get the kid's attention and we pulled in. I was starving, I don't know why, I'd just had breakfast.

While I was wolfing down two excellent hotdogs, I read Sara's latest communiqué:

CONFIDENTIAL

22 May
Report
From: Agent S.S.
To: V.D. (Ha ha)
(From notes taken on stake-out)
5.45 p.m. Contacted P. ('Petey') Bolden.
Explained the caper.
He said yes.
From whence comes my power over men?
6.30 p.m. He arrives in his father's Corvette.
I make my glib farewells, and then
We cruise the school neighborhood.
6.45 p.m. Check out the phone (my idea)
It works.   Expenses: 00.10
Two Cokes to go for disguise purposes.   Expenses: 01.20
6.55 p.m. Park about fifty yards south of school on Victory.

Slouch and sip sodas
And listen to radio, i.e.
Adopt role of typical teenager
In all its grotesquerie
And lack of imagination.
7.15 p.m. Allow Petey a kiss and a
Quick grope.
Anything to keep the dope
Happy.
7.25 p.m. Suspect in uniform & funny hat
Drives off in gray
1982 Chevrolet
And proceeds past us heading north on Victory Boulevard.
Allow Petey another kiss for disguise purposes only.
Allow five minutes to pass, as instructed, then proceed to
Phone booth (see above).
7.35 p.m. Call in report to V.D.   Expenses: 00.10
Return to stake-out
Strictly against orders
Due to (choose one) (a) brilliant flash of female intuition
(b) standard female curiosity
(c) Petey's being afraid to go home as he took the car without
His father's permission
(d) a poet's thirst for Experience.
And aren't you glad we did,
Tall, and in the dark, handsome??
7.45 p.m. (about): I see what looks like the suspect's car
Stopped for the light just across the street from us.
'Petey, start the car.'
He starts.
'Petey, if it's him, hit him.
'I'll make it up to you . . . somehow.'
From whence comes my power over men?
It was him. Crash! Grind!! Scrape!!!
Anger and tears,
Cops and whoopsy-doo, my dear,

A hell of a hullabaloo, I fear,
Two smashed fenders I also fear.   Expenses: Millions,
                                                 probably

Then, irate Father,
Then, sobbing Mother,
Then, phone call to Agent In Charge of Case (my idea)
Then, proud Father,
Then, beaming Mother,
Then, home to empty house
& supper of soup & cold roast beef.
Over and out,
Sez   Total
Sara.   Expenses: 01.40
                                   plus millions

'What was that?' the kid asked me when I'd finished reading it.

'God only knows,' I said. What a twerp. As if I cared what she had for supper.

I paid the bill and we hit the road again. When we were getting close I waved him back so we wouldn't arrive at the same time.

Art's condo turned out to be in a right fancy development indeed, there were eight or ten redwood residences laid out irregularly around a large patio and pool, with stables and a riding track complete with little jumps visible at the back. I was a few moments early but I spotted Art's car, with Art in it, parked some fifty yards farther on. I pulled in behind him, not too close, got out, went over, tapped on the window, then, when he unlocked the door, slipped into the bucket seat beside him.

'Nice day,' I said.

'It had to be you,' he said, giving me a look of loathing. 'A house painter, for Christ's sake.'

I gave him my second-best smile, took out my gun and held it in my lap in one hand while I checked him out for armaments with the other. I didn't find any.

'Grow up,' he said. 'Do you think I'm nuts?'

'Yes, I do, Art,' I told him. 'I think you have to be nuts if you go around torching places and killing people in this day and age. Nuts sums it up perfectly.'

'I didn't do shit,' he said. 'And you can't prove I did, neither.'

'Maybe not,' I said, 'and maybe so.'

'Maybe not,' he said. 'Who the fuck are you, anyway?'

'Good question,' I said. 'I'm surprised you didn't ask it earlier if you really wanted to know.' I saw him glance at the gun I was holding so I tossed it on his lap. 'It's what they call a Police Positive.'

He jumped a mile. 'Look out, for Christ's sake!'

'Don't worry, pal, it's not loaded,' I said. 'I wasn't sure I could stand the temptation.'

'Take the Goddamned thing,' he said, and tossed it back to me. I took a casual peek over my left shoulder and saw the willing boy disappear into one of the condos. Two kids on skateboards went careening past the car. A lady with a headful of hair curlers went by on the other side of the street.

'If there's anything I hate,' I said. 'How's Dev these days?'

'Dev who, I don't know any Dev.'

'Dev. Everybody knows Dev. Head of security at St Stephen's. St Stephen's. That school just across from where your place of business used to be.'

'Funny, funny,' he said. 'Maybe I seen him around, get to the point, will ya?'

I took out the envelope that had the coke in it and passed it to him.

'Ever seen this before?'

He looked inside, looked closely at one of the glassine bags, then said, 'Nope.'

I put it away carefully, then took out the envelope with the fake twenties in it and handed that over.

'How about this?'

He checked it out, then said, 'Money is money, who knows?' I retrieved it and tucked it away too.

'Ever heard of a kid called Les La Rosa, or Micky Spritz, or Paco De Leon, or Harold Hall?'

'Who knows, I see kids all day, who knows who they are?'

I sighed. I enjoyed it so much I did it again.

'Art,' I said, 'don't make me any madder than I am already because I'm already mad enough to kick your fat face in. Those four kids and a few more worked for you. They sold illegal substances to minors til someone knocked over their stashes last night.'

'I know nothin' about it,' Art said.

'How come your face is always red?' I asked him. 'Are you embarrassed about something?' I heard a car draw up and park some way behind us and hoped it was my favorite Little Person. Then I heard the willing boy's bike start up; as he passed us he did a wheelie, then he chugged off down the hill; I assumed that the acrobatics were the favorable sign I'd been hoping for.

'Kids today,' I said, not for the first time.

'Listen, pal,' Art said, 'unless you got something more interesting to say I'm taking off.'

'You got a short attention span, you know that, Art? But OK, maybe this'll interest you. A few minutes ago a messenger boy delivered a package to your house. While he was there your charming wife let him inside briefly, who knows why, maybe to use the john, maybe to phone in. Anyway, and here's the really interesting part, what he did was hide five grand's worth of nose candy in your nice new condo.'

'You're shittin' me,' said Art.

'Why,' I remarked, 'isn't that one of those new-fangled car phones I see right there between us? Why don't you give the old girl a call and find out?'

He took a couple of deep breaths, gave me a nasty look, switched on the phone and went on giving me a nasty look until the operator had connected him.

'Deb? It's me. I'm right outside the fuckin' house is where I am. Listen, did you just let some messenger kid in? Oh, he did, eh? You dumb bitch.'

I cut him off there before he could say anything else to her. When he started to climb out of the car, I said, 'I wouldn't, Art. Take a look at who's parked in front of your place.'

He looked.

'That's a policeman, that is,' I said. 'Small, but every inch of him a cop. Also, he hates pushers. Also, he's got a warrant in his tiny hand. If you get back in the car I'll tell you why he's not up there already turning your place over.'

Art sat back down heavily.

'Door,' I said.

He slammed the door closed.

'He's waiting for a call from me on your new-fangled phone is what he's waiting for, Art, telling him either to go ahead and bust you or forget about it. Want to get busted, Art? With your record it'll be a long time before you grill another cut-rate wienie, unless of course you make cook in the slammer.'

'Up yours,' Art said. He reached for the phone again; I caught his wrist and began bending it back until sweat popped out on his big fat red face.

'Going to be good?'

'All right, all right, for Christ's sake,' he said. I let go of him.

'Listen, pal,' I said. 'Would you believe I'm not even interested in you? I was hired to do something about Dev, not you. I figure we're even, you and me. You fired my place and I sent yours into the fourth dimension or maybe it was the fifth. As for that kid, that poor, dumb kid, I know that was an accident, you probably did him a favor, even his mother said that.'

'I heard he was some kind of moron,' Art said, rubbing his wrist.

'Right,' I said. 'What happens to you, I couldn't care less, it's good ol' Dev I'm after. Did he tell you the FBI was sniffing around after him?'

'He mentioned it.'

'They haven't bothered you, have they?'

'Not so's I've heard.'

'How do you think I got on to you, think that one over, pal. Who wants to have the heat off him, who might even cop a plea and walk?'

'That fucker Dev,' Art said.

'Here, read this.' I passed him the work of literature I'd typed back at my place after wrapping his present so tastefully. 'I put it all in short words to make it easier for you.'

He managed to read it all the way through without moving his lips, but you could see it was a struggle. Or maybe I'm just being mean again.

'What does "under no duress" the hell mean?' he asked at one point.

I told him. What he was reading was a short statement which affirmed that Devlin was the middleman in the traffic, that he accepted bribes for looking the other way, and that he also accepted a regular supply of horse as part of his end.

'Hell, it's not even legal evidence,' I said mendaciously. 'I just need it to get a hold on the bastard.'

'I sign and you call off the bust on my house?'

'As God is my witness,' I said, looking him straight in the eye.

The dope signed it. I put the paper away in an inside pocket.

'How do you work this thing, anyway?' I asked him, indicating the car phone. He turned it on and got the operator. I told him the lieutenant's call sign and he passed that along. After a minute, thanks to yet another miracle of modern technology, I was through.

'Conyers,' he said.

'Any time, Shorty,' I said, then hung up. 'Amazing invention, eh? By the way, don't look behind you whatever you do.' Of course he looked behind him immediately and saw the midget heading our way. While his attention was thus diverted I slipped the two envelopes from my right-hand pocket on to the floor under the seat and when Art started clambering out of the car, added the gun and a clip of ammunition. Then I hastily got out my side.

'Mr Wetmore?' Lieutenant Conyers said when he was close enough. 'A pleasure. I have here a warrant that may interest you.'

'You lying bugger,' Art said to me.

'No one's perfect,' I said to him. 'Anyway, there you go, jumping to wrong conclusions again. What's the warrant for, Officer? His brand-new redwood condo?'

'Why, no,' said Conyers. 'His almost brand-new car. I have reason to believe, in evidence received, that you are illegally transporting drugs, counterfeit money and an unlicensed firearm, with ammunition. All three of these are capital charges in the state of California. I hope for your sake your fingerprints aren't on any of them.' No, they were on all of them.

I was keeping a close eye on Art, knowing his history, so I dodged the first roundhouse right he threw at me but he caught me in the ribs with a good left hook and then battle was joined, as some mother-in-law said once. Art was big, heavy and slow; so was I but I was bigger and heavier. He hurt me some but I hurt him more and finally I measured him properly and decked him with a solid, almost straight right thrown from the hip. The lieutenant, of course, merely backed up a few steps and watched. Once he said, 'Hit him in the bread basket,' but I'll never be sure who he said it to.

When Art was finally down, I kicked him once, as hard as I could, in the groin. He screamed; tears ran down his fat face.

'Timmy,' I said. 'The moron. His name was Timmy.'

Then the midget cuffed him, took out a small, printed card and read him his rights, and, when he could walk again, led him back up the hill. Art stopped once to spit out some blood and parts of his bridge-work.

'Messy,' I said.

CHAPTER TWENTY - FOUR

A peach of a day, I mused, as I cruised down Balmoral toward the freeway. A peach of a Southern California day. I fiddled with the car radio and finally got Barbara Mandrell wondering why she always picked the wrong man. Because you ain't looked in my direction recently, I told Barbara.

Back at my place, I got out of that foolish safari jacket and into a superb early Hawaiian number, almost a collector's item, transferred Art's confession to my wallet, picked up the roll of film I'd shot at the school the night before and tootled over to my friend Wade's. A peach of a day, I mused, as I tootled.

Wade was out lying in his hammock, as usual, puffing on a garish waterpipe, the kind you buy at the last moment at North African airports for someone else. The gigantic mutt dozing in the shade under the hammock looked as stoned as his master; it opened one eye briefly, then closed it again.

'If it's like, work, like, man, forget it,' Wade said. 'I've retired. I've gone to a far, far better place than planet Earth.'

'Where have you gone to?' I asked him reverently.

'It has no name,' he said dreamily. 'It is known only by a number.'

'May I know the number?'

'No, you may not,' he said, inhaling a long, gurgling hit of what smelled like Nepalese. 'No one over six feet high is ever allowed to know the number.'

'Excuse me for asking, master,' I said humbly. 'And excuse me for bringing up a subject as crass as dinero, but do they use money where you are?'

'They do,' he said. 'Their money is butterflies.'

'That must be good stuff,' I said. I tossed the roll of film on to his weedy chest. 'Two contact sheets and right away, please, and I will pay you in butterflies of any denomination you wish, as in two twenties and one ten. Do they have time where you are?'

'They do,' Wade said. 'They measure it in sighs.'

'See you in thirty sighs,' I said, and got out of there. His cat was sunning itself on my car roof and didn't get off until I was turning out of the driveway.

I found a post office not far away that had a copy machine and made a couple of dupes, then had a late lunch at the same greasy spoon near Wade's I'd breakfasted at a few days earlier. Their pot roast was awful, so was their apple pie. I knew I should have had the banana cream, it's always awful so you're never disappointed.

All right. Back to Wade's, where the scene was unchanged except my contact sheets were in an envelope in one of his seemingly lifeless hands. I withdrew them gently and told him his butterflies were in the mail.

'Where I am, we are not allowed emotions,' Wade said without opening his eyes. 'Except, occasionally, deep pity.' He stroked his skimpy goatee complacently.

Home again. A weak brandy and ginger ale to wash away the taste of the over-cooked pot roast. I stowed away in my security box the original and one copy of Art's statement and one of the contact sheets. Then I puttered around a while making sure the place was more or less tidy for Mom. I'm not saying I cleaned the oven and the bathroom mirror and waxed the kitchen linoleum, but tidy it was. Then I collected the bits and pieces – I was going to say, of my life, but I'll go into that another time – the bits and pieces I was going to need shortly, and drove over to St Stephen's to look for Dev. I did not muse on the way.

Tracking him down took some doing as the school was officially closed, it being a Saturday, but luckily there were lots of kids around practicing various sports and one of the coaches finally let me in one of the side doors. Dev was in the otherwise empty gym sitting in a corner on a fold-up chair.

He was wearing an old warm-up jacket and a pair of shorts. His artificial leg started just below the knee; he was unbuckling it as I walked over to him. On the floor beside him were two small barbells of the kind used for strengthening forearms and a heavy bar on which he was resting his good leg. His prosthesis was finished in a smooth, skin-colored plastic instead of the metallic skin I might have expected.

'Hi, Dev,' I said. 'Want to shoot a few baskets?'

He finished unbuckling his leg, held it up, then began wiping it down with a clean towel he had thrown over one shoulder. The fold of skin over the butt of the amputation looked red and sore.

'Dirt gets in,' he said, 'no matter how careful you are.' He kept his eyes on the job, away from mine. 'I've got four of these things, you use them for different purposes, you know?'

I bent down and tried to lift the heavy bar and managed to raise one end of it a couple of inches.

'Oof,' I said. 'They've taken Art away to a far, far better place where he will not have a name anymore. He will have a number, however.'

'It wasn't my idea,' Dev said, still engrossed in his polishing. 'I would like you to know that.'

'OK,' I said.

'I tumbled you right away, though,' he said. 'I did that, and I did tell him you were poking around, but that's all.'

'OK,' I said. I took a look around. 'They sure got a lot of stuff here they never had in my day. All we had was two hoops, a couple of ropes and some wooden bars.'

'And some dirty mats,' he said. 'Don't forget those.' He began doing a series of exercises with his bad leg, lifting it as far in the air as he could, holding it, and then relaxing. The effort made the veins in his neck stand out like cables. 'I do that fifty times twice a day.'

'To each his own,' I said.

'Have you got my smack?' he asked me. 'I need it. I'm going to need it more tonight.'

'I got it.'

'Did you blow up Art's too? You must have. How did you do it?'

'Chicken soup,' I said.

'Was that you with Bobby too? Must have been. What was that all about?'

'I felt like dressing up,' I said. I picked up one of the small barbells and pumped it a few times. 'Do you think I could ever have muscles? If I did this regularly?'

He shrugged. 'Miracles have happened.'

'Actually, what I was on about was this.' I handed him one of the duplicates of Art's signed statement. 'I figured he'd turn on you if I gave him half a chance, so I did.' Then I gave him a copy of the contact sheet of the roll of film I'd shot in his apartment and the boys' locker room. He looked at them almost without interest, then started to pass them back to me. I said, 'Keep 'em, I got plenty of copies.'

'I had a desk job with the military police in Can Tho,' Dev said. 'I did a pal a favor and got caught and was transferred to a combat division of the Fourth. The best man I had was Corporal William Lynch, I don't know how many times I hauled his black ass out of the shit but it was nothing to the number of times he saved mine. Two weeks or so before Tet we were patrolling a valley that was so beautiful it was like some kind of Shangri-La, it made you cry. Were you ever in the army?'

'Briefly,' I said. I went over to the window and looked out. A pick-up game had started on the soccer field. On one of the tennis courts, two boys were playing against four girls.

'Briefly, yeah,' he said. 'Well, briefly, we killed some villagers who probably had no more to do with the war than Little Orphan Annie, and Willie lost it and fragged me – or maybe he didn't lose it, who knows? Then he carried me four klicks back to camp on his back. When I started getting better, except for the pain, they took me off morphine, so he used to get smack for me. You explain it.'

I couldn't so I went on looking out the window instead. One of the boys playing tennis set himself for an overhead smash, missed the ball by a mile, then collapsed dramatically. His partner bent over him with exaggerated concern.

'Willie was the first guy I ever saw giving an officer a black power salute instead of the regulation one,' Dev said after a moment. 'Later, they were all doing it.'

'I heard,' I said.

'You ever been to Ireland?'

'No. I used to sit outside an Irish bar Friday nights and wait for my pop.'

'I was going, like John Wayne in *The Quiet Man*. I've still got some family there. In Cork. That's in the south, on the sea.'

I strolled back over to him. 'Well, don't book your ticket yet,' I said, 'you got things to do first.'

'Only too true,' he said. He pushed himself off the chair with one hand, then seemed to lose his balance, so I put out a hand to steady him. He showed his gratitude by swinging the tin leg in a vicious arc, catching me right on the temple. It didn't seem to hurt that much but I started going down. He gave me another one for luck right in the same place. I hit the floor like the dumb, overweight slob I was. He was just lining up a third shot when I passed out.

I don't think I was unconscious longer than a moment or two. When I started focusing again I could see Dev had his leg strapped back on and was bending over the heavy bar. Funny time to pump a little iron, I remember thinking foggily. With a grunt of effort he snatched the bar up to the chest position, then took a couple of deep breaths, then, wobbling a bit, got it up over his head. I was beginning to get the idea but I couldn't seem to get any words out. I did think about moving rapidly somewhere out of the way but I couldn't get that together either.

If you think three years in a closed prison is a long time, try thirty seconds on a wood floor watching two hundred pounds of cast iron wobble over your head with some mad-eyed Paddy staring at you all the while. Finally he let the bar slam down; dust exploded from between the floorboards; it missed my tender cranium by a good six inches.

'My poor old mother, she always said I was too soft-hearted for my own good,' Dev said, sitting heavily down in the chair again. 'So I'll go no more a-roving after all.'

'Only too true,' I said after a few minutes when my mouth began doing what my brain told it to. 'Just another senti-mental Mick, that's you.' I sat up part way; after a few more minutes the room stopped going round and round. Blinking didn't help much but it was the traditional thing to do so I blinked for a while.

'Now what, I wonder,' Dev said.

'Now you start cleaning up the mess you and your friends have made of this school.'

'I don't know if I can,' he said. 'I don't know if I want to.'

'Oh, you want to.' I sat up a little more. 'Otherwise you won't get to see the Old Sod til you're more like Barry Fitz-gerald's age than Big John Wayne's. For Christ's sake, talk about throwing away the key. I've got you by the balls, Irish. "School Security Cop His Students' Connection". "What Really Went On During Recess". Jesus.'

'All right, all right, I get the message.'

'You're getting off easy is what you're getting, Irish.' I dug out his smack and tossed it to him. 'Here. Have a good time. I use Demerols myself.'

'So do I til it gets bad,' he said, 'which is about half an hour after I wake up.'

'Excuses, excuses,' I said. He almost smiled. 'Look at it like a problem in tactics, then what would you do?'

'About cleaning up this place? First of all I'd get myself an army.'

'You got an army,' I said, 'in fact you've got two of them. One's the rifle club, the other's your gung-ho all-American cadet corps, how many troops does that make?'

'About thirty and sixty which is ninety,' he said.

'I bet there's more, too,' I said, 'if that's not enough for you. I bet there's America First clubs and karate clubs and Four Fs and girls' wrestling clubs and God knows what all. Hell, you'll probably wind up outnumbering the civilians. So have yourself a hit and a good, long think, Paddy me boy, about ways and means. I'll get on to the vice-principal so he can start working from his end on any possible legal problems and hassles with parents and all the rest, then you can get together with him so you'll be all ready to go for assembly Monday morn.'

'Two assemblies,' he said, 'Monday morn. The school's too big for one.'

'Who cares?' I said. 'So long as it gets done. Then in say a year from now if the school's clean not only will you be able to pop off to County Cork and that horrible black beer they drink and peat fires and that homemade white lightning they brew but I'll help you pack. Maybe I'll even come over and visit you sometime and we can have a hearty laugh over the good old days.'

'Sure,' he said. 'Sure. I can't wait. I don't suppose I get my money back too.'

'Don't worry,' I said. 'It'll go to a good cause.' This time he did manage a tired smile.

I left Irish sitting there in the empty gym, in the Celtic twilight of his days, and took myself out into the California sunshine after rinsing my poor, mistreated face at a water fountain I passed. I sat in the grass beside the soccer field for a while watching tomorrow's leaders at their play. They looked a pretty scruffy lot to me but maybe that was merely an old man's jealousy. Maybe there was no maybe about it. However it was still a peach of a day as I told Mr Lowenstein in so many words when I got through to him about an hour later from my office.

'A peach of a day, Vice,' I said. I had my feet up and Betsy up and was drinking a root beer from Mrs Morales. Maybe

Sara was right after all, maybe Mrs Morales had put on a little around the hips.

'What's so peachy about it?'

'Hang on to your mortar board, Grumpy,' I said. 'I've got some good news and some bad news.'

'What's the good news?'

'We got 'em all,' I said. 'The outside man, the inside man and the runners. Art we got on at least three capital charges, assault, pushing, and funny money. We also got him on contravention of the firearms act but that's only six months or five hundred bucks in California. The assault was on me. We'll never get him for my office or Timmy, the only witness was an Armenian, and that's not a joke, son. We got Dev tied up so tight that if he doesn't take charge of your clean-up crusade he'll be in serious trouble too. We got evidence on most of the kids involved and if you have a quiet word with one of your students, Robert Santee, you'll probably get a few more names. Finally, I did my little best to start a war between the two major drug syndicates in town; if it doesn't break out soon I'll have to drop them an anonymous letter or two and make sure it does. O K so far?'

'Holy Toledo!' he said.

'Language,' I said. 'The bad news is, there goes the rest of your weekend.'

'That I can live with,' he said. 'We were going to spend the night with my in-laws in Encino, and believe me it takes a good excuse to get out of that. Do you know what my mother-in-law puts in her chili? Leek tops and raisins.'

I told him if he obliged with his home address I'd get something to him in writing or at least in typing, in a couple of hours. He obliged, thanked me more than profusely, then hung up happily. I switched on and went to work, one carbon. I laid it all out, the names of the kids, what I found in the locker room and where, what I found in Dev's room and where and why. I didn't bother telling him that Irish had almost brained me, nor did I provide any details about the unfortunate end to Art's brave venture into the fast-food business. I decided that I'd better keep a few other tidbits to myself as well, such as my thrilling career as an FBI agent. Someday, though, the whole truth could be told.

I added an appendage (a), a neatly itemized list of my expenses, which had been considerable if not astronomic what with truck rentals and Benny and funny money and willing messenger boys and Sara's pathetic contributions and odds and ends of wardrobe. Was a cat trap a legitimate expense? Foolish question. Then I calculated the per diems I had coming and listed them. Then I added an appendage (b), some general suggestions about school morale, handling the press if necessary, patrols and monitors and so on, but figured that Dev could do a better job than me on the details, especially now that he was a willing boy too. A show of force Monday morning at the assemblies, I suggested, with the stage crammed with every uniformed eager-beaver type the school could produce. Public expulsions, I suggested. I even, God help my reactionary soul, suggested some kind of a dress code.

As soon as a willing girl this time from the messenger service sped off into the murk with the report I put away things, locked up and went home to bathe my bruises and don some gladrags as it was, after all, Saturday night. And I had been mildly sensational all day, if you took my word for it.

By six thirty I was more or less bathed, pilled, aftershaved and resplendent. I automatically started to call up Mae, then caught myself. Whoops. So I made myself a large drink and watched a bit of one of my favorite TV programs, a Mexican variety show in which the girls were costumed as pineapples. Then I thought Evonne might like to hear the latest developments so I gave her a call. She was out back watering her garden, she told me on her portable phone.

'Beat it!' she said loudly. 'Off! Out! You little bastard!'

'Well!' I said. 'That's a fine way to talk to someone who's spent all day risking his life and being sensational.'

'Not you,' she said. 'It's the neighbors' miserable cats, they eat my parsley.'

I told her I had serious cat problems as well, what a coincidence, how about getting together that evening to compare notes and enjoy a celebratory drink or two or three.

'I can't,' she said, 'and it's all your fault, I have to get together with the boss. Do you know how much has to be done before Monday?'

'Ah, blast,' I said.

'Look, why don't you come over tomorrow evening, I'll cook us something on my tiny barbecue that never did work right.'

'Make mine rare,' I said. 'T T F N.'

O K! But that left tonight. I called Linda, no answer. I called Mavis, whose number was scribbled on a cocktail napkin from Hal's Hickory House. A man answered and said she was in Reno for the weekend spending his money. O K. I figured I might give that twerp Sara a break and take her to an under-twenties drug orgy somewhere but there was no answer at her place. Maybe Benny had another aunt I could check out.

O K. So I'd cruise a while, maybe have a quick one at the Corner Bar, see what was going down, then check out Sandy's dump, maybe see if Mario's house wine had gotten any better due to some miracle of secondary fermentation.

It was later, much later, that evening, that peach of an evening.

I was not only feeling no pain, I was not only feeling a great deal of happiness, but I was feeling that the answers to those elusive truths that have troubled Man since the dawn of history, like why nurses have the reputation they do, were just a bar away, maybe only a drink. I was way the hell up Ventura near Glendale at the time, just idling, singing along with the radio and wondering why I hadn't decided to be a wonderful country singer instead of merely a wonderful human being when I espied a neon sign that promised every-thing a wonderful human being would ever want – Drinks, Eats, Games, Girls, Music, Parking.

I pulled smoothly into the alley alongside and parked next to a low-rider that had a front bumper a good inch off the ground. A guy blowing weed by the back door ignored my cheerful wave of greeting. I more or less tacked around to the front and made a casual entrance. The joint turned out to be a Mexican beer-only cantina but I guess beer is Drinks and microwaved tacos are Eats and pool is a Game and the apparition behind the bar was almost a Girl and what was coming from the jukebox was undoubtedly Music of some south of the border kind.

What the hell. I think someone said that once, too. What the hell. Great expression, though, whoever said it; short and pithy. What the hell.

I was on my second Corona and working on my high-school Spanish with the drunk next to me when I had an eerie feeling as if someone with a very large and very cold hand had suddenly grabbed the back of my neck. Being normally about as mystic as Sandra Dee I figured that either someone with a very large, very cold hand *had* grabbed me by the back of the neck or I'd flashed on something in the mirror that would repay a second and closer look fast. So I looked, and saw him; at least I thought it might be him, a young Latino shooting pool who, the last time I'd seen him, if it was him, was at Martha's when he was trying to ensure that from then on I'd be in the soprano section of the choir. When I peeked again a few minutes later I caught him looking at me, but I still wasn't sure.

'Caballeros?' I loudly asked the drunk beside me who was looking unhappily down at two burritos he'd ordered.

'Por allá,' he mumbled, waving vaguely toward the back of the bar. I arose and headed that way, weaving a little more than I really had to. When I was out of sight of the pool table I nipped out the back door, ran up the alley and was just in time to catch the bastard nipping out the front door.

'Buenas noches,' I said with a friendly grin.

'Buenas,' he said with a friendly grin.

'Qué tal, amigo?'

'Pues, bien, como siempre,' he said. 'Hasta luego, eh?'

'Momento, compadre,' I said. 'Take off your shirt.'

'No comprendo,' he said, but I suspected he'd comprendoed because he held his hands innocently out in front of him.

'Camisa,' I said. 'Off.'

When he went for the back of his belt I knew it was him all right and when he pulled out the knife I had my bean bag already cocked and I caught him a good one right on that nerve in the upper arm that you always tried to find when you are giving another kid, especially a brother, a knuckly. The knife dropped to the street. He started to take off but I caught him in two strides and threw him into the alley. When he got up I beat the shit out of him, then beat some more shit out of him, then kicked him a bit, then took his wallet and knife and got the hell out of there. The guy blowing weed by the back door didn't even wave me goodbye.

When I stopped for a light a few blocks away I checked out the wallet; the cheapskate had only about sixty bucks in it, which I kept. The wallet and the rest of its contents, which included a picture of some virgin or other and a lubricated rubber, I tossed out a while later. I did keep his ID to give to Shorty.

A peach of a day, a peach of an evening, a peach of a noche.

CHAPTER TWENTY - FIVE

Alzheimer's disease is a devastating illness of the aging.

The cause is not known, nor the cure, nor even any effective ongoing treatment. It affects the centers of the brain that control the memory and personality and is progressive and irreversible. The sufferer commonly asks the same question over and over and usually loses control of some bodily functions as well. My Mom had it.

I drove over to Tony's about eleven Sunday morning to pick her up. She wasn't quite ready so I spent some time with the kids in the backyard telling lies about my job. They didn't mind, they liked lies. I didn't mind, I liked them, occasionally. The boy, Martin, was ten, the girl, Martine, nine and they were both soccer freaks; their father had built them a half-size goal behind the garage and they wanted me to take a turn being goalie. I said my multi-million-dollar contract with Manchester United prohibited me from playing on the amateur level due to possible injury.

When Mom was finally settled in the back seat of the car with her bag beside her and her knitting bag beside that, I gave the kids a wink, waved to Tony and his missus and took her home. The rest of the day I didn't do much, I got Mom settled in, talked to the Vice on the phone a couple of times. He reported that he and Dev were making progress, and how, they had lists ready of those students who were going to get the chop and those to be put on probation, Evonne had letters to their parents all ready to go, and all concerned were looking forward to extremely interesting assemblies Monday morning, with, as I'd suggested, everyone conceivable who had a uniform marching out on stage for starters, and did I want to be there?

'Thanks but no thanks,' I said. 'The only thing that would get me back to that hotbed of sex and drugs would be to carry Miss Shirley's books home.'

'I had a good laugh at some of the expenses you claimed,' he said.

'I'm pleased to hear it,' I said. 'After all, is not humor the best medicine?'

The afternoon passed; I read a while and ironed a couple of shirts, Mom knitted and watched golf on television. When evening was nigh I made sure the beeper that kept Mom in touch with Feeb was pinned on her blouse and working, then took my leave. Mom, who knew just about everything else, didn't know that I forked over a hundred dollars a month extra to her friend Feeb for services rendered above and beyond the normal duties of a landlady. Hell, cheap. The beeper had been cheap, too, thanks to you know who. On the way to Miss Shirley's I stopped at the Arrow for two bottles of Martini Brothers Gamay. Aunt Fat'ma wasn't there but a plateful of her halvah was. I was licking the stuff off my teeth for a week.

Monday morning early I stopped by Mrs Martel's to order some special stationery. I had that letter of thanks from the FBI to the Bolden boy to write, also I wanted to send Timmy's mom a certified check that would use up three quarters of Dev's cash and thought it might make it easier for her if it came with a nice letter from, say, the California Association of Unwed Mothers.

Back at the office I called Syd, the happy used-furniture hustler, and spent the rest of Dev's money on an air-conditioning unit. All right! Do not the spoils belong to the victor, at least some of them? Then I wasted a little time leafing through a catalogue of video games; rubbing out peasants was beginning to pall slightly, you know how it is. I'd already decided I wouldn't call Evonne up, at least not until noon, I didn't want her to think I was too easy. And I won't bother telling you at this time how we got on Sunday evening, some things are too personal to be gossiped about willy-nilly, but I can reveal Evonne has a middle name, Beverly, a brother in Biloxi called William and that she puts Tabasco sauce on her baked potato.

Then someone phoned me, a long-distance operator wanting to know if I would accept a collect call from Davis, California. Would I ever, not often do you get a call from one of the missing bits and pieces.

The caller was a Mrs Doris Lillie and she had seen my ad and might be able to tell me something about the child. How was she, anyway?

'Fine,' I said, 'but determined and none too happy.'

There was a sigh from Mrs Lillie. 'I know,' she said. 'I can imagine. Heck. I don't know if I'm doing the right thing or not but it feels right.'

'Speaking for the girl,' I said, 'it would certainly help her to know who she is, all other things being equal.'

'I can't argue with that,' Mrs Lillie said. 'Well. Now what?'

I said I could be in Davis the following afternoon if that was convenient. It was. She asked me to please come by myself as she wasn't sure she could manage the girl too. I said I understood.

As soon as Mrs Lillie hung up, I called Sara's apartment. She answered the phone herself with her customary bored 'Yeah?' When she found it was me, she said, 'What's up, Sherlock?' I told her I had hot news and to get her little buns moving in my direction.

'I'm on my way, V.D.,' she said.

I went back to the catalogue. I had just narrowed my choices down to either a detective game which would probably be too easy for me or a sort of treasure hunt when the kid slouched in the door, cool as could be but a little out of breath. She was attired that day in a pair of camouflage overalls worn over a torn net undershirt, red sunglasses and a red and white bandana tied like Aunt Jemima's on her dopey head. She plopped herself down on the edge of the desk and said, 'OK, Doc, tell me the worst, I can handle it.'

I told her. She clenched one fist and waved it in the air. 'Banzai!' she shouted. 'Now we're gettin' somewhere!' She leaned over and ruffled my hair.

'Cut that out,' I said.

'Of course I'm going with you,' she said.

'Oh no you're not.'

'Why not?'

'Because the lady said I should come alone.'

'Don't give me that line,' she said. 'I can wait in the car.'

'You can't come anyway,' I said.

'Why not?'

'I don't want to be seen walking around with you, that's why not.'

'How do you think I feel about you? It's like being with the Hulk,' she said.

We glared at each other.

'That cat's here again,' she said after a minute. 'Dunno what it sees in you.' I turned around and told the cat to beat it. It just looked at me. I finally had to get up and chase the thing out.

'How're we getting there?'

'We're not,' I said. 'I'm getting there.'

'Oh, give it up,' she said. 'Give it a rest. You know perfectly well I'm going. If we took that jalopy of yours it'd take a year.' I had to agree with her there. 'Anyway I don't like driving too far, I get car sick, I'll puke all over you. We'll have to fly.'

'Oh no we won't,' I said. 'I don't like flying, I get air sick, I'll puke all over you.'

'Bet you're just scared,' she said. 'Big chicken.' What a pest.

'Well, maybe I am scared,' I said. 'Maybe I've got good reason to be. Maybe I was in a crash once. Maybe twice.'

'Were you?' she asked interestedly. 'When?'

'Some war or other,' I said. 'I forget . . .'

'What'll we do then, hitch-hike?'

'Ever heard of trains?'

'Pops, no one takes the train.'

'We do,' I said. 'You'll love it.'

'I'll bet,' she said. 'If there even are any.'

'I'm just about to find out, aren't I,' I said, 'if you'd shut up for once in your life.'

I called Amtrak. After I'd listened to recorded music for a while a lady told me the good news – there were trains to Sacramento which was near Davis leaving twice daily. The one that followed the Valley north departed at three forty-five a.m. and the one that took the scenic coastal route left early in the afternoon but took longer. Then she told me about connections and such. It all sounded fairly laborious. I knew that flights left regularly from L A X and Burbank and only took about an hour and were cheap, too, because the competing airlines were always having price wars, but I was not going to fly, so there.

'All aboard,' I told Sara. 'We leave tomorrow morning at a quarter to four.'

'Holy moly,' she said. 'Too bad they didn't have a train that left early. Is that it? Is that our only choice?'

'No, that is not our only choice,' I said, with commendable patience. 'We could take the scenic coastal route but that takes thirteen hours, and thirteen hours with you would drive anybody nuts. Got any money, or bread, as you call it?'

'What for?'

'For your ticket, that's what for.'

'I got ten dollars,' she said. 'Almost. Is it much more than that?'

'Just a trifle,' I said. 'That'll probably take you as far as Bakersfield. You ever been to Bakersfield?' She shook her Technicolored head. 'Not a nice town to be stuck in.'

'So put the rest on the bill, big shot,' she said. 'What are you giving me such a hard time for anyway?'

I thought about it for a moment. 'I don't know, maybe I just don't believe in happy endings.'

'Maybe I do,' she said.

'In front of Union Station, tomorrow morning, three thirty,' I said. 'That's on North Alameda, downtown.'

'See you there,' she said.

'Your folks going to give you any trouble?'

'No,' she said. 'Even if they do.'

'Do me a favor,' I said. 'If you've got anything halfway presentable to wear, wear it?'

'Same to you,' she said. 'With bells on.'

She left, swinging what hips she had. What a twerp. Shortly after, I tidied up my desk, put away what had to be put away, locked up and drove home. I had a word with Feeb on the way in. She said Mom was fine, she'd beeped once but had forgotten why by the time Feeb had arrived. In the early days Mom would get upset when something like that happened but now she laughed it off. I told Feeb I was off to Sacramento for a day on a job, could she manage? No sweat, said Feeb. I was glad I'd leveled with the old battle-axe about the fire in my office.

Mom cooked us lamb chops and baked potatoes for supper. The chops were done to a turn but the potatoes were a little hard, she'd forgotten to light the oven. No sweat, said I, and gave her a kiss. I made some instant mash instead. Later we watched a *Magnum, P.I.* Now there was a guy with a wardrobe I could relate to.

Three thirty, in front of Union Station, on North Alameda. I'd just bought the tickets, $58 for each round trip. A brand-new 'Vette with a smashed right front fender stopped five feet in front of me and guess who got out. The 'Vette took off. She came over to me and twirled to show off her traveling outfit.

'Love it, dear,' I said. 'It's so you.' She was wearing a sort of late 50s party frock made out of blue felt, with appliqués of musical notes on the skirt. On her thin legs, green fishnet stockings. On her feet, hiking boots. Thrown over her shoulder, the tattiest bit of fur since the last of the buffalos. On her head, a 'Welcome to L A' sun visor. She was dragging by one strap a small, orange backpack.

'Come on, will you?' We got on a waiting bus and found two seats together at the back.

'Funny train,' she observed. 'Don't they usually run on tracks?'

'Bus to Bakersfield,' I said. 'Train to Stockton. Bus to Sacramento.'

'Now you tell me,' she said. 'Can you smoke in here? I'm a nervous wreck. You should see a shrink about your fear of flying, then we wouldn't have to go through all this boring drek.' Legally or not, she lit up one of her imitation stogies and stared out of the window at what excitements downtown L A before dawn had to offer, i.e. a passing wino in a sleeveless overcoat buttoned up to his neck. He glanced up through the darkened window at us. Poor mother, I thought. However there are attractions in giving up completely, maybe he was thinking the same right back, poor mother.

It's roughly two and a half hours northwest on Interstate 5 to Bakersfield; we both dozed off, there's not a lot to see on that route even in daylight. We had time for a coffee, a stretch and a leak in the old Bakersfield train station before boarding. A few of the locals' eyes popped when they took in the full beauty of my companion's get-up but they stopped popping when they looked at mean old me.

By six thirty we were ensconced in a smoking section right next to the club car so madame could puff her lungs out if she wanted to and the train was heading up the Valley to Hanford, Fresno, Madera, Merced and all points north. Sara dozed off again, her polychromatic head against my shoulder. I hoped the dye wouldn't rub off on my suede jacket. I thought about this and that, trains are good for thinking. I thought I might write a slim monograph on my bits and pieces observations someday. Once when we were a family Mom and Pop and Tony and I had taken a train somewhere but I couldn't remember where. I know there were cows and horses because Tony and I were on opposite sides of the train counting them but if you saw a graveyard you had to start all over again. Once Aunt Jessica and I almost took a train to Carmel. Sara stirred in her sleep and reached out with one hand. I put mine in hers and she grasped it like a baby grasps a proffered thumb or finger.

After a while she woke up and produced some peanut-butter and honey sandwiches from her pack and we ate those. Then she produced a deck of cards and we played gin on the little table that comes down from the back of the seat in front. Can you believe the poor thing had never heard of the technique of fishing for a card that you needed, like throwing a ten of spades you didn't need, trying to lure the ten of hearts out of her, which you did need? Pathetic. True, she beat me two games out of three, but hell, anyone can win if they get the cards. Then, I don't know, maybe it was the train, trains are not only conducive to musings but can also invite or allow confidences much like candlelight does. Or perhaps it was being away for a while in a temporary limbo, like on a ship. She was trying to remember some boring card trick someone had once taught her and the cards spilled all over our laps for the umpteenth time and I tickled her, accidentally, I can assure you, picking them up.

'You know, sometimes you're almost human,' she said. 'But the rest of the time, forget it. What's your problem, anyway, aside from being huge? Me, I was a bed wetter.'

'Well, I wasn't,' I said. 'I haven't wet a bed in months.' Then, to my surprise, I found myself telling her about it, or part of it, anyway, and I never tell anyone anything. It must have been the train.

I told her that one Saturday night when I was sixteen and Tony was fourteen, we were living in Davenport then, I'd come home from a movie and found Tony behind the wheel of a strange car right in front of our house. He was drunk as a skunk. He had the car door open and was throwing up in the street. I was the older brother, see, the bad one. He was the younger brother, the good one. Although I didn't want to believe it I guess I knew by then that Pop was dying, he died later that year from the type of emphysema you get from handling asbestos board all your life although they didn't know what it was then.

'Hey, they probably didn't even know what germs were yet when you were a kid,' Sara said.

'Me and Pop didn't get on too well. I was a goof-off at school and a smart-ass at home, when I could get away with it. Tony got the good marks. Pop liked him. I got Tony up the stairs and into bed without anyone seeing us and figured I'd better move the jalopy he'd stolen as it wouldn't be too smart leaving it right in front of our house. I'd just gotten it started up when the cops came. So what was I going to do? Tell them Tony had been joyriding, not me? I shut up, which is what you should do once in a while instead of making uncalled-for jokes about my advanced years. I shut up. It turned out Tony had hit someone, some half-blind old lady, and put her in the hospital. I got sent for two years to a farm down south near Springfield that was part of the juvenile reform system. If you ever should want to know anything at all about weeding raspberry bushes, ask me. Or hoeing melons.'

'O K,' she said. 'How do you hoe a melon?'

'The hard way,' I said. 'With a hoe that's too short for you. Ah, what the hell, it was all a long time ago, I don't know why it still matters.'

'Me too,' she said. 'It was just as long ago for me and it still matters. So then what happened? Come on, come on.' She dug her knuckles in my arm a couple of times. I pretended it hurt.

'Ouch!' I said. 'Cut it out. They got me a job, what do you think happened? I was on probation for a year, I sorted mail.

Then I got a job as a bouncer at a rock club, or what passed for a rock club in Davenport.'

'Bet you were a good one,' she said. 'Being big and dumb.'

'Adequate,' I said. 'Then after a while my goody-goody brother takes an exam and becomes a police cadet. No problem, top of his class and all that. Then after a while I get offered a more or less respectable job as a sort of chauffeur–bodyguard for this kid who used to sing at the club but had started to make it; he was pretty good, too, but I had to be licensed to get insured so I put the squeeze on Tony to pull my sheet so I could get legal again. Then after a while I hit this Hell's Angel monster during a riot at some dump in Baton Rouge, I hit him with his own chain and he fell off the stage and hit his head and was in a coma and when he came to his lawyer claimed he'd suffered brain damage and I claimed he never had enough brains in the first place to damage and I got three years this time in the Louisiana penal system. They didn't have any raspberry bushes or melons but that's about all I can say for it. Course when I got out the employment agencies weren't exactly clamoring for my services so I started working repos with Charlie the Fish. You know that thing that cops do when they question someone, you see it in the movies all the time, one guy plays the good guy and his partner the bad guy, Mutt and Jeff they call it in Chicago, well me and Charlie had our own system. I played the bad guy and he played the worse.'

'Then what?'

'Then I came to California and lived happily ever after.'

'Want a Coke?' she said. 'My treat.' She went off to get them. At train prices I figured that would leave her with about twenty cents out of her almost ten dollars. Serve her right. I used the Coke to wash down a Demerol, as my leg was starting to act up. Then I took a nap.

'Hang in there, kid,' I told her just before I dropped off. 'You're doing good so far, considering.' She slurped the last of her Coke as noisily as possible, a nuisance to the bitter end.

CHAPTER TWENTY - SIX

We weren't far out of Modesto, Sheriff Gutes' old manor, when Sara started getting jittery again. She made me go over the whole conversation with Mrs Lillie and became even more convinced she was her real mom. I still wasn't sure but I didn't think so.

'But don't they always do that?' she said, shaking my arm. I donm't know when she'd decided the best use for me was a walking punching bag. 'I mean, a woman goes to the doctor, "I have this friend who's in trouble," she says, but it's her really, isn't it? I mean I understand if she wants to get a look at me first to see I'm not a total freak.' I didn't bother saying (a) Mrs Lillie didn't want a look at her and (b) she was a total freak. So I looked out the window instead to see if there were any cows or horses to count. There weren't so I counted illegal workers in the tomato fields instead, there were plenty of those.

'They grew a lot of poppies around here til the turn of the century, did you know that?' an old geezer in the seat across the aisle from me said.

'No,' I said.

'And eucalyptus,' he said. 'Know what they used them for?'

'Feeding silkworms?'

'Railroad ties,' said the old-timer. After a moment he added, 'Hunt's. Hunt's owns all them tomatoes. Know what he uses them for?'

'Yes,' I said. 'Watery catsup.'

We changed over in Stockton to an air-conditioned (like my office was soon to be) bus and shortly thereafter were heading north up the Interstate again. My ward alternated between moods of depression and bursts of energy. During one of the latter she wanted to talk about why a mother would ever give her child up, let alone dump it somewhere like a dead cat in a bag. She wondered where her name came from, was there a tag on her bootie saying, this is Sara, please care for her and love her? I did see her problem; it wouldn't make it any easier to get together with her mom whoever she was if Mom was still riddled with guilt and Daughter furious with blame. I told her about Timmy's mom – a young girl, liked a good time, had a mentally defective child, no husband to help, what would have happened if she hadn't taken off and left Timmy with her friend, probably an institution. Did Sara really imagine all mothers gave up their children for selfish reasons, surely some of them at least must be thinking of the child, too, even putting the child first. Little Sara brightened at this line of reasoning; all in all she was going pretty good for an airhead, and the occasional toot of weed she snuck in the washroom that she thought I was too square to notice didn't seem to hurt either. I was only surprised she didn't roll up right there in her window seat and offer the old geezer across the aisle a bit or pass the roach back to the couple behind us who spent the whole trip loudly playing Yatzie.

Sacramento is only about fifty miles from Stockton so we weren't on the bus long; it was coming up to noon when we found ourselves outside the bus station in the old, downtown area of the state capital. We weren't expected at Mrs Lillie's until later so we took a stroll, saw the newly restored legislature in all its finery, sat in the adjoining park for a while, watched the winos at their sad play, had some lunch, Sara surprisingly eating twice as much as me and you know I don't stint myself when the dinner bell rings, then strolled back near the station where I'd spotted a car rental agency.

Davis is a smallish town some fifteen miles west of Sacramento out Highway 80. It would be even smaller if the University of California–Davis, with its well-known vet school, wasn't situated there. We turned off 80 and found Chestnut Drive by asking directions of one of the millions of cyclists who seemed to have their own private bike lane on every street in town, it looked like rush hour in Canton. We found Mrs Lillie's house, a modest affair with an avocado tree in the front yard. Across the wide street a large, empty park waited in the noonday sun for mad dogs or Englishmen.

I parked in front of the house and we sat there a minute getting our nerves up.

'I'm gonna puke,' Sara said.

'Don't give me that shit,' I said kindly. 'By the way, I've seen something highly suspicious.'

'What?'

'There are no chestnut trees on Chestnut Drive.'

'I'm still gonna puke,' she said.

'Take a deep breath instead.'

'Do I look OK?' She poked at her multicolored mop and straightened her sun visor.

'Terrific,' I said. I licked one finger and ran it nervously over my arched eyebrows. 'How about me?'

'I'm scared, Vic.' She grabbed my arm with both her hands.

'I knew you'd chicken out,' I said. 'That's why I didn't want to bring you.'

'Up your ass, buster,' she said, clambering out of the car. I hadn't even bothered trying to talk her into waiting outside for me, to have come all that way and be so close and to be made to wait was too mean even for me. So I got out and followed her up the flagstone path by the driveway. She started out confidently enough but then slowed up and stopped. I took her hand and pulled her the last bit.

'Don't forget, act ladylike,' I whispered to her and received a small grin in return.

The door was opened just as we got to it by a pleasant-looking woman in a nurse's uniform. She was frowning with worry. Sara was squeezing my hand and staring down at her boots, she couldn't bear to look.

'Sara?' the woman said. 'Sara?' Sara snuck a look at her. 'I'm Doris Lillie, I was a friend of your mother. God almighty, you look just like her.'

Mrs Lillie's eyes began to water. Before we all broke into tears out there in the yard, I said, 'Should we come in, Mrs Lillie? I'm Victor Daniel, the large but kindly investigator who you telephoned.'

She apologized and bustled us in. I didn't like it. What I didn't like was Mrs Lillie saying, 'I *was* a friend of your mother.' I know it could have meant she had been a friend at one time and they just weren't friendly anymore but it more likely meant something else.

Mrs Lillie led us down a hall past two bedrooms and a bathroom to the small, crowded sitting room at the back of the house. Through the picture window I could see well-tended rows of beans, carrots, onions and lettuce and a row of my old favorite, gone but not forgotten, raspberry bushes. Sara did well, she kept herself together until we were sitting down on what looked like a do-it-yourself sofa, then she put it to Mrs Lillie.

'Where is my mother, please?'

Mrs Lillie looked at me for help; I didn't have any.

'She's dead, dear,' she told the girl gently. 'I'm terribly sorry.'

Sara burst into tears. I pulled her into my shoulder, I mean there are times you just don't fuss about what wet mascara will do to almost new suede.

'I knew it,' she said, her voice muffled. 'I knew it.'

'Sure you did.'

'I did! I knew it all along! Or else she would have gotten in touch with me.'

'Sure she would have, babe.' I held her skinny frame until her tears shuddered to a stop, then Mrs Lillie took her off to wash her face and I got up to sneer out of the window at the raspberries. Be damned if I didn't see a row of melons too. Then I sneered at a large, framed photograph that shared a side table with a rubber plant and a silver dish full of mints, an expensive studio shot complete with back lighting of a handsome glamor boy in a naval lieutenant's uniform. Then I stole a mint and, as there were still noises coming from the bathroom, peeked into a manila folder that was on the coffee table in front of the sofa. I assumed Mrs Lillie had put it there in preparation for our visit. Inside were some old photos of her and what had to be Sara's mom as student nurses, then the two of them at a graduation ceremony and a handful of assorted other holiday snaps, several of which had glamor boy in the middle of the two girls. After a quick look I put them away again, it was none of my business now, if Mop-Head wanted to tell me about it she would, if she wanted to hug her secrets to herself, why not?

The girls came back freshened up, Sara pale but calm. When Mrs Lillie went into the kitchen area to put the water on for coffee, I asked the kid how she was doing. She made an 'up yours' gesture with two fingers so I guessed she was doing all right. I told the ladies as they had a lot to talk about I'd take myself out for some air, about two hours' worth, if that was O K with them. They didn't put up any protests so I left.

I sat under a tree in the park for a while, watching two teenage lunatics play Frisbee in the 90-degree heat, got an orange Popsicle from a passing ice-cream truck, then followed my unerring sixth sense or maybe seventh and wound up in the nearest bar. Home is the hunter.

When the appointed two hours were up I made my way leisurely back to Chestnut Drive. Although I wasn't lost I stopped yet another cyclist to ask for directions as she was so mouth-watering, so incredibly cute, she was that cheerleader I never did meet at college because I never went to college and I probably wouldn't have met her even if I had, her eyes were blue, her hair was sun-streaked blond, her legs were tanned and her T-shirt damp and tight.

'Second on the right, sir,' she told me. Sir – that'll learn me, but probably it won't.

When I got back to the house I rang and was let in. Sara was ready to go; she had the manila folder tucked tightly under one arm.

'Hubby not home yet?' I asked Mrs Lillie.

'He's out of town,' she said shortly. The house had felt like he was out of town a lot.

Doris Lillie and Sara hugged each other at the door. Mrs Lillie and I shook hands.

The piece of junk I'd rented wasn't too hot as I'd parked under the avocado tree, but it was hot enough. When we got in I asked Sara, 'What now, kid? Want a bite to eat, want to stay here for the night?'

'I want to go home,' she said in a low voice. 'Please.'

'Sure, babe.'

'I just phoned home. Mom said she was glad I phoned and to come right on home.'

'You got it, kid.'

We passed a hospital on the outskirts of Davis, I'll be damned if it wasn't St Mary's. I didn't bother pointing it out to the twerp. In a minute or two we were back on 80 East heading towards Sacramento.

'Can't we fly?' Sara said after a while. 'I want to go home.'

Oh, Jesus, I knew it was coming, I just knew it, I felt sick already. But all I said was, 'Sure, babe, no sweat,' just like any other wonderful, tender and considerate human being would. I patted her head – well, she'd patted mine once – she had it halfway out the window to get the breeze like dogs do but cats are too stupid to do.

'You're not really afraid of flying, hot stuff like you?'

'You kidding?' I laughed. 'I was just thinking of you, I was just thinking a few peaceful hours on a train up here might help you to get your wooly head together.'

We picked up 5 again, followed the Sacramento River south for a bit, then out east to the airport. Air-Cal got us on a flight almost immediately despite my prayers that the God-damned runways might be fogged up or something. They even accepted my credit card without demur. I had never flown before. There, I've said it. All my life I'd avoided it by one ruse or another and some of the ruses were masterpieces. I don't know where the fear came from in the first place but it sure came. However, it is funny what you can do when there's no possible way out or when you really want to. I once knew a guy, Rickey, Rickey the hairdresser, called Henri de Paris when he was working, who had a complete, absolute, pathological fear of driving a car. He couldn't have driven to his mother's funeral and he was a total Mommy's boy. So he met a girl one night at a party in the Valley right near where he lived. She phoned up the next morning to ask him out to her place in the wilds of Topanga Canyon for the day. He took one driving lesson, rented a car and got there a half hour early. As for flying, hell, it wasn't that bad once you threw up the beer from that bar in Davis and the bar sausage and the pickled eggs and a Hot-Stik or two and the bar nuts and the peanut-butter and honey sandwiches from the train and God knows what else. And a guy can always drop a couple of Demerols and never look out of the window and it only lasted an hour, but I will add this – it'll be a mighty cold day when I do it again, and I don't mean next Christmas.

Sara was pretty quiet during the nightmare flight until we were about ten minutes out of LA and then it came out in a flood. Her mother was a colleen called Mary Heather McBride who had left Dublin age seventeen to go and live with an aunt and uncle in Oakland. Aunt and uncle had promptly placed her in a Catholic nurses' training college in San Francisco where she shared a room with her best friend Doris. Sara showed me a picture of the two girls together, the one I'd already seen, both girls smiling proudly in their new uniforms and student nurses' starched caps.

Mary McBride got pregnant in her second year, she would have been nineteen then, father unknown to anyone but herself. In her fifth month of pregnancy Mary was given sick leave; she'd had pneumonia as a child and indeed continued to suffer the after-effects. Her best friend Doris' widowed mother then owned and lived in the house on Chestnut Drive which Doris took over when her mother retired to Sun City, Arizona. The baby was delivered in that house by Doris' cousin, a resident instructor at the nurses' college who had served his internship at St Mary's in Davis and who still was an occasional consultant there. Doris assisted at the birth. The child, Sara, was left at St Mary's by Doris with the slightly comforting knowledge that her cousin could ensure the child was properly cared for. The name Sara had not been given to the child by her proper mother. Mary McBride died from a type of bronchial pneumonia the following year without having seen her child again. The father never came forward. The end.

Sara put the pictures away carefully in the folder, then managed to squeeze the folder into her backpack.

'How's all that grab you?' she said. 'Eh?' She gave my arm another unnecessary thump. I hoped she'd never hire me to find her father, I didn't think glamor boy would be much of one.

We caught a bus from L A X that took us downtown within a block or two of the parking lot where I'd left my car, which I ransomed, then I drove her home.

'It's been,' she said. She got out, gave a little wave, then disappeared into her apartment building. It was a warm evening. I sat there for a moment listening to the engine ping. Then I drove home to my mom.

For once, quite a tidy week, all things considered. Where did I go right?

A couple of days later the following report or poem or whatever it was arrived in my mailbox; like the others it had again been delivered mysteriously by hand in dark of night.

CONFIDENTIAL

28 May
Report
From: S.S.
To: V.D. (Ha ha)
Enclosed is ten dollars ($10.00) on account.
Spend it on clothes.
Drove by St Stephen's Hi School.
Jock types with armbands were checking every car
Going in and out of newly fenced
Parking lot. Large sign –
EMERGENCY MEETING – ALL PARENTS –
    TONIGHT AT 7.30.
TV news mobile unit parked outside front door.
Uniformed guard at front door.
Boy
Are you *stoopid*,
To change the subject.
No one's gonna put a 14-year-old boy in jail in the first place.
And in the second, how could your pop like you more
If you did something terrific (for once) but never even told
    him
About it??????????????????????????????
So
You did it all for nothing, *stoopid*.
Tried to scribe a poem about your pop and my mom –
One of my rare failures.
See ya,
Sez Sara
XXX
P.S. Flown anywhere recently?

> And if I laff at any mortal thing,
> 'tis so I do not weep.

This well-known saying can best be attributed to (choose one):
(a) Vince Lombardi. (b) Mary, Queen of Turkey. (c) V. (for
    Victor) Daniel.

FOR THE BEST IN PAPERBACKS, LOOK FOR THE

In every corner of the world, on every subject under the sun, Penguin represents quality and variety – the very best in publishing today.

For complete information about books available from Penguin – including Pelicans, Puffins, Peregrines and Penguin Classics – and how to order them, write to us at the appropriate address below. Please note that for copyright reasons the selection of books varies from country to country.

In the United Kingdom: Please write to *Dept E.P., Penguin Books Ltd, Harmondsworth, Middlesex, UB7 0DA*

If you have any difficulty in obtaining a title, please send your order with the correct money, plus ten per cent for postage and packaging, to *PO Box No 11, West Drayton, Middlesex*

In the United States: Please write to *Dept BA, Penguin, 299 Murray Hill Parkway, East Rutherford, New Jersey 07073*

In Canada: Please write to *Penguin Books Canada Ltd, 2801 John Street, Markham, Ontario L3R 1B4*

In Australia: Please write to the *Marketing Department, Penguin Books Australia Ltd, P.O. Box 257, Ringwood, Victoria 3134*

In New Zealand: Please write to the *Marketing Department, Penguin Books (NZ) Ltd, Private Bag, Takapuna, Auckland 9*

In India: Please write to *Penguin Overseas Ltd, 706 Eros Apartments, 56 Nehru Place, New Delhi, 110019*

In Holland: Please write to *Penguin Books Nederland B.V., Postbus 195, NL–1380AD Weesp, Netherlands*

In Germany: Please write to *Penguin Books Ltd, Friedrichstrasse 10–12, D–6000 Frankfurt Main 1, Federal Republic of Germany*

In Spain: Please write to *Longman Penguin España, Calle San Nicolas 15, E–28013 Madrid, Spain*

In France: Please write to *Penguin Books Ltd, 39 Rue de Montmorency, F-75003, Paris, France*

In Japan: Please write to *Longman Penguin Japan Co Ltd, Yamaguchi Building, 2–12–9 Kanda Jimbocho, Chiyoda-Ku, Tokyo 101, Japan*

CRIME AND MYSTERY IN PENGUINS

Call for the Dead   John Le Carré

The classic work of espionage which introduced the world to George Smiley. 'Brilliant . . . highly intelligent, realistic. Constant suspense. Excellent writing' – *Observer*

Swag   Elmore Leonard

From the bestselling author of *Stick* and *La Brava* comes this wallbanger of a book in which 100,000 dollars' worth of nicely spendable swag sets off a slick, fast-moving chain of events. 'Brilliant' – *The New York Times*

Beast in View   Margaret Millar

'On one level, *Beast in View* is a dazzling conjuring trick. On another it offers a glimpse of bright-eyed madness as disquieting as a shriek in the night. In the whole of Crime Fiction's distinguished sisterhood there is no one quite like Margaret Millar' – *Guardian*

The Julian Symons Omnibus

The Man Who Killed Himself, *The Man Whose Dreams Came True*, *The Man Who Lost His Wife*: three novels of cynical humour and cliff-hanging suspense from a master of his craft. 'Exciting and compulsively readable' – *Observer*

Love in Amsterdam   Nicolas Freeling

Inspector Van der Valk's first case involves him in an elaborate cat-and-mouse game with a very wily suspect. 'Has the sinister, spellbinding perfection of a cobra uncoiling. It is a masterpiece of the genre' – Stanley Ellis

Maigret's Pipe   Georges Simenon

Eighteen intriguing cases of mystery and murder to which the pipe-smoking Maigret applies his wit and intuition, his genius for detection and a certain *je ne sais quoi* . . .